DISCARDED

MORE PRAISE FOR LOIS WINSTON'S
ASSAULT WITH A DEADLY GLUE GUN

"You think you've got trouble? Say hello to Anastasia Pollack, who also happens to be queen of the one-liners. Funny, funny, funny—this is a series you don't want to miss!"

—Kasey Michaels, *USA Today* bestselling author

"Anastasia Pollack is as crafty as Martha Stewart, as feisty as Stephanie Plum, and as resourceful as Kinsey Millhone."

—Mary Kennedy, author of *The Talk Radio Mysteries*

"What a treat—I can't stop laughing! Witty, wise, and delightfully clever, Anastasia is going to be your new best friend. Her mysterious adventures are irresistible—you'll be glued to the page!"

—Hank Phillippi Ryan, Agatha Award-winning author

"Fans of Stephanie Plum will love Lois Winston's cast of quirky, laughable, and loveable characters. *Assault with a Deadly Glue Gun* is clever and thoroughly entertaining—a must-read!"

—Brenda Novak, *New York Times* bestselling author

D0067088

ASSAULT
WITH A
DEADLY
GLUE GUN

OTHER BOOKS BY LOIS WINSTON

Talk Gertie to Me
Dorchester Love Spell, 2006

Love, Lies and a Double Shot of Deception
Dorchester Love Spell, 2007

FORTHCOMING FROM LOIS WINSTON

Mop Doll Murders
the second book in the Anastasia Pollack Crafting Series
January 2012

AN ANASTASIA POLLACK CRAFTING SERIES

ASSAULT
WITH A
DEADLY
GLUE GUN

Lois Winston

Milton-Union Public Library
West Milton, Ohio

FEB 11

MIDNIGHT INK
WOODBURY, MINNESOTA

Assault with a Deadly Glue Gun: An Anastasia Pollack Crafting Mystery © 2011 by Lois Winston. All rights reserved. No part of this book may be used or reproduced in any manner whatsoever, including Internet usage, without written permission from Midnight Ink, except in the case of brief quotations embodied in critical articles and reviews.

First Edition
Second Printing, 2011

Book design and format by Donna Burch
Cover design by Lisa Novak
Cover illustration © Marc Tobin
Editing by Connie Hill

Midnight Ink, an imprint of Llewellyn Worldwide Ltd.

Library of Congress Cataloging-in-Publication Data
Winston, Lois.
  Assault with a deadly glue gun / Lois Winston. — 1st ed.
      p. cm. — (Anastasia Pollack crafting series)
  ISBN 978-0-7387-2347-1
  1. Single mothers—Fiction. 2. Periodical editors—Crimes against—Fiction.
  3. Handicraft—Fiction. I. Title.
  PS3623.I666A96   2010
  813'.6—dc22   2010035320

This is a work of fiction. Names, characters, places, and incidents are either the product of the author's imagination or are used fictitiously, and any resemblance to actual persons, living or dead, business establishments, events, or locales is entirely coincidental.

Midnight Ink
Llewellyn Worldwide Ltd.
2143 Wooddale Drive
Woodbury, MN 55125-2989
www.midnightinkbooks.com

Printed in the United States of America

DEDICATION

In memory of Karen Davenport,
amazing critique partner, friend,
and Anastasia's biggest fan.

ACKNOWLEDGMENTS

My everlasting gratitude to the following people who played a part in making the Anastasia Pollack Crafting Series a reality:

To Carolyn Grayson for suggesting I write a crafting mystery and Denise Dumars for finding Anastasia a home.

To Terri Bischoff, Midnight Ink acquisitions editor, for offering Anastasia that home and to all the other members of the Midnight Ink team for the various roles they played in making Anastasia look her best.

To authors Mary Kennedy, Kasey Michaels, Brenda Novak, and Hank Phillippi Ryan for taking time out of their busy lives to read *Assault With a Deadly Glue Gun* and provide such awesome praise.

To my fellow founders of Liberty States Fiction Writers: Gail Freeman, Melinda Leigh, Caridad Pineiro, Kathye Quick, Michele Richter, Rayna Vause, and Anne Walradt for their friendship and support through all those ups and downs. You ladies totally rock!

And finally, to Rob, Chris, Scott, Jen, Megan, Jack, Zoe, and Chase for filling my life with love.

ONE

I HATE WHINERS. ALWAYS have. So I was doing my damnedest not to become one in spite of the lollapalooza of a quadruple whammy that had broadsided me last week. Not an easy task, given that one of those lollapalooza whammies had barged into my bedroom and was presently hammering her cane against my bathroom door.

"Damn it, Anastasia! Hot water doesn't grow on trees, you know!"

Some people can't start the day without a cigarette. Lucille Pollack, Monster-in-Law from the Stygian Swamp, can't start hers without a sludge load of complaints. As much as I detest cigarettes, I'd much prefer a nicotine-puffing mother-in-law, as long as she came with an occasional kind word and a semi-pleasant disposition. Unfortunately, marriage is a package deal. Husbands come with family. And mine came with a doozie to end all doozies.

My mother-in-law is a card-carrying, circa 1930s communist. When she met me, it was hate at first sight. I bear the name of a dead Russian princess, thanks to my mother's unsubstantiated Romanov link—a great-grandmother with the maiden name of Romanoff. With Mama, the connection is more like sixty, not six, degrees of separation, and the links are coated with a thick layer of rust. But that's never stopped Mama from bragging about our royal ancestry, and it set the tone for my relationship—or lack of it—with my mother-in-law from Day One.

I suppose I didn't help the situation by naming one of my sons Nicholas and the other Alexander, even if they were named after my grandfathers—Alexander Periwinkle and Nicholas Sudberry.

"My kingdom for a bedroom door lock," I muttered. Not that I had much of a kingdom left. So it would have to be a really cheap lock.

"About time," said Lucille as I exited the bathroom amidst a cloud of warm steam. "Some people have no consideration of others." Raising one of her Sequoia-like arms, she waved her cane in my face. "Those boys of yours have been camped out in the other bathroom for half an hour doing what, I can't imagine."

Lucille always referred to Nick and Alex as *those boys*, refusing to use their given names. Like it might corrupt her political sensibilities or something.

"Three minutes," she continued ranting. "That's all it takes *me* to shower and all it should take any of you. I'm the only person in this house who gives one iota of concern for the earth's depleting resources."

She landed an elbow to my ribs to push me aside. Manifesto, her runt-of-the-litter French bulldog—or Mephisto, the Devil Dog, as the rest of the family had dubbed the Satan-incarnate canine—followed close on her heels. As he squeezed past me, he raised his wrinkled head and growled.

As soon as they'd both muscled their way into the bathroom, my mother-in-law slammed the door in my face and locked it. God only knows why she needs her dog in the bathroom with her. And if he does know, I hope he continues to spare the rest of us the knowledge.

My Grandma Periwinkle used to say that honeyed words conquered waspish dispositions. However, I doubted all the beehives in North America could produce enough honey to mollify the likes of Lucille. After eighteen years as her daughter-in-law, I still hadn't succeeded in extracting a single pleasantry from her.

Of all the shocks I sustained over the past week, knowing I was now stuck with Lucille topped the list. Two months ago, she shattered her hip in a hit-and-run accident when an SUV mowed her down while she jaywalked across Queens Boulevard. Her apartment building burned to the ground while she was in the hospital.

Comrade Lucille put her political beliefs above everyone and everything, including common sense. Since she didn't trust banks, her life savings, along with all her possessions, had gone up in flames. And of course, she didn't have insurance.

Homeless and penniless, Lucille came to live with us. "It won't be for long," my husband Karl (Lucille had named him after Karl Marx) had assured me. "Only until she gets back on her feet."

"Literally or figuratively?" I asked.

"Literally." Karl liked his mother best when two rivers and an hour's drive separated them. "I promise, we'll find somewhere for her to live, even if we have to pay for it ourselves."

Trusting person that I am—was—I believed him. We had a moderately sized nest egg set aside, and I would have been more than happy to tap into it to settle Lucille into a retirement community. Lucille had recovered from her injuries, although the chances of her now leaving any time soon were as non-existent as the eggs in that same nest.

Unbeknownst to me—formerly known as Trusting Wife— Karl, who handled the family finances, had not only cracked open, fried, and devoured our nest egg, he'd maxed out our home equity line of credit, borrowed against his life insurance policy, cashed in his 401(k), and drained the kids' college accounts.

I discovered this financial quagmire within twenty-four hours of learning that my husband, who was supposed to be at a sales meeting in Harrisburg, Pennsylvania, had dropped dead on a roulette table at the Luxor Hotel in Las Vegas. The love of my life was a closet gambling addict. He left me and his sons totally broke, up the yin-yang in debt, *and* saddled with his mother.

If he weren't already dead, I'd kill him.

Without a doubt, a jury of my peers would rule it justifiable homicide.

With Ralph, our African Grey parrot, keeping a voyeuristic eye on me from his perch atop the armoire, I dried myself off and began to dress for work.

They say the wife is always the last to know. For the past week I'd wracked my brain for signs I might have missed, niggling doubts I may have brushed aside. Even in retrospect, I had no clue of impending cataclysm. Karl was that good. Or maybe I had played my role of Trusting Wife too well. Either way, the result was the same.

Karl and I hadn't had the best of marriages, but we hadn't had the worst, either. We might not have had the can't-wait-to-jump-your-bones hots for each other after so many years, but how many couples did? That sort of love only exists in chick flicks and romance novels. Along with the myth of multiple orgasms. Or so I'd convinced myself years ago.

Besides, after working all day, plus taking care of the kids, the shopping, the carpooling, the cooking and the cleaning, who had the energy to put into even one orgasm most nights? Even for a drop-dead-gorgeous-although-balding-and-slightly-overweight-yet-still-a-hunk husband? Faking it was a lot quicker and easier. And gave me a few extra precious minutes of snooze time.

Still, I thought we'd had a pretty good marriage compared to most other couples we knew, a marriage built on trust and communication. In reality what we had was more like blind trust on my part and a whopping lack of communication on his. Most of all, though, I thought my husband loved me. Apparently he loved Roxie Roulette more.

Could I have been more clueless if I'd tried?

The theme from *Rocky* sang out from inside the armoire. Dead is dead only for the deceased. The widow, I'm learning, becomes a multi-tasking juggler of a thousand and one details. Our phone hadn't stopped ringing since the call from the hotel in Las Vegas.

But this wasn't the home phone. I opened the armoire and reached for the box of Karl's personal items the funeral director had given me. No one had bothered to turn off his phone. The display read *Private Call*. "Hello?"

"Put Karl on."

"Excuse me?"

5

"Don't play games with me, Sweet Cheeks. Hand the phone to that slippery weasel. Now."

"I'm afraid that's not possible."

"Make it possible. You tell him Ricardo's run out of patience, and *he's* run out of time."

As an auto parts salesman for a national wholesaler, Karl dealt with his share of lowlife Neanderthals, but Ricardo sounded lower than most of the run-of-the mill Neanderthals in the auto industry.

I wasn't in the mood for any macho-posturing *Soprano* wannabe. "If this concerns an order you placed, you'll have to get in touch with the main office in Secaucus. Karl passed away last week."

Silence greeted my statement. At first I thought Ricardo had hung up. When he finally spoke, I wished he had. "No kidding?"

"Your sense of humor might be that warped, but I can assure you, mine isn't."

"This his missus?" He sounded suspicious.

"Yes."

"Look, I'm sorry about your loss," he said, although his tone suggested otherwise, "but I got my own problems. That *schmuck* was into me for fifty G's. We had a deal, and dead or not, he's gotta pay up. *Capisce?*"

Hardly. But I now sensed that Ricardo was no body shop owner. "Who are you?"

"Let's just say I'm a former business associate of the deceased. One you just inherited, Sweet Cheeks. Along with his debt."

I glanced at the bathroom door. Thankfully, Lucille's three-minute shower was running overtime. I lowered my voice. "I don't know anything about a debt, and I certainly don't have fifty thousand dollars."

Although both statements were true, after what I had recently learned about my husband's secret life, he probably did owe Ricardo fifty thousand dollars, the same fifty thousand dollars the casino manager in Las Vegas said Karl gambled away shortly before cashing in his chips—literally—at that roulette table.

But what really freaked me out as I stood half-naked, in nothing more than my black panties and matching bra, was the thought that there could be other Ricardos waiting to pounce. Lots of other Ricardos. Behind my husband's upstanding, church-going, family-oriented façade, he had apparently hidden a shitload of secrets. What next?

Ricardo wasn't buying into my ignorance. "I happen to know otherwise, Sweet Cheeks, so don't try to con me. I'll be over in an hour to collect."

There are five stages of grief. I'd gone through the first stage, denial, so fast I hardly remembered being there. For most of the past week, I'd silently seethed over Karl's duplicity. With each new deceit I'd uncovered, my anger grew exponentially. I knew Stage Two, anger, would be sticking around for a long time to come, sucking dry all the love I once had for my husband.

Ricardo became that proverbial last straw on my overburdened camel's back. "You'll do no such thing," I screamed into the phone. "I don't know who you are or what kind of sick game you're playing, but if you bother me again, I'm calling the police. *Capisce?*"

Ricardo's voice lowered to a menacing timbre. "I wouldn't do that if I were you, Sweet Cheeks." The phone went dead. Along with every nerve in my body.

And I thought I had problems before?

"*If you have tears, prepare to shed them now,*" squawked Ralph. "*Julius Caesar.* Act Three, Scene Two."

No *Polly wants a cracker* for this bird. Ralph spouts Shakespeare and only Shakespeare, thanks to several decades of listening to Great-aunt Penelope Periwinkle's classroom lectures. When Aunt Penelope died two years ago, I inherited the parrot with the un-canny knack for squawking circumstance-appropriate quotes.

Could have been worse. At least Aunt Penelope wasn't a closet rap queen with a bird who squawked about pimpin' the hos in the 'hood. I'm also grateful Ralph is housebroken, considering his ability to pick the lock on his cage.

"I've already cried enough to replenish New Jersey's drought-lowered reservoirs, Ralph. So unless you know of some way to transform tears into twenties, I've got to move on and figure a way out of this mess."

He ignored me. Ralph speaks only when *he* wants to, and right now his attention had turned to grooming himself. Like I said, I hate whiners, but jeez! How much simpler life would be if my only concern was molting feathers.

TWO

LUCILLE DIDN'T YET KNOW about the financial ramifications of Karl's death. Coward that I am, I'd spent much of the last week putting off what promised to be one of the more pleasant tasks—and I mean that with all the sarcasm I can muster at six-thirty in the morning—of my widowhood. Whether this Ricardo creep turned out to be a crank or the real thing, the time had come to impart the gory details of how Lucille Pollack's darling son Karl had drained our savings and plunged us into a shitload of debt.

I confronted her as soon as she came out of the bathroom. She accepted my penniless state about as well as Mephisto the Devil Dog takes to cats.

"I don't believe it!" She sat down on my bed and clutched Mephisto tight enough for the dog to whimper and squirm. "Karl would never get involved in gambling. I know my son."

"Right." Good old Saint Karl. "Believe what you want," I told her, "but here's the deal: Either you start paying for room and board, or you can find somewhere else to live because thanks to that son you know so well, I can't afford to support you."

"So you wash your hands of me and toss me out on the street? How typical!"

"I never said that."

I took a deep breath and told myself to count to ten thousand. How could she believe I was that cruel? "You have several options."

Besides her Social Security, Lucille received a meager pension from her years as an editor at *The Worker's Herald*, the weekly newspaper of the American Communist Party. The pension had covered her now-a-pile-of-burned-rubble, rent-controlled Queens apartment. Social Security paid for her other living expenses.

Rent-controlled apartments were a dying breed in New York and nonexistent in New Jersey. Between the two monthly checks, Lucille might be able to afford another apartment, but she'd have little left to live on. For all their Workers Unite and Power to the People propaganda, *The Worker's Herald* offered shit in the way of benefits to its retirees.

"There's always senior-citizen housing," I suggested. I didn't tell her that I doubted many would welcome Mephisto the Devil Dog, even those that did allow pets. Aside from Lucille, Mephisto had never met a human he didn't immediately grace with a menacing growl.

"I will *not* live with prattling idiots who sit around all day watching soap operas, playing Canasta, and complaining about their aches and pains. If my son were alive—"

"But he's not, and I'm in this mess because of him, no matter what you want to believe. I know there's never been any love lost between us, but I'm not the villain here. Karl left me with a mountain of debt and without two nickels to rub together. So either you contribute or you leave. It's as simple as that."

Neither option appealed to her. Karl had promised to subsidize a new apartment once her doctors gave the okay for her to live on her own again. Even though I'd hoped she'd opt to leave, no matter how much she despised me, she had it better here than she'd have it on her own, and she knew that.

"How much?" she finally asked.

I named what I thought was a reasonable monthly figure to cover her expenses.

"Outrageous!" she bellowed. "You're no better than a slum lord!"

"*The lady doth protest too much, methinks*," squawked Ralph. "*Hamlet*. Act Three, Scene Two." Both Mephisto and Lucille growled at him. Ralph squawked back a mimicking growl.

My domestic skills would never win me the Good Housekeeping Seal of Approval, but my home didn't exactly qualify as a slum. I pulled the phone book off the bottom shelf of my nightstand and tossed it on the bed. "Fine. You'd better start calling rental agents."

With a harrumph, she pushed the directory aside, lowered Mephisto to the floor, and stood. "For that kind of money, I want more room. I'll move into the apartment above the garage. I need my privacy."

She needed her privacy? This coming from the woman who'd stuck her nose into every millimeter of our lives every nanosecond of the day since she moved in? "Even if you could manage the stairs, which I don't think you can, I'm afraid that won't be possible."

"You don't need all that space. You can move your things into the basement."

"I plan to," I said. "I'm renting out the apartment. You'll have to stay where you are."

"Absolutely not. It's too small."

"For what? You lost everything you owned when your apartment burned to the ground."

She offered no rebuttal. Her entire argument had been an exercise in pushing my buttons. Argument for the sake of argument. Standard Lucille discourse.

"By the way," I said to her departing back, "that amount includes cut-rate kibble for Mephisto. If the rest of us have to live on mac and cheese to get by, he's going to have to make do without his gourmet canned cuisine."

She stopped, pounded her cane on the carpet, and glowered at me over her shoulder. "His name is *Manifesto*, and he has a delicate constitution."

So delicate that he'd scarfed down an entire doorstop-heavy fruitcake several weeks ago when no one was looking. At least Mephisto's thievery had spared the rest of us from dealing with the annual Christmas gift from Hell.

"We all have to make sacrifices," I told her.

"Don't you lecture me about making sacrifices, missy. I lived through the Great Depression. A depression brought about by greedy *capitalists*, I might add. I know all about making sacrifices. Unlike *some* people."

Then she launched into one of her very own communist manifestos, which set an orchestra of percussion instruments pounding between my temples.

Over the years I've tried my damnedest to foster a congenial relationship between me and my mother-in-law. Lucille had pulverized all my attempts under her size-ten orthopedic heels. At least I knew I wasn't the sole beneficiary of her wrath. The Daughters of the October Revolution, all of whom have similar curmudgeon-like personalities, are the only people I ever recall warming up to my mother-in-law—probably because they're all as curmudgeonly as she is.

"I'm late for work," I said, interrupting her dissertation of all that's wrong with the world. This time I closed the door in her face.

———

I tried not to think about Ricardo's phone call as I made my way to work. Maybe it was a crank call. One of Karl's lowlife Neanderthal clients with a warped sense of humor. *And maybe pigs really can fly, Anastasia.*

Sitting astride a winged Miss Piggy would have been a preferable mode of transportation at the moment. Making the daily rush hour trek to and from work had been somewhat tolerable while I still owned my Camry. My new state of pauperdom had forced me to sell the comfortable silver car with its multitude of amenities back to the dealer. In its place I'd purchased a used, stripped-down, bottom-of-the-line, eight-year-old mud-brown Hyundai.

The balance of the money from the car sale had paid for shipping Karl's body back from Nevada and the cremation expenses. Cremation is cheaper than burial, and after what my husband had done to me and his kids, we didn't need the expense of a cemetery plot. If anyone wanted to visit Karl in the future, they could talk to the urn on the bookcase shelf.

I'm not a large woman, barely five-two. And as I've mentioned previously, I don't like to whine. Although, I suppose that's hard to tell lately. Anyway, years ago I learned to accept the God-dealt genes that landed me Mama's stubby legs, Grandma Sudberry's below-the-navel spread, and Grandma Periwinkle's training bra-sized boobs, making me a height-challenged, cellulite-dimpled, flat-chested brunette Bartlett pear.

And although I refuse to take responsibility for the additional ten pounds I haven't been able to shed since the birth of my last child—thanks in part to both my Carbo Junkie Gene and my Chocoholic Gene—I still managed to squeeze into a size eight. On good days. Still, in the sub-sub compact Hyundai, I felt like The Incredible Hulk shoehorned behind the steering wheel.

After an hour of creeping along Routes 24, 78, and 287 at a pace slower than the average snail, I pulled into the parking lot of Trimedia's new headquarters, situated in the middle of a former cornfield in Morris County. Builders planned an entire business complex for the area, but at present our only neighbor was the new parking lot and commuter rail stop built across the road to accommodate the expected influx of corporations fleeing New York.

Prior to September 11th, we were located in lower Manhattan, an easy commute for me via public transportation. Our building had sustained minimal damage from the terrorist attack, and after a short stint in temporary offices, we'd returned to our headquarters. However, a few months ago our new owners were lured across the Hudson by cheaper real estate and huge tax incentives.

Few staff members at *American Woman* were happy about the move, but then again, even fewer were happy about any of the changes Trimedia had instituted since gobbling up the family-owned Reynolds-Alsopp Publishing Company—least of all our former owner, Hugo Reynolds-Alsopp.

Hugo remained publisher in title only. The real power now rested in the hands of the Trimedia Board of Directors, a parsimonious group of bean counters who sacrificed editorial content for the almighty bottom line.

I worked in a cat-claw-cat environment, but unlike most of my coworkers at *American Woman*, I was content in my position as crafts editor. I had no desire to scheme and plot my way up the monthly magazine's editorial ladder to the Holy Trinity, better known as Decorating, Beauty, and Fashion.

None of my coworkers seemed surprised to see me Monday morning. Publishing deadlines wait for no one. Our motto is much the same as the mail carriers': Neither rain, nor sleet, nor snow, nor hail—or in my case, recent widowhood—will keep us from getting our issues out on time.

Besides, thanks to Trimedia's Simon Legree–like benefits package, I'd already used up my yearly allotment of personal leave days. And it was only the end of January.

After dumping my coat in my cubicle office, I grabbed my notes and headed for the conference room. The last Monday of each month was the day we planned the issue five months down the road and gave status reports on the progress of the other issues in the works.

I arrived to find all the usual suspects, minus Marlys, already gathered around the battered and chipped walnut conference room table. Our building might be spanking brand new, but Trimedia's bean counters had saved a bundle by moving all our crappy old furnishings from lower Manhattan to the cornfield.

Marlys Vandenburg was our fashion editor and resident *Prima Donna*. Rumor had it, she got her job, not because of her experience in fashion but from her gold medal performance in bed—the bed of our former owner, Hugo Reynolds-Alsopp. Marlys kept her own hours and got away with it because, according to another rumor, now that Hugo had lost control of the company, she was performing her bedroom gymnastics for the chairman of the Trimedia Board of Directors.

I poured myself a cup of brewed high test and took my seat on the Bottom Feeders side of the table. The food and health editors were to my left. The travel and finance editors, plus the one editorial assistant the five of us shared, were to my right.

Across the table sat the decorating and beauty editors, their individual editorial assistants, and Marlys's assistant. Naomi Dreyfus, our editor-in-chief, sat at one end of the table. Hugo, who still attended editorial meetings, commanded the chair at the opposite end.

"I suppose we might as well get started," said Naomi, scowling at the empty butternut faux-leather upholstered chair usually occupied by Marlys. "You'd think she'd make an effort to show up on time at least once a month." She directed this last comment, along with a bitter purse of her lips, toward Hugo.

Naomi and Hugo had been an item for years until Marlys came along. Now they barely spoke to one another. Another rumor flying around the office suggested Marlys had recently set her sights on Naomi's job.

Hugo lowered his thinning gray head to avoid eye contact with Naomi. He had aged considerably since losing the company and had lost the dapper patina that had attracted beautiful women for most of his sixty-plus years. His hair needed a trim, his suit a good pressing. A series of small stains marred his custom-made shirt and striped silk tie, as though he had dribbled his morning coffee and either hadn't noticed or no longer cared.

Now that Marlys had given him the boot, I suspected he regretted walking out on Naomi. The statuesque Naomi, with her well-bred patrician features, cultured tones, Swiss boarding school education, and trademark silver chignon, exuded class. Without the aid of any plastic surgeon, she looked years younger than her actual age of fifty-nine. Naomi was a true silk purse. Next to her, the twenty-five years younger Marlys, for all her designer duds and hours spent at the most chic Manhattan spas, came across as a sow's ear.

The rest of us certainly regretted the day Hugo hired Marlys, especially Erica Milano. Erica was Marlys's personal slave, although technically her title was assistant fashion editor.

"I have everything covered," Erica said, her voice little more than a whisper directed at the shocking pink folder on the table in front of her. One of her hands fidgeted with a corner of the folder. The thumb and index finger of her other hand picked at the rubber end of a pencil stub.

Erica put in sixteen-hour days, doing all of Marlys's work while Marlys took three-hour, four-Cosmopolitan lunches and all the credit. Unfortunately, Erica was a doormat, and Marlys, who owned a closet full of Christian Louboutin boots, took extreme pleasure in tramping their trademark red soles all over Erica.

Marlys had even bullied her milquetoast assistant into running personal errands for her during her lunch hour.

Naomi forced a smile. "Of course you do, Erica. You always do. And we appreciate your dedication to your job. I have to wonder why we even bother to pay Marlys a salary." Again, she leveled an icy green glare at Hugo.

Around the table, the others traded surreptitious glances. Erica was fashion editor in all but name, Marlys in name only. Too bad Erica lacked the backbone—and the looks—to steal the job away from her bitch of a boss. Poor Erica. As long as she carried around an extra thirty pounds and refused to apply to her own body the same design sense and style she used in the pages of *American Woman*, she'd stay hidden away in a Trimedia cubicle.

The magazine couldn't risk the ridicule of the press. A fashion editor had to look the part. And if nothing else, Marlys looked the part.

One by one, each of us gave our status reports for the issues in progress, pinning copies of layouts and photos up on the cork-covered wall behind me. The Holy Trinity got a bird's-eye view. We Bottom Feeders needed to twist in our seats. When we had covered each department, we moved on to planning the July issue.

"I'd like to do a Lazy Days of Summer theme," said Naomi, "focusing on a patriotic color scheme."

Her half-Chinese, half-Irish assistant Kim O'Hara, pushed a lock of straight auburn hair behind her ear and rose to pin some swatches and photos to the wall in the space allocated for the next issue.

"Any ideas?" asked Naomi.

"Denim and bandanas are making a comeback," said Jeanie Sims, our decorating editor. She rifled through one of the file folders in front of her and extracted several catalogue sheets which she handed Kim to add to the wall.

"Furniture manufacturers are showing denim upholstered sofas and chairs. We could accent with red and white bandana throw pillows?" She glanced my way.

"Envelope pillows," I suggested, "along with a few patchwork pillows using both denim and bandanas."

"Good," said Naomi. "What else?"

I thought for a moment. "We could bring the theme outdoors onto a patio for placemats, napkins, a tray. Maybe a denim hostess apron?"

"*Denim hostess apron?*"

Everyone turned as Marlys Vandenburg breezed into the room and made a production of settling herself into the chair next to Erica. Her derision sounded in her voice and showed on her face.

She wore a calf-length handkerchief dress of vermillion-colored raw silk. A plunging neckline showcased an enormous tear-drop shaped diamond nestled between her breasts. Somewhat smaller matching diamonds hung from each ear. A diamond clip pulled back her chin-length platinum layered haircut on one side of her face.

I glanced at Hugo. Was that drool I noticed on the corner of his mouth?

Naomi didn't bother to conceal her annoyance. "Nice of you to join us, Marlys, even if you are three hours late. And a bit overdressed."

"As I'm sure you're well aware, previews for Fashion Week began today. I had an interview at Cartier first thing this morning. Didn't Erica mention that?" She glared at her assistant.

Erica's eyes grew wide, her voice squeaked in protest. "But I didn't know."

Marlys, who stood nearly six feet in three-inch stilettos, literally looked down her nose as she graced Erica with a sneer. "You would if you did your job properly."

Her lips turned up into a too-saccharine sweet smile as she fingered the expensive bauble between her breasts. "Beautiful, isn't it?" she asked no one in particular. "The diamonds are from Cartier's newest collection. On loan to me for a late dinner with Emil Pachette this evening. He's agreed to give me an exclusive."

"An exclusive what?" I asked, unable to resist. Titters sounded around the room.

Cloris McWerther, our Food editor, elbowed me in the ribs. "Naughty Anastasia," she whispered.

"You're just jealous I beat you to the punch," I whispered back.

"An exclusive *interview*," snapped Marlys. "I don't suppose someone like *you* has ever heard of Emil Pachette, but he's the brightest new star to hit the fashion scene in a decade. By this time next year everyone will be wearing couture from the House of Pachette."

She turned to Naomi. "And if we weren't exiled to this godforsaken no-man's-land, I'd have time to return home to change before my dinner date. Or perhaps you expect me to show up wearing *denim*?"

Not that Marlys had ever shown up for work on time when we were located in Manhattan, but Naomi chose not to mention that fact. "Let's get back to the issue," she said.

"Just a minute," said Marlys. "What's this about tacky hostess aprons? That's so seventies. What's next? Palazzo pants? Do it yourself disco balls?" This time I was the recipient of one of her sneers.

Marlys considered my monthly contributions to the magazine a waste of editorial space. In her effort to grab more pages for herself, she'd launched a campaign to eliminate my department. Luckily, Hugo and Naomi had fought for me and the value of the craft section to our readers. However, I had no reason to believe she'd given up her quest now that we had new owners. Especially if the rumors about her current bed partner were true.

Given my dire financial situation, I should have restrained my sarcastic tongue. I couldn't afford to lose my job. Too bad I hadn't thought of that before I gave Marlys one more reason to hate me.

Naomi gave her a brief recap of our plans for the July issue.

Marlys's voice rose two octaves. Her face suffused with a color akin to her dress. "Denim and bandanas? Over my dead body! Where do you suggest we hold the fashion shoot? Dogpatch?"

She slapped her hand onto the table. "We are *not* featuring denim and bandanas. I won't allow it."

Naomi sat back in her chair and steepled her fingers under her chin. Somehow she managed to keep her voice calm and controlled as she spoke, but I'm sure the effort nearly killed her. "I happen to be the editor-in-chief of this magazine, Marlys. I make the decisions, not you."

"We'll see about that." Marlys rose from her chair and stormed out of the conference room, slamming the door behind her.

As the rest of us squirmed nervously in our chairs, Naomi snapped at Hugo. "I want to thank you from the bottom of my heart, Dr. Frankenstein."

Hugo grimaced. "I'll see if I can talk some sense into her."

"And if you can't?"

He cleared his throat, straightened his skewed tie, and pushed away from the table. "I'll think of something."

THREE

AFTER HUGO LEFT THE meeting, we continued planning the July issue, everyone ignoring Marlys's objection to denim and bandanas. Hugo never returned, but lunch arrived about half an hour later. We continued to work as we nibbled on club sandwiches, a monthly company perk that we all expected to lose once the bean counters discovered that Naomi tapped into miscellaneous expenditures to pay the deli each month. The meeting finally broke up shortly before two-thirty.

Once back in my cubicle, my cell phone rang before I even had a chance to flip on my computer. I didn't recognize the number on the display. "Hello?"

"Hello." Something about the way those two syllables rolled off the guy's tongue sent a flooding warmth through me. Or maybe I'd just experienced my first hot flash. Two plausible possibilities (although I certainly hoped I was too young for the latter). Whichever the culprit, though, the thought of either sent a chill down my spine that immediately readjusted my estrogen levels.

"I'm calling about the apartment you have for rent," he continued.

Aside from having to replace my semi-luxurious sedan with an aging clunker, the second casualty of getting booted off Mount Upper Middle–class was the realization that I'd need to supplement my income. Sharing a house with Lucille was bad enough. Sharing a cardboard box with her and two teenage boys was far worse. That meant giving up my home crafts studio over our detached garage.

The end of last week I reluctantly placed an ad in the *Star Ledger*. Having missed the deadline for the weekend edition, the ad appeared for the first time in this morning's issue.

"Would you like to see the apartment this evening?" I asked.

"Actually, I'd like to see it now. I'm scheduled to leave on a seven-thirty flight tonight and won't be back for a few days. The apartment sounds perfect. I'd hate to lose out to someone else."

I glanced at my watch and did some quick mental gymnastics, factoring travel time back and forth and the hours of work I still needed to put in on the wedding spread scheduled for tomorrow's photo shoot. Three dozen peach, pink, and white satin birdseed roses sat in a vase on the corner of my counter, but I still had to create several pairs of bridal and bridesmaid tennies for the second part of the article.

It was going to be tight, and I'd have to work late, but I couldn't risk losing out on a possible tenant. Besides, if I timed things right, he'd be gone before Lucille returned from her afternoon Kommie Koffee Klatch. Thank God for the Daughters of the October Revolution, their weekly Lower East Side meetings, and Lucille's improved health, which enabled her to take the train into Manhattan.

"I'm at work, but I can meet you at the apartment in an hour," I told him.

"Great."

I gave him directions.

"Thanks. By the way, I'm Zachary Barnes."

"Anastasia Pollack."

"See you in an hour, Anastasia Pollack."

After I hung up from Zachary Barnes, I noticed the flashing message light on my office phone. I tapped in my code to retrieve the message.

"Given your recent widowhood, I'm cutting you a break. You have until tomorrow. Don't make me regret my generosity. Don't call the cops, and don't *ever* hang up on me again if you know what's good for you, bitch. *Capisce?*"

Maybe I'd watched too many episodes of *The Sopranos*, but something told me this guy meant business. Might have been his uber-mafia-like accent. Or the repeated click-click-click of what sounded like a gun cocking. Not that I'd ever heard a gun cock except on TV or in the movies but what else would make that scare-the-living-wits-out-of-me sound?

I *capisced* all right. This was no crank caller as I'd hoped. The likelihood of a crank caller having both Karl's cell phone number and the direct line to my office was about as likely as Miss Piggy sprouting those wings and sailing toward the clouds.

I was now convinced that on top of everything else, Karl had gotten himself mixed up with a loan shark. And I'd be the one wearing the cement Manolos if I didn't pay up.

But how could I? Thanks to Karl, I didn't have an extra fifty cents, let alone fifty thousand dollars. I sank into my desk chair and stared at my blank computer screen, willing it to offer up some answers. It didn't comply.

"Marlys! Where are you, you goddamn fucking bitch-whore? You can't hide from me. I'll rip your fucking heart out and shove it down your fucking throat!" The shrieking outrage of Vittorio Versailles, the Franco-Neapolitan fashion designer whose creations were a favorite of the celebrities on Mr. Blackwell's Worst Dressed List, boomed from the direction of the elevator bank. A moment later, I heard him pounding down the corridor in search of the woman who had minced and mangled him in our latest issue.

In our business, egos often clash. Harsh words and not-so-mild expletives were frequently hurled. Jealousies abounded. Wild histrionics regularly pierced the normal frenzy of our workplace. Only the players changed from day to day and confrontation to confrontation.

I poked my head out in time to see Vittorio, his face a deep purple that clashed against his skin-tight burgundy jumpsuit, charge down the hall toward Marlys's office. He waved a copy of our latest issue over his head. An entourage of eight anorexic men, all dressed head-to-toe in die-cut aqua suede, followed at his heels.

"Looks like Vittorio saw the slice-and-dice Marlys did on him," said Cloris, stepping out from her office directly across the hall from mine. She gave me an odd look. "You okay?"

"Sure, why?"

"You look like you're about to cry."

I pasted a smile on my face. "I'm fine."

"Sure you are, sweetie." She broke the ears off a chocolate bunny and handed them to me. As food editor, Cloris received samples for review on a daily basis. She ate them all and still maintained a size two figure. I hated her.

I hadn't told anyone at work about my financial situation and wasn't about to now. And I certainly wasn't going to say anything about the message I'd just received. I changed the subject back to Vittorio. "I can't believe I'm about to say this, but for once I agree with Marlys. Vittorio's designs belong in a circus."

"On the clowns," said Serena Brower, our travel editor. She and Daphne Jervis, our shared editorial assistant, joined us. We watched as Vittorio and his group stormed into Marlys's corner office.

"What do you have against clowns?" asked Daphne.

The three of them laughed. I joined in with a forced and half-hearted chuckle.

They were still laughing a minute later when Erica, tears streaming down her cheeks, ran out of Marlys's office and headed for the ladies' room.

"Uh-oh," said Cloris.

"Whose turn is it?" asked Serena.

I sighed. "Mine."

"If only she'd listen to us and file a complaint against that bitch," said Daphne.

Erica and Daphne had been hired the same day, and Daphne could just as easily have been assigned to Marlys. At first Daphne resented Erica winning out on the choicer assignment, but her resentment soon disappeared when she saw how Marlys treated Erica. Now she thanked her lucky stars for her position as assistant to us Bottom Feeders.

"This is harassment," said Daphne. "It's illegal. Erica should exercise her rights."

But Erica didn't have the backbone to say boo to Marlys, much less take legal action against her. She suffered Marlys's wrath, then dissolved into tears at least once a week. I headed for the ladies' room, hoping I could calm her down quickly. I had bigger problems than a sniveling, spineless assistant who wouldn't stand up for herself to worry about—like a threatening loan shark and a prospective tenant I couldn't afford to stand up.

Entering the restroom, I found Erica locked in a stall, her gulping sobs sounding from behind the pink metal door. "Want to talk about it?" I asked.

"She blamed me!" she wailed between snuffles. "Do you believe that? She told him I typed up her notes wrong, and she didn't see the mistakes until after the issue was printed because I proofed the bluelines while she was out of town. She didn't even have the guts to tell him to his face that she deliberately trashed him!"

"Did he believe her?"

Everyone knew Marlys was out to get Vittorio after he snubbed her in Milan last summer. She had waltzed into the House of Versailles, demanding the kind of freebies reserved for the editors of *Vogue* and *WWD*. We were a second-rate general women's magazine sold at supermarket check-out lines. Vittorio knew it. He had laughed in her face and bounced her out on her liposuctioned butt.

Erica sniffed back a mucousy sob. "I don't know. I ran out before he said anything, but he looked like he was about to strangle both of us."

As if on cue, we heard Vittorio's booming voice passing outside the ladies' room. "You won't get away with this, Marlys. Your days are numbered, bitch."

It took me ten minutes to talk Erica into unlocking the stall and another ten minutes before she had calmed down sufficiently to wash her tear-stained, puffy face. "I hate her," she said.

I placed my hand on her trembling shoulder. "So I guess this means we can rule you out as president of the Marlys Vandenburg Admiration Society, huh?"

She jerked away. "Don't make fun of me!"

"I'm sorry. I was just trying to cheer you up."

"Well, you didn't." She headed back to the stall, slammed the door and relocked it. "Go away, Anastasia. Just leave me alone."

———

I arrived home forty-five minutes later to find Zachary Barnes standing in my driveway, staring up at the apartment above the garage. He looked exactly like a guy with a voice like his should look: like someone had dumped the genetic components of Pierce Brosnan, George Clooney, Patrick Dempsey, and Antonio Banderas into a pan and baked up the epitome of male perfection.

I wasn't sure whether this was a good thing or a bad thing, given my current situation. Luckily, my recent tumble into pandemonium, thanks to my own deceitful, dearly departed, drop-dead-gorgeous-although-balding-and-slightly-overweight-yet-still-a-hunk husband, had inured me to all males in general and drop-dead-gorgeous hunks in particular. I doubted any woman had ever had to fake an orgasm with the stud standing before me. If I hadn't already sworn off men for the rest of my life, recently widowed or not, I'm certain I would have been reduced to drooling and babbling like some hormone-riddled sixteen-year-old.

Instead, I assumed my most professional, forty-something demeanor, introduced myself, then led him up the flight of stairs on the side of the garage and into the second-floor apartment.

"Perfect," he said after taking a quick peek into each of the three rooms, bathroom, and closets. "I'll take it. I'm assuming you want first and last month's rent plus references?" He reached inside his well-worn brown leather bomber (the hunk jacket of choice) and produced a folded sheet of paper and a checkbook.

I stared dumbly at him, my mouth refusing to work.

"Is something wrong, Mrs. Pollack?"

I shook my head, forcing my jaw to loosen and allow words to exit. "No, I ... I'm ... this is happening much quicker and easier than I anticipated. That's all."

What I had really been doing was mentally calculating how many rent checks it would take to get the *Capisce* thug to go away. What proof did I have that Karl even owed Ricardo money? However, did a loan shark really need proof? Was there a Society of Loan Sharks with a set of rules and code of ethics that had to be followed to maintain their certification? Highly unlikely. These guys made up their own rules. And broke legs—or worse—when the *schmucks* who did business with them didn't pay up.

I may never have come up against a loan shark before, but I do live in New Jersey, and I do read the newspapers. I was in deep shit. *Thank you very much, Karl.*

Zachary Barnes was staring at me. "The apartment is for rent, right?"

"Yes. Of course. Absolutely." I snatched the sheet of references from his hand and gave them a cursory glance. "Freelance photo-journalist?" His contacts included an editor at *National Geographic* and the president of the World Wildlife Federation.

He tapped the paper with his index finger. "They'll vouch for my integrity."

The connection suddenly clicked in my brain. Zachary Barnes. Photo-journalist. *The* Zachary Barnes. "I'm sure they will," I said, "but why would *you* of all people want an apartment over a garage in a New Jersey suburb?"

This guy was on the A-list of every club in Manhattan. He dated models and celebrities. Correction. He *was* a celebrity, albeit a minor one, who'd been mentioned numerous times on Page Six and in other gossip columns. This guy enjoyed the nightlife of Manhattan. The only nightlife he'd find in Westfield, New Jersey, was high school basketball, PTA meetings, and Tuesday night Bingo at the Catholic church.

He combed a hand through his hair, the kind of hair heroes in romance novels always have—thick and wavy and the color of bittersweet chocolate with just a hint of gray at the temples.

"Look," he said, "all I want is a quiet place to crash and work. I'm fed up with pushy publicists forcing me to be seen every night, not to mention interfering neighbors who think I'm running a meth lab."

"A meth lab? Hey, I've got two teenage sons." I shoved his references back at him. "I can't have a junkie living on my property, no matter who vouches for your character." A loan shark breathing down my neck was enough of a crime connection for this working mom.

"Chill, lady. I'm not running a meth lab. I don't do drugs of any kind. Never have."

Right. I raised an eyebrow. "Never?"

He grew sheepish. "Okay, so I smoked a little pot in college. Didn't everyone?"

"But never inhaled?"

That caused him to chuckle, which brought out a nice set of laugh lines around his eyes and the corners of his mouth. Why is it that guys with wrinkles look sexy, but when women get wrinkles, they just look old?

And why on earth was I thinking of such things when my life was turning to week-old crap? Maybe my brain decided I needed a shot of serotonin to give me a brief respite from the more pressing problems of newly acquired poverty and how to avoid being fitted for cement Manolos.

I gave myself a mental slap upside my head. I couldn't afford to lose this guy. "Then why do your neighbors think you're running a meth lab?"

"Because Mr. and Mrs. Can't-Mind-Their-Own-Business are a pair of geriatric nut cases who don't know the difference between a meth lab and a darkroom."

Darkroom? And here I thought those were assigned to the antiquities section of the Smithsonian, along with typewriters and adding machines. Didn't photographers use digital cameras nowadays? All the photographers who worked for Trimedia did. But I decided this was not the time for such a discussion. Maybe Mr. Zachary Barnes was an old-fashioned purist. What did I care as long as he paid his rent on time?

"Last night," he continued, "the cops raided my apartment and ruined three days worth of work when they barged in and turned on the lights while I was developing film. And that wasn't the first time. It's been an ongoing problem."

He glanced at his watch. "Now I have to fly back to New Mexico to reshoot those three days in less than twenty-four hours in order to meet my deadline."

He indicated the apartment with a sweep of his arm. "A place like this is ideal. No neighbors and easy access into the city."

He looked at me.

I looked at him.

"Hey, I'm desperate here. You've got to believe me," he said.

I did. After all, I had my own geriatric nut case living under my roof, didn't I? Besides, going head-to-head in a Who's More Desperate contest, I'd win hands down. I needed Zachary Barnes and his rent check a hell of a lot more than he needed my apartment. What I couldn't believe was my good fortune in finding a renter so quickly. But then again, maybe I deserved a slight nod from the Karma gods and goddesses, given the lollapalooza of a quadruple whammy they'd recently dropped on my head.

I reached into my purse and handed him the standard lease agreement form I'd purchased at Office Depot. His check for two months' rent would make a nice dent in the enormous stack of past-due bills sitting on my desk—bills that I, as Trusting Wife, had assumed Karl had paid. Silly me to take my husband at his word.

Or maybe I should wait with the bills and offer the money to Ricardo as a down payment. How long would the gas and electric company carry me before shutting off the power? Weren't there some laws against doing that in winter? And what were the odds of a loan shark accepting a payment plan?

"Sign on the bottom line, and the apartment is yours, Mr. Barnes. When would you like to move in?"

"Zack," he said, extending his hand. "And how does Saturday sound?"

"Saturday works for me." I shook his hand. "And it's Anastasia."

"You've saved my life, Anastasia."

Actually, he'd saved mine, but I wasn't going to let him know that. I also wasn't going to mention the geriatric nut case living mere feet from his new apartment.

I wondered how he felt about communists.

———

An hour later I pulled into a space under one of the parking lot lampposts at Trimedia. The dashboard clock read six-thirty, thanks to an overturned eighteen wheeler on Route 287 that had me stuck in traffic for two additional hours. The parking lot was empty except for Marlys's silver Jaguar, which surprised me, considering her big date of this evening. Maybe it was a midnight supper.

I stepped from the car and stretched. My lower back ached from sitting so long. The Hyundai's seats were sub-standard, hard and non-ergonomic. As I entered the steel and glass structure, using my magnetic ID to release the lock, I made a mental note to investigate seat pads. Or maybe those beaded things that are supposed to give added support.

Scratch that. I had to reprogram my attitudes. Find creative ways to make do instead of solving problems with dollars. After all, I was a crafts designer and editor. Maybe I could make a seat cover with some old macramé beads I had stored in the basement.

As I walked down the vacant hallways, passing one unoccupied office after another, the staccato rhythm of my heels against the Terrazzo floor echoed in the eerie silence. I don't often stay late; however, when I do put in overtime, I enjoy the calm silence that blankets the otherwise tumultuous environment that is *American Woman*.

Tonight, though, disquiet permeated the emptiness surrounding me. Disquiet and the distinct odor of hot glue. A prickly shiver crept its way up my spine, raising the tiny hairs at the back of my neck. I shivered, hugged my arms to my chest, and hurried around the corner to my own office.

The last thing I expected was to find Marlys sitting at my computer. She stared at the blank screen, her fingers poised on the keys. "Marlys? Can I help you with something?"

She didn't answer.

"Marlys?" I stepped into the cubicle and placed my hand on the chair's headrest. The chair swiveled around, the keyboard moving off my desk and hovering in the air under Marlys's fingertips.

FOUR

MARLYS STARED STRAIGHT AHEAD. She had ignored me plenty of times in the past, staring through me as if I were made of cellophane, but this time was different. The macabre scene sent a truckload of the willies careening through my stomach. Marlys wasn't just ignoring me this time.

Marlys was dead.

Just to be sure, I forced myself to reach for her wrist, hoping to find a pulse. After all, I'm no Quincy. Medical examiner isn't listed in my Trimedia job description.

Besides, only yesterday I had read about a dog who was run over by a car, shot by the responding cop to put it out of its misery, then stuck in a morgue freezer. And damned if that mutt didn't survive. You never know.

So I tamped down the squeamy ickies running riot through my own body and gingerly fingered Marlys's suspended wrist in the hope of discovering a beat. Her skin turned white under my searching touch, and no matter where I placed my fingers along the usual pulse points, I felt no signs of life.

The hot waxy smell of melted glue permeated the small office. Still plugged in, my hot glue gun lay on the counter next to the computer monitor. Its nozzle, caked with remnants of vermillion-colored silk, continued to disgorge grayish-white globs.

Strings of glue hung from Marlys, the chair, and the keyboard. Whoever had killed her had been in no rush to leave. He—or she—had taken the time to glue Marlys's body into my chair and attach her fingers to my keyboard.

I also noticed that he—or she—had taken the time to remove the Cartier diamond necklace, matching earrings, and hair clip.

For all I knew, the killer could still be lurking somewhere in the building. If my glue gun was still disgorging globules, he couldn't have finished his task too long ago.

At that thought, my knees buckled, and I grabbed for the first thing within reach to steady myself. Not a bright move, the nearest object being Marlys's shoulder. Her head slumped toward me, her hair prickling the top of my hand as if a thousand-legger had scampered across it.

I yelped as I jerked away and ran for the nearest exit as fast as my linguini legs would carry me.

Three flights of stairs later, huffing and puffing, thanks to my aversion to any form of exercise more strenuous than racing around Macy's during a three-hour sale, I pushed open the door and sprinted for the safety of my car.

I fumbled in my coat pocket for my keys. My hands shook like a wino with the DTs. Between rapidly panting breaths, I stabbed in the dark for the lock.

Of all the nights for the damn lamppost bulb to burn out! Or had it? I hazarded a quick glance upward as the key slid into the slot. The lamp was shattered. Jagged edges of glass glistened in the dim glow of a half-moon. Broken glass littered the ground. My heart galloped into my throat. Yanking open the door, I jumped behind the wheel, locked myself inside the Hyundai, and started the engine.

I had to call the police, but I wasn't about to wait for them in a dark parking lot with a killer on the loose. With my foot pressing the gas pedal to the floor, I sped out of the parking lot. Taking each turn on two wheels, I didn't slow down until I came to a well-lit twenty-four-hour Quickie Mart about a mile down the road.

Leaving the motor running, I grabbed for my cell phone and punched in the three digits.

"9-1-1 operator. State your emergency, please."

"M … m … murder." Even though I could barely get out the word, I couldn't shake the ghoulish image of Marlys's blank stare and creepy pose filling my head. "In my office," I added.

"Where are you, Ma'am?"

I stared at the sign above the store, the letters not making any sense to me. *Where am I?* I'm in some crazy alternate reality. People like me don't find dead bodies glued to their desk chairs. Then again, people like me don't get calls telling them their husband dropped dead in Las Vegas when he was supposed to be in Harrisburg. And people like me don't get threats from loan sharks owed money by that same dead husband. Obviously, this was all one very long nightmare, and if I concentrated hard enough, I'd wake up soon. The sooner the better.

"Ma'am? Are you still there?"

The operator's question snapped me out of the murder in-
duced stupor. I told her my location. "But that's not where the
dead body is."

"And where's that?"

I gave her the office address. "I was too scared to stay. I didn't
know if the killer was still in the building."

"Okay, ma'am. I'm sending a squad car to meet you. Stay where
you are, and I'll remain on the line until the officers arrive." Her
calm voice attempted to soothe my jangled nerves. She wasn't suc-
ceeding.

I had seen dead bodies before, most recently my own husband's,
but I had never stumbled across a murder victim. I doubt most
middle-class working mothers do—unless they happen to work in
law enforcement. Which I didn't.

Besides, a dead body in a casket reposes peacefully. Cushioned
in satin, the deceased's hands are either folded across his chest or
placed comfortably at his sides, his eyes closed. You can pretend
he's sleeping. Marlys definitely wasn't sleeping.

When a black and white cruiser pulled into the parking lot
three minutes later, I felt safe enough to end the call. I unlocked
my car, left the motor running, and stepped out into the frigid
night.

"Mrs. Pollack?" asked one of the officers, a giraffe of a man. I
had to crane my neck to see his face.

I nodded—as best I could with my head cricked back to my
shoulder blades.

"I'm Officer Garfinkle." He indicated the driver of the cruiser.
"This is Officer Simmons."

I had heard that shock can make normally sane people do really stupid things. I can now vouch for the truth of that statement. I glanced first at Officer Garfinkle, then at Officer Simmons, a squat, beefy-muscled black man with a shaved head and a gold stud in his left ear.

"Simmons and Garfinkle?" The hysteria I had fought back since finding Marlys's body erupted with a force equal to when Vesuvius buried Pompeii. Tears streamed down my cheeks, but not from crying.

I couldn't stop laughing.

The officers exchanged glances. Garfinkle sighed. "Mrs. Pollack, have you been drinking?"

I waved the question away with a flick of one hand while my other arm clutched my torso. "I'm sorry," I said, fighting to regain control.

I knew I'd pass a Breathalyzer test hands-down. A sanity test might be another story. Brushing the stream from my cheeks, I took a deep breath and tried to explain. "I ... it's been ... I didn't mean ... first a dead body and now Simmons and Garfinkle." I slapped my hand over my mouth and fought back another gush of hysterics. "And me standing in a *Hazy Shade of Winter* on my very own *Bridge Over Troubled Water*."

Simmons cocked his mouth into a wry grimace. "We're used to it."

I gasped, the laughter dying on my lips mid-chortle. "To murders?"

"The reaction to our names," said Garfinkle.

"What makes you so sure the victim was murdered?" asked Simmons.

Odd as it seemed to me, I suppose from the officer's viewpoint the question was legitimate. We weren't in Newark or Camden. We were out in the middle of nowhere. Surrounded by cornfields. Or what would become cornfields after spring planting.

"We don't get many murders around here," said Garfinkle. "This would be the first in over three years. If it is a murder."

I exhaled, my breath forming a cloud in the icy night air. "That's a relief, but you've got one now, and it's certainly not your run-of-the-mill murder."

Garfinkle raised his eyebrows. "Meaning?"

"Meaning, Officer, I doubt you've ever seen anything as bizarre as what I found in my office."

Simmons took a step closer to me and placed his hand on my upper arm. "We'd like you to accompany us back to your office, Mrs. Pollack. We have a forensics team on the way that will meet us there."

I rubbed at my quickly numbing arms. I was afraid they'd ask that, but someone needed to let them into the building, and I was the nearest someone—besides being the person who had discovered the body. They probably had a gazillion and ten questions to ask me. I turned to step back into my car, stumbling as I reached for the door.

Garfinkle grabbed for my other arm, nearly lifting me off the blacktop. "Would you like one of us to drive, ma'am? You look a little rattled."

A little? Any more rattled and I could pose as a baby's toy.

———

Less than fifteen minutes later a forensics team descended on my office. From the hall, flanked by Simmons and Garfinkle, I watched the technicians do their *CSI* thing—which bore little resemblance to the Hollywood version. Not surprising. I've seen plenty of television sitcoms set in magazine publishing houses. All of them were as realistic as *SpongeBob SquarePants*.

"So how do you think she died?" I heard one of the homicide detectives ask one of the evidence collectors. "I don't see any outward trauma."

"You're not gonna believe this one." Wearing a rubber glove, the technician unplugged my heavy-duty—emphasis on the *heavy*—hot glue gun and started to drop it into a plastic evidence collection bag.

"No, don't!" Everyone in the room spun around to face me. I pointed to the glue gun. "That nozzle is extremely hot. It'll melt a hole in the bottom of your bag."

Rather than appreciating the fact that I stopped him from contaminating evidence, the forensics investigator took offense. He dropped the gun into the bag and sealed it. "You telling me how to do my job, lady?"

I waved a hand at the bag. "Heaven forbid. You obviously don't need me, so I'm out of here. The front door will lock behind you when you leave."

I turned on my heels. One of the detectives placed his hand on my shoulder to stop me. "Garfinkle, why don't you take Mrs. Pollack down to the lobby so she can sit down?" he said. "We'll be with you shortly."

As we headed down the hall, Simmons to my left, Garfinkle to my right, I heard the unmistakable sound of plastic shattering against the Terrazzo floor. An extremely annoyed "Shit!" followed.

Simmons and Garfinkle exchanged glances, then stared at me. I offered them an I-told-him-so smile.

A few minutes later, two detectives joined us. "I'm Detective Batswin," said the woman who had asked about the cause of death.

She stood nearly six feet tall, dressed in a conservative dark-gray suit with a powder-blue-and-white pinstripe oxford shirt. She wore her silver-streaked sable hair tied back off a face devoid of make-up except for a slash of peach gloss across her lips. A long loop of liquid silver earrings that swayed as she spoke were her only adornment.

With a tilt of her head she indicated the man who had stopped me from leaving. "This is my partner, Detective Robbins."

I nodded to both of them, keeping my lips pursed tight for fear of letting loose another eruption of laughter. This was getting too weird. Simmons and Garfinkle as uniformed officers. The dynamic duo of Detectives Batswin and Robbins. Holy Spoonerisms, Gotham City! What was next? Woodstein and Bernward waving press passes?

"Can you tell us your connection to the deceased and how you happened to discover the body, Mrs. Pollack?" asked Robbins.

A compact middle-aged man who looked like he'd be more comfortable in sweats or jeans than his navy blue serge suit, he stood nearly a head shorter than his partner. The fluorescent lights of the lobby sparkled off his polished head. His Scooby-Doo tie suggested a sense of humor hidden behind steely gray eyes and a grim expression.

I explained why I had come back to the office. "I didn't expect anyone else to be here this late. Especially Marlys. I was surprised to see her car in the parking lot."

"Why is that?" asked Batswin.

"This morning she mentioned she had a dinner date in Manhattan."

"Was she meeting her date here?" asked Robbins, taking notes on a small pad with a stub of a pencil. Just like in every cop show I'd ever seen. Were all police budgets so tight that cops couldn't afford regulation size pencils, let alone PDAs?

"I was under the impression she was meeting him in the city."

"Do you know his name?"

"Some new designer. I can't remember. One of the other staff members might. Or Marlys's assistant. I wasn't paying much attention at the time."

"Why is that?" asked Batswin.

"Because Marlys is always bragging about her celebrity connections. I tune it out."

"You don't sound like you cared for her very much," said Robbins.

I laughed. "No one liked Marlys. Except Marlys. She collected enemies the way my kids collect video games and baseball cards."

When both detectives raised their eyebrows and glanced sideways at each other, I realized my mistake. "Look, in the past week I've lost my husband and discovered I'm in debt up the wazoo. Marlys and I didn't get along. That's no secret. She didn't get along with any of her co-workers. But she's way down on my pain-in-the-butt list. I didn't kill her."

Robbins paused taking notes and trapped me with that steely-eyed stare of his. "We didn't suggest you did, Mrs. Pollack."

Refusing to blink, I eyed him back. "I'm glad we have that cleared up, Detective."

"Can you think of anyone who hated Marlys enough to kill her?" asked Batswin.

I could think of a long list of people who probably dreamed of boiling Marlys in oil every night, but I also knew them well enough to know they weren't killers. Hugo had neither the strength nor the temperament. Naomi wouldn't stoop to something as low class as murder. And Erica was too much of a wuss to say boo to her boss, let alone whack her.

That left Vittorio Versailles. And he *had* threatened Marlys in front of an office full of witnesses. I mentioned to the detectives how he and his entourage had stormed into our offices earlier in the day.

"Anyone else?" asked Batswin.

"I suppose whoever wanted the diamonds."

"What diamonds?" both detectives asked in unison.

"They were on loan from Cartier. Marlys was wearing them this morning. A necklace, earrings, and hair clip."

"You mentioned your debt," said Batswin.

"For godsake, Detective, do you think if I took the diamonds, I'd be telling you about them?"

"Stranger things have happened, ma'am."

I rolled my eyes.

"You aren't planning any trips, are you, Mrs. Pollack?" asked Batswin.

"Does a trip to the supermarket count?"

"Cute. Don't leave town," said Robbins. "We'll be in touch."

A snappy rejoinder about how I didn't live in this town, let alone this county, probably wouldn't be an appropriate response at the moment. Not when I suspected that Detectives Batswin and Robbins had already mentally placed me on their Who Killed Marlys Vandenburg List. So I kept the comment firmly sealed behind my closed lips.

I wondered if the Dynamic Duo would even bother questioning Vittorio Versailles. Why should they? My big mouth had already handed them both motive and opportunity. As for method, it didn't take a Ph.D. in Forensics to figure out my glue gun had played some part in Marlys's murder.

Detective Batswin reached into her pocket, pulled out a business card, and handed it to me. "If you think of anything else, here's where you can reach me."

———

By the time I arrived home, it was nearly two in the morning. In less than five hours I had to turn around and head back to the office—if I'd even be allowed in my office. None of the cops had said anything one way or the other, but I suspected I'd find lots of yellow crime scene tape blocking the entrance to my cubicle tomorrow morning.

And I still had work to finish up before tomorrow's scheduled photo shoot. If there'd even be a photo shoot. At the moment, I was too tired to care.

I pulled into my driveway, expecting to find a darkened house. Instead every window was lit up like Rockefeller Plaza at Christmas.

A not-very-welcoming committee greeted me when I opened the front door.

FIVE

"ANASTASIA, WHERE IN THE world have you been at this ungodly hour?"

"Mama!" My mother enveloped me in one of her all-consuming embraces, my nose and mouth smothered by her eggplant-colored nubby wool suit. I twisted my head to gulp in some air, the wool scratching against my icy cheek.

"My poor baby. So young to be a widow!"

I stepped out of her bear hug and stared at her. "You know?"

"The boys told me." She jutted her chin toward the sofa where Lucille sat camped out in all her angry glory, the Devil Dog on her lap. "That despicable woman tried to keep me from entering the house."

"No one in her right mind comes calling after midnight," said Lucille. "She woke me out of a sound sleep. And scared Manifesto half to death the way she wouldn't stop pounding at the door."

Ignoring Lucille, Mama turned to me and launched into an accusatory tirade. "Why didn't you call? You had our itinerary in case of an emergency. If Karl dying doesn't qualify as an emergency, I don't know what does!"

Seamus O'Keefe, Mama's current husband, had taken her to Ireland several weeks ago to meet his family. I wanted to call her—would have called her—if I could have called her. "Because you mailed me your dry cleaning claim check instead of your travel schedule."

Mama's face glazed over in puzzlement. "Did I? So that's what happened to it. I turned the apartment upside-down looking for that damn piece of paper. Good thing the cleaner knows me. You remember that nice Mr. Wong, don't you, dear?"

"Focus, Mama."

"At this hour? You want coherent conversation, I need eight hours sleep." She shook her head to dismiss the birds from her brain. "Anyway, like I said, it was a good thing my grandsons woke up or I'd have frozen to death on your doorstep. That nasty taxi driver zoomed off the moment I stepped out of the cab."

She motioned toward Alex and Nick who were camped on the living room carpet. They both seemed to be enjoying this family farce far too much. Who needed reality TV? "You guys should get back to bed," I said. "Tomorrow's a school day."

"And miss the good stuff?" asked Nick.

I pointed in the direction of their bedroom. "Now!"

Mama blew them a kiss. "Sweet dreams, my knights in shining armor."

"'Night, Grandma."

"'Night, Mom."

Both pointedly ignored their other grandmother. Not that I blamed them. I'd like to ignore the old battle axe, too. However,

I'm the parent—the only one they had left—so I had to act like one. I cleared my throat, the universal Parent Signal.

"Good night, Grandmother Lucille," they sing-songed from halfway down the hall.

Lucille didn't even bother to respond with her usual, "Hmmph!"

"Saved me from frostbite or worse, those two sons of yours did," continued Mama. "Not to mention trying to find a hotel at this ungodly hour, not that I had any way to get to one. Can you imagine? Barred from my own daughter's home by Comrade Lucille!"

My mother, a lifelong member and past social secretary of the Daughters of the American Revolution was convinced my mother-in-law, president of the Greater New York area chapter of The Daughters of the October Revolution, was plotting to overthrow the government. Considering the total membership of The Daughters of the October Revolution consisted of thirteen semi-crippled female octogenarians, I found the threat negligible. Mama thought otherwise.

"We don't have room for her," said the Comrade in question. With one hand she clutched the lapels of her ratty gray robe to her throat. Her other hand rhythmically petted the growling Devil Dog curled up on her lap. With her closely cropped head of steel gray hair, her large ears, wrinkled skin, and perpetual scowl, my mother-in-law bore a more than striking resemblance to her bulldog. And right about now she looked two seconds away from echoing one of his deep, menacing growls.

I followed Mephisto's slit-eyed doggy grimace to the object of his own growl. Catherine the Great, my mother's extremely corpulent white Persian cat, crouched in attack mode on the fireplace mantle.

Mama had feigned innocence when I accused her of an ulterior motive in naming the cat, but I knew she knew it would annoy the hell out of Lucille. Anything smacking of Czarist Russia launched Lucille into seethe mode. I suspected Mama was trying to provoke the old bat into a stroke.

"Braaaawk!" Ralph kept watch over the interlopers from the relative safety of the top of the bookcase. Luckily, he could take wing faster than Catherine the Great could pounce, thanks to her over-indulgent mistress.

I glanced around the room; a queasy feeling tiptoed its way into my stomach. "Where's Seamus?"

"Dead."

"What!"

"*He's dead*," said Ralph, with a squawk for emphasis. "*Troilus and Cressida*. Act Five, Scene Ten."

"Honestly, Anastasia, when are you going to get rid of that filthy flying rat?"

I glared at Ralph, daring him to comment further. He glared back but kept his beak shut. Sometimes Ralph seemed smarter than all the rest of us put together, and I suspected he knew it.

I turned back to my mother. "Forget Ralph, Mama. What happened to Seamus?"

"That damn parrot of Penelope's will outlive us all. What is he? A hundred years old by now?"

"Mama! Can we *please* get back to Seamus?"

With her classic Talbots fashion sense and chin-length, L'Oreal-enhanced natural strawberry blonde waves, on a good day Flora Sudberry Periwinkle Ramirez Scoffield Goldberg O'Keefe bore a striking resemblance to Ellen Burstyn as the older Doris in *Same Time Next Year*.

Today was not a good day.

Seamus's death and jet lag had taken their toll on my mother. She still looked like Ellen Burstyn, but more like the lonely widow Sara Goldfarb in *Requiem for a Dream*.

Mama's face became a haggard mask of resignation. She inhaled deeply, releasing the breath in a dramatic sigh. "Face it, Anastasia. When it comes to men, I'm cursed." She collapsed onto one of the two overstuffed easy chairs that flanked the bay window. "He *had* to kiss that damn Blarney Stone! I told him it was dangerous, but would he listen to me? No!"

I'd never been to Ireland, let alone Blarney Castle, but I assumed they had certain safeguards in place for such a popular tourist attraction. "He fell?"

"No, no, no. He suffered a fatal cerebral aneurysm when he leaned backward to kiss that damn stone. Died instantly. And on our six-month anniversary!"

Poor Seamus. So much for the luck of the Irish. And poor Mama.

Flora Sudberry Periwinkle Ramirez Scoffield Goldberg O'Keefe had a knack for losing husbands. With Seamus gone, she was fast approaching Liz Taylor territory. In truth, Mama didn't lose them so much as they wound up dying on her in a succession of odd circumstances. My own father had drowned while scuba diving in the Yucatan on their twenty-fifth anniversary.

A year and a half later, Mama remarried. Husband Number Two, an adventure-seeking daredevil, lasted four months before the bulls gored him to death as he raced through the streets of Pamplona.

Number Three made it to their first anniversary. Barely. Highly allergic to shellfish and having forgotten to bring along his epinephrine, he asphyxiated after inhaling the aroma from a sizzling platter of shrimp that a waiter carried past their table.

Number Four lost his footing at the Grand Canyon and plunged to his death during their honeymoon.

So now Mama was once again widowed. A temporary situation. Mama was the kind of woman who needed a man. And whenever Mama was between husbands, she came to stay with us.

Except that every other time Mama had camped out at *Casa Pollack* during a husband-hunting campaign, we hadn't been stuck with Lucille. If I bunked them together, would either still be alive tomorrow morning?

The grandfather clock in the hall bonged two-thirty. Mephisto growled.

Catherine the Great hissed.

Ralph squawked.

Lucille glared a SCUD missile at Mama.

Mama countered with a Patriot missile aimed back at Lucille.

Batswin and Robbins suspected me of murder.

Ricardo wanted his fifty grand, or else.

A multi-species World War III was about to erupt in my living room.

How lucky could one slightly overweight, more than slightly in debt, middle-aged widow get?

King Solomon would have thrown his arms up in defeat if he'd had to figure out sleeping arrangements at *Casa Pollack* that night. Nick had already doubled-up in Alex's room, sleeping on the trundle. That left the trundle under the twin in his room, where Lucille now slept, and my master bedroom with its queen-size bed and attached bathroom.

Call me selfish, but having already lost my husband and my financial security last week, I wasn't about to give up half my bed this week. Not even to my mother.

I took a mental deep breath and laid out the sleeping arrangements. "Mama, I'm afraid you and Lucille will have to share a room."

"Absolutely not," said Lucille. She grabbed her cane and pounded it into the carpet. Mephisto yelped. "She can sleep with you. My room is too small."

I refused to let my mother-in-law boss me around in my own home. Comrade Lucille could share. Like a good communist. "No." I turned to my mother, "Mama, I'm sorry."

Her jaw dropped, her eyes widened in horror. "Anastasia, you can't—"

"I'm the one paying room and board," said Lucille, her voice rising several octaves. "That entitles me to a room of my own."

"Paying?" Mama's brow wrinkled. "You mean she's not just visiting?"

"Unfortunately."

"That woman's *living* with you?" Mama's shrieked question did wonders for the headache that had begun the moment I walked in the house—ratcheting it up from a quartet of percussionists to the entire New York Philharmonic pounding out the *1812 Overture*. At glass-shattering decibels. I quickly explained about the fire. And Lucille's life savings going up in flames.

Mama turned on Lucille. "Wake up and smell the twenty-first century, you stupid old Bolshevik cow. The Depression ended over sixty years ago. Ever hear of FDIC? Banks have been safe for decades."

Lucille pounced on Mama. "Capitalists like you caused the Depression. It happened once; it can happen again. FDIC or no FDIC. Ever hear of Enron? Or Tyco? Or WorldCom?"

That was hitting below the belt. Mama had heard of all three. She'd lost much of her retirement savings because of them. And Lucille knew it.

"Enough!" I grabbed my mother's suitcase and marched down the hall. On my way to what used to be Nick's room, I grabbed a set of fresh sheets, a blanket, and a pillow from the linen closet. Behind me I heard Mama and Lucille continuing their political knock-down, drag-out boxing match.

Forget détente. I needed an Iron Curtain between their beds.

After dumping Mama's suitcase and the linens, I headed for the kitchen. Yanking open the freezer door, I grabbed a bag of frozen peas, a spoon, and the last carton of Ben and Jerry's I'd be able to afford for Lord knew how many decades. After settling into bed, I placed the bag of peas across my pounding forehead, closed my eyes, and savored a large spoonful of Chunky Monkey.

———

Thirty minutes later I was basking on a deserted, sunny beach in Maui. Sipping a frozen pina colada, I sank my toes into the warm sand and my mind into the latest of Janet Evanovich's Stephanie Plum books.

As I inhaled the rich scent of orchids, the ground began to rumble and shake. An angry Kilauea yanked me off the sand and out of REM sleep.

I glanced at the illuminated digital display on my alarm clock. With a groan, I rolled over to confront the volcano. "Mama, please, I have to get up for work in a few hours. I can't have you sleeping with me."

"I simply cannot share a room with that woman!" she said, burrowing under the blankets beside me. In the process she appropriated more than her fair share of both the mattress and the quilts.

"Do you know that woman snores like an elephant? And so does that damn dog of hers. Except when he's growling at Catherine the Great. I'm afraid he'll attack my poor precious if I doze off."

The aforementioned corpulent pussy jumped on the bed, settling her royal rump in my face. In less than three minutes both Mama and Catherine the Great were snoring loud enough to rattle the windows, and I was wide awake.

I yanked my pillow out from under Catherine the Great, grabbed one of the quilts off the bed, my portable alarm clock from the nightstand, and headed for the den. With luck, Ralph would be asleep and not wake from the nocturnal intrusion into his domain. I could do without Shakespeare at three in the morning.

As I made my way down the darkened hall, I spit cat hairs from between my lips. Mama was missing the entrepreneurial venture of a lifetime. Catherine the Great shed enough fur to provide Dolly Parton with an unending supply of wigs, which would in turn provide Mama with a steady income—something she sorely needed, given her penchant for marrying men who lived way beyond their means and left her with little besides short-lived memories.

For the next several hours I tossed and turned on my makeshift bed. The den couch had seen better days a decade ago. A replacement had been at the head of my home improvements list for ages, but something more pressing always bumped it back to Number Two. Or Three. Or Thirty. Like a leaky roof. Or a dead washing machine.

Or a gambling husband.

Besides a lumpy couch keeping me awake, thoughts of extortion and murder raced through my veins and my brain like a triple-shot espresso. Every time I closed my eyes, I saw a dead Marlys, heard a threatening Ricardo. Saw the crime-fighting duo of Batswin and Robbins jabbing their accusatory fingers in my face. And I still had no idea what I was going to do when Ricardo demanded his money a few short hours from now.

A discordant orchestra made up of Mama and Lucille and Mephisto and Catherine the Great played in the background. Above the din of their grumbling and griping and growling and hissing, Ralph squawked, "*Help, ho! Murder! Murder! Othello*. Act Five, Scene One." Eyes open or closed, the nightmare pounded in my head.

I tossed and turned and tossed some more. Finally, out of sheer exhaustion, my brain called it a night—or a morning, considering the late hour—and drifted me back to the sands of Maui.

A moment later the alarm clock screamed the arrival of six A.M.

SIX

"Mom! We're gonna miss the bus," yelled Alex a short time later. "Grandmother Lucille's set up base camp in the bathroom."

"For a change," added Nick.

"And Grandma Flora's taken your bathroom hostage," continued Alex.

"Tell me about it," I muttered. The moment I'd stepped out of my bathroom in search of clean underwear, Mama had commandeered the commode, locking herself in and taking my hairdryer and make-up prisoner.

I pounded on the door. "Mama, are you coming out any time soon?"

"I don't think so, dear. Having a bit of a problem this morning."

Lord, please don't let me have inherited Mama's internal plumbing, I prayed as I headed for the other bathroom. One working mother, two elderly women with an assortment of semi-dysfunctional bodily functions, and two hormone-driven studmuffin teenagers definitely required more than two bathrooms and a forty-gallon hot water heater.

I pounded on the door of the hall bathroom. "Lucille, the boys need to get in there." She didn't answer. I tried the knob. Locked.

I pounded harder. Mephisto's bark echoed off the tile. "Lucille!"

"Leave me alone. I'm busy!" A sound better left to the confines of the bathroom punctuated her statement. The Devil Dog yelped.

"She cares more about that dog than she does us," said Nick.

"We don't choose our relatives," I said, as much as I wished otherwise.

"I'll bet Dad was secretly adopted," said Alex.

"Or maybe stolen at birth," offered Nick. "He was nothing like her. Ever."

In truth Karl had been the complete opposite of his mother in both appearance and personality, not to mention political persuasion. Then again, had Karl been more like his mother, I never would have married him, and I wouldn't currently be treading water in the middle of piranha-infested Lake Titicaca. Pun intended.

Karl had inherited all his genes from his father. Or so I assumed. According to my husband, his father had walked out on them shortly after knocking up his mother. No one had seen or heard from Isidore Pollack since.

Another sound best left undescribed erupted from behind the door.

"What's she doing in there?" asked Alex.

"I'm not sure I want to know."

"We need another bathroom," said Nick.

I offered him a wry, caffeine and sleep deprived grin. "I'll add it to my list."

"Sorry, Mom," he mumbled. I hadn't yet told my sons the full extent of our financial problems, but I did have to tell them something of the situation. Our lifestyle had to change and change fast. They'd taken the news as best as can be expected from typical teenage boys, which is to say not well at all.

I dreaded having to tell them all that I'd left out. Like their now nonexistent college accounts. Only a year and a half away from college, Alex had his heart set on Harvard. Until last week, I believed we'd have no trouble swinging the steep Ivy League fees. Today we couldn't even afford the local community college. Coward that I am, I kept putting off the college discussion. But now that Lucille knew the extent of our pauperdom, I knew I had to tell my kids soon.

Nick fixed his gaze on a dust bunny that had taken up residence between the carpet runner and the baseboard. Or maybe it was one of Catherine the Great's hairballs. Something else I didn't want to know at six-thirty in the morning. Cleaning came last on my to-do list right now. Not that it had ever ranked all that high, but there are just so many hours in the day, and a girl's got to juggle and prioritize.

And delegate.

As soon as they decamped from the bathrooms, I'd assign Mama and Lucille cleaning and laundry detail. I didn't dare ask them to take over the cooking. Either they'd burn the house down or we'd all wind up with a case of food poisoning. Possibly both.

I placed my hand on Nick's shoulder. "We'll get through this."

"How?"

"I haven't a clue, but we will. Meanwhile, go use the bathroom in the apartment above the garage."

"I thought we were going to rent that out."

"We are. As of Saturday. And don't worry about the bus. I'll drive you both to school."

The phone rang as the boys headed toward the back door. "I'll get it," Alex yelled.

A moment later he called out, "Hey, Mom, it's for you. Some guy. Says it's important."

I grabbed the phone, placed my hand over the mouthpiece and pointed to the back door. "Hurry up," I told the boys. I waited until they closed the door behind them before speaking into the phone.

"Hello?" As much as I hoped it was that guy from Publisher's Clearing House telling me I'd won a million dollars, I knew immediately it was my not-so-friendly neighborhood loan shark.

"Got my money?"

"I told you, I don't have your money."

Ricardo made a noise that sounded halfway between a *tsk* and a kiss. "And I happen to know otherwise. Check your safe deposit box recently?"

"Look, for all I know Karl never even met you. What proof do I have that he owed you any money?"

"My word."

I snorted. "Since when is the word of an extortionist worth anything?"

"Extortionist?" His tone grew more menacing. "Look, lady, I staked that no-good weasel husband of yours to fifty G's. I know for a fact he got the dough to pay me back. Now I want it, and I intend to get it. *Capisce*?"

61

"And I'm telling you I don't have it. Karl left me with nothing but debt."

"Then you'd better find some way to get it. And remember, Sweet Cheeks, you tell the cops, and you live to regret it. Get my drift?"

I clenched the receiver so tightly that my knuckles turned white and my fingers throbbed. "Stop threatening me!"

"No threats, Sweet Cheeks. Facts. By the way, those are two handsome looking kids you got there. Spittin' image of their old man. Sure would be a shame if they lost those good looks."

"No!" I clamped a hand over my mouth to stifle my strangled cry. My words came out in a choked whisper. "Leave my sons alone. Please! You'll get your money. I just need some time."

"You got a week."

"That's not enough!"

"One week." The phone went dead.

———

Marlys's murder aside, I couldn't wait to get to work. Another day of backstabbing office politics would seem like a week at The Golden Door Spa compared to dealing with widowhood, pauperdom, and getting shaken down by a loan shark—not to mention dealing with Lucille and Mama.

Some sadist had yanked me out of my dull but normal life and plunked me down in the middle of a Janet Evanovich novel. What would Stephanie Plum do? I pondered this question on my drive to work. Stephanie never had to worry, though. No matter how big the mess she found herself in, good old Janet would write her a happy ending. No such luck for me. My problems were real. They weren't about to disappear with the stroke of a pen or click of a keyboard.

By the time I arrived at work, an hour late and with damp hair, speculative gossip circled the halls of Trimedia. Half the staff crowded around the entrance to my cubicle. They scattered like cockroaches as I approached. All except Cloris and Daphne.

"Did you hear?" asked Daphne. Her wild mane of Nicole Kidman red curls bounced on her shoulders as she bounced on the balls of her Payless mock alligator pumps. "Someone killed Marlys last night. Here. In your office."

That last bit of information seemed a tad redundant, considering, as I'd suspected, yellow crime tape barred the entrance to my cubicle. "I know," I told her. "I found the body."

"Shut up!" she shrieked.

"You didn't!" cried Cloris.

I gave them a quick recap of my late-night adventure after returning to the office.

"Ewww!" Daphne hugged her arms around her chest and shivered, whether from her belly button-showcasing ivory lace crop-top or from revulsion was anyone's guess. "That's too weird."

"Someone sure has a sick sense of humor," said Cloris. "Who do you think did it?"

"Marlys had more enemies than friends. I'd imagine there's a long list of people who hated her."

"But enough to kill her?" asked Daphne, her wide-eyed gaze fixed on my nearly empty office. The police had confiscated my computer, my desk chair, all my supplies, and—worst of all—the three dozen satin birdseed roses scheduled for this morning's photo shoot.

A thin coating of black fingerprint powder dusted the empty counters and shelves. Was I expected to clean up the mess or could I cajole the janitor into tackling the chore? "Do you think crime scene cleanup is included in the janitor's job description?" I asked.

"Don't count on it," said Daphne. "Those guys are unionized."

Have I mentioned how low a priority cleaning is on my to-do list?

"We all need to pull double Erica shifts," said Cloris, a flaky croissant poised in front of her mouth. "She's shaken up something awful. That poor kid is about to have a nervous breakdown."

Just what I needed with everything else going on in my life, more Erica babysitting duty.

I eyed the croissant, my salivary glands kicking into overdrive. Not only hadn't I had time to dry my hair, I hadn't even downed my eye-opening morning cup of java, let alone breakfast. "Got any more of those?" I asked.

Cloris took a bite and spoke around the mouthful of flaky pastry. "Two dozen in the break room. Compliments of *Cuisine a Go-Go.*" Several crumbs landed on the forest green Kiss the Cook chef's apron that covered her 32AA bosom. One by one, she picked them off and popped them into her mouth. Cloris hated waste.

"*Cuisine a Go-Go?*"

"I kid you not. It's a new take-out franchise. Non-traditional fast food. Mostly French. You should try the escargot burger."

"Thanks but I'll pass."

She grinned. "Okay, so maybe escargot burgers won't catch on in Peoria—or even New Jersey—but the croissants are to die for."

"Not the best turn of a phrase under the circumstances," I said.

"Right. Sorry."

I scowled in the direction of my empty cubicle. Hopefully, Naomi could juggle the photo schedule. After all, it wasn't every day I found a dead body sitting at my computer. Besides, Batswin and Robbins had kidnapped my projects and supplies, and there was a croissant in the break room calling my name. Both extremely legitimate reasons why I couldn't go ahead with the scheduled photo shoot.

"So tell me about Erica," I said, making a beeline for the break room. Anything to take my mind off Ricardo, Marlys, and my other problems.

"She's worried the police will think she did it," said Cloris as she and Daphne followed behind me. "They've been questioning her in the conference room for over twenty-five minutes."

"I expect they'll question all of us," I said.

"For nearly half an hour?" asked Cloris. "They must suspect something. With me it was slam, bam, thank you, ma'am. In and out in no time."

"Me, too," said Daphne. "I don't think I was in there more than two minutes. But you know how Marlys treated Erica. If the cops get wind of that from anyone, Erica becomes *Suspect Numero Uno*."

"As soon as the police question her, they'll realize Erica isn't capable of squishing an ant, let alone whacking her boss," I said as we entered the break room, an oversized, dingy closet of a space, outfitted with a compact sink, mini-refrigerator, microwave, chipped Formica table, and four rickety plastic chairs.

I grabbed a Styrofoam coffee cup off the shelf above the microwave. "Besides, I'm pretty sure the police already have a suspect."

"Who?" they both asked at once.

I lifted the coffeepot off the burner, filled the cup with the last of the brew, and took a huge swig before I answered. "Me."

"Shut up!" cried Daphne, giving me a hard jab to my upper arm. The coffee cup flew from my hand, spattering over the counter and floor.

"Sorry! Didn't mean for that to happen." She ripped off enough paper towels to sop up all five Great Lakes and went to work on the mess.

I stared at the now empty coffeepot. *My kingdom for a cup of caffeine!*

"I'll make a fresh pot," offered Cloris, noting the desperation that I'm sure had telegraphed its way from my caffeine-starved corpuscles to my face. She pulled out the basket of used grounds and dumped them into the trash. "In need of a fix, huh?"

I grabbed a croissant, collapsed into a chair, and pushed a few strands of damp hair behind my ear. "Desperate enough to suck on unground beans."

"I don't get it," said Daphne, trashing the coffee-saturated paper towels. "Erica, I can understand. But why you, Anastasia?"

"Yeah, why you?" asked Cloris. "Naomi I could understand. She sure had reason to want the bitch dead. Not to mention Hugo after the way she walked out on him after he lost control of the company."

"Or Vittorio Versailles," added Daphne. "Remember how he threatened to kill her yesterday? But not you, Anastasia. Why would the police suspect you?"

"Yes, do tell."

I turned toward the entrance of the break room. Detective Batswin filled the doorway.

SEVEN

MOMENTS BEFORE, THE CROISSANT had sent my salivary glands into flood mode. Now my mouth had transformed into the Kalahari. During an extended drought. I forced myself to swallow. "Detective Batswin."

She wore the same tailored gray suit from last night, but she had traded the pinstripe shirt for a solid white one and the silver earrings for a pair of dream catchers. The long black and white feathers, falling nearly to her shoulders, echoed the light and dark shades of her hair.

"I think you and I need to have another chat, Mrs. Pollack."

I glanced at Cloris and Daphne. Both had gone as white as over-bleached poltergeists. They cast worried glances at each other, then at me.

"I'll bring you some coffee when it's done brewing," said Cloris.

I mumbled my thanks, then feeling like a dead woman walking, trailed Detective Batswin down the hall to the conference room.

Detective Robbins was waiting for us. Mighty Mouse had replaced Scooby-Doo as the crime-fighting cartoon character tie of choice, but the detective's grim expression of last night remained in place.

"Have a seat, Mrs. Pollack," he said, indicating the chair normally reserved for Hugo. He and Batswin settled in at either side of me.

My clammy hands knotted into a perfect facsimile of a mutant pretzel, my breathing on hiatus for the unforeseeable future, I waited for the good cop/bad cop interrogation to begin. Over the years I've seen my share of *Law & Order* episodes. I knew the routine.

Batswin began. "We found something interesting on your computer, Mrs. Pollack."

"Excuse me?"

This was the last thing I expected to hear. Besides company memos and work-related e-mails, my computer contained nothing other than design and word processing files for past, current, and future issues. Trimedia had a strict policy against using company computers for private net surfing or e-mails. Playing Tetris or FreeCell or Solitaire, even after hours, was grounds for immediate dismissal.

"Who's R?" asked Robbins.

"I have no idea."

He removed a sheet of paper from a manila folder and passed it face-down across the table.

I picked it up and turned it over.

From: R
To: Anastasia Pollack
Subject: 50Gs
Friday. Or else.

I gasped, dropping the paper as if it were as blistering as the wax from my hot glue gun. How had Ricardo gotten my work e-mail addy?

More importantly, how was I going to explain his threatening message to the two very suspicious detectives now glaring at me?

Trapped.

No way could I lie my way out of this situation. Karl was the poker face in our family, not me. If I ever tried to fib my way through a polygraph, the needle would leap around so frenetically, it would break off and fly clear across the room, impaling Mighty Mouse to Robbins' thick chest. Reluctantly, I realized I had no choice but to tell Batswin and Robbins about Karl and Ricardo.

Before I could begin, though, there was a light rap at the door. Robbins rose to answer it.

Cloris entered with a tray containing three cups of coffee. Her questioning eyes, filled with a combination of blatant curiosity and genuine worry, scoured my face. "You okay?" she mouthed, as soon as she had positioned herself with her back to Batswin and Robbins.

I reached for some coffee and wrapped my sub-zero digits around the Styrofoam. My trembling hands caused a tidal wave of java to slosh ominously within the cup. Biting down on my lower lip, I shook my head ever so slightly.

Her eyes bugged out. As she scurried from the conference room, I regretted the silent communication that had passed between us. Cloris was my closest friend at Trimedia, but that friendship had never been tested by such juicy gossip as Anastasia getting grilled by the cops.

Once the door clicked behind Cloris, I took a deep swig of caffeine before plunging into an account of the events of last week. I doubt Batswin and Robbins expected to hear anything so bizarre. But then again, they were cops. And this was New Jersey.

"But I didn't kill Marlys," I said in conclusion.

I glanced from Batswin to Robbins and then back to Batswin. They both stared at me, Batswin's expression just as grim as Robbins's.

"You have to believe me."

Neither looked all that convinced.

"And I didn't take the diamonds," I continued. "I'm the one who found the body and called the police, remember? I'm the one who told you about the diamonds in the first place. Why would I be stupid enough to tell you about them if I took them to pay off Ricardo?"

"To cover your tracks?" suggested Robbins.

At that moment I felt like pounding my head on the battered conference table. Maybe I shouldn't have told them anything. Too late I thought about the need for a lawyer—not that I could afford one.

And forget court-appointed counsel. Over the years, I'd read and seen enough news accounts, not to mention all those *Law & Order* episodes, to figure out that court-appointed attorneys were as effective as mosquito repellant in January—in Siberia.

Besides, I don't think the court appoints representation until after a person's been formally charged with a crime. So far, at least, I was lucky in that respect. Although my current predicament had driven my normally rational and focused brain to digress into the land of irrelevant minutia.

But if I had refused to speak before consulting an attorney, wouldn't Batswin and Robbins take that as an admission of guilt? Or at least that I knew something I wasn't telling them?

I asked the question I dreaded hearing the answer to. "Do I need to call a lawyer?"

"Do you?" asked Robbins.

The man had a maddening habit of answering my questions with ones of his own. My entire body, let alone my voice, quaked like the California coastline after a seismic shift of the San Andreas Fault. "Are you going to charge me with Marlys's murder?"

Batswin shook her head. She removed a sheaf of papers from a beat-up leather satchel sitting on the chair next to her. "Not for now. I'm still trying to decide whether or not to believe you, Mrs. Pollack."

Instead of taking comfort in her statement, the blood in my veins turned as cold as a Slurpee. Her *not for now* hung ominously in the air above me like a craft knife suspended by a frayed strand of embroidery floss. Any moment the strand would break, and the knife would fall. Piercing one of my vital organs.

Detective Batswin spent the next eon rifling through the pages. Then she glanced up and trapped me with her nearly ebony eyes. "My gut suggests you're telling the truth, but that could just be the tasty memory of last night's tequila and enchiladas."

Several of the frayed floss fibers split, and the knife dropped lower, dangling precariously above my heart. I saw through her. She expected me to drop my guard. Make a mistake. Then she'd swoop in for the kill. Or in this case, the arrest. But I had no guard to drop. I didn't murder Marlys.

"I'm curious," said Robbins. "Since you've already admitted you intend to pay off this Ricardo, where did you plan to get the money?"

I told them about renting out the apartment over the garage. "If I can't get him to leave me alone, I'm hoping he'll allow me to pay off the debt over time."

Robbins and Batswin exchanged incredulous expressions, their eyes nearly rolling out of their heads. "And you really believe he'll go for that? Accepting a grand or two when he's owed fifty? And what about interest? Have you got any idea how much loan sharks charge?"

I hadn't thought of that. "I'm showing good faith."

Robbins slammed his hand on the table, rattling the coffee tray. And me. "What you're showing is two tons of stupidity, Mrs. Pollack."

My voice strangled in my throat as it rose several octaves. "Damn it! He threatened to hurt my kids."

Batswin steepled her hands in front of her on the table and spoke in a modulated, unemotional tone that set off alarm sirens inside me. "Most likely, you're dealing with organized crime. Loan sharks around here are usually connected to the mob. They don't want to hear excuses."

"Show up with only partial payment," added Robbins, his voice as grim as his words, "and you'll be wearing cement mukluks before the day is out."

Suddenly my shoes felt much heavier than the pair of Nine West black pumps I had slipped into that morning. I fought back an uncontrollable urge to check my feet. I knew Batswin and Robbins were serious, not just trying to scare the shit out of me. This is New Jersey where cement shoes come in all styles and sizes.

"We can help you," he added.

"How?" And what would they want in return?

"We'll put a tap on your phone. When this Ricardo creep calls to set up a drop, we'll nab him."

"I don't live in this county. It's out of your jurisdiction, isn't it?"

"You let us worry about the details," said Batswin.

It sounded so easy, so simple. And that's what scared me. "But what if something goes wrong? What if he gives you the slip? What if you arrest him and some slick lawyer gets him off? What happens to my kids, then?"

"You've been watching too much television," said Robbins. "We're not as incompetent as Hollywood portrays us."

"And I'm not that gullible, Detective. I also read the newspapers."

Robbins leaned in close, his palms and forearms flat against the table, Mighty Mouse dangling from his neck as if the mouse were about to swoop down and save the day. Robbins' stormy gray eyes narrowed, his voice grew menacing. "We don't need your permission, Mrs. Pollack. Extortion is a crime. We can get a court order to tap your phone."

"This is a nightmare," I moaned.

"Then end it," said Batswin.

They gave me no choice. "All right."

"We'll supply you with the fifty thousand dollars," said Robbins.

Marked bills, no doubt. Meanwhile, between now and the time they caught Ricardo, they'd hear every word spoken over my phone line.

Which was probably the reason they were so eager to help me get rid of Ricardo. They expected to glean information about Marlys's murder from listening in on all my private conversations.

Dumb cops. All they'd hear is carpooling arrangements, teenage pseudo phone sex, Fantasy Baseball player trades, and The Daughters of the October Revolution plotting to take over the world.

But if Batswin and Robbins could rid me of Ricardo, at least I'd have one less two-thousand-pound gorilla sitting on my chest. I'd also have the money from the apartment rental to pay the overdue utility bills.

Now if I could only cajole the Dynamic Duo into taking Lucille…

As I left the conference room, I paused, my hand on the doorknob, and turned to face them. "Do you know yet how Marlys died?"

Batswin shook her head. "We're still waiting for the lab results."

I opened the door to find Erica hovering on the other side.

EIGHT

ERICA HUGGED HER MIDSECTION, her face a pastiche of worry and fear. Grabbing my arm, she hurried me down the hall to the empty break room. "What did they say?" she asked after closing the door behind us. Her nervous whisper quaked around snuffles and tears as she poured coffee for both of us. "Did they ask about me?"

"No, why?"

She placed the coffee on the table, then dug in her pocket for a used tissue. Choking back a panicked sob, she collapsed into one of the plastic chairs, her voice muffled by her fists and the crumpled tissue she pressed against her face. "I think they think I had something to do with it. They questioned me for nearly an hour."

"They're questioning all of us, Erica. That's how they do their job."

Tears spilled onto her cheeks and bounced into her lap, raining dark blue spots on her stone-washed denim jumper. "But everyone knows how Marlys treated me, how I hated her," she wailed.

"I think they're quickly learning that lots of people hated Marlys. Do you have an alibi for last night?"

"I was with Dicky. Except for when he left for a few hours to meet with a client. But I didn't tell the detectives about that. I was too scared."

"Dicky?"

A deep scarlet suffused Erica's pale cheeks; a shy smile tickled the corners of both her mouth and eyes. "My boyfriend," she mumbled.

"Erica!" I plunked into one of the other plastic chairs that surrounded the rickety, coffee-stained Formica table.

Erica had a boyfriend? We all assumed she went home every night to an empty apartment and microwavable meals-for-one. She had never mentioned a boyfriend. Hell, Erica had never mentioned having a date.

It was nice to know that someone's life was picking up, unlike mine, which had recently received a royal flushing down the toilet. "How long has this been going on?"

"A few months."

"Why have you been keeping him a secret?"

"I didn't want Marlys to find out. You know how she is ... was. She'd say he's a real loser if he's going out with me. He's not, though. Dicky's a very successful businessman. He's a financial advisor and owns his own company with lots of employees."

Her slight smile blossomed into a sheepish grin. She spoke into her lap. "And he really likes me."

"I'm happy for you, Erica."

She blew her nose in what was left of the tissue. "I guess I don't have to hide my relationship with Dicky anymore. Now that Marlys is gone."

"Relationship? This sounds serious."

"I guess you could say that." She averted her eyes; her cheeks deepened to the shade of a cooked lobster. "We're living together."

"Really?"

"Does that shock you?"

"Why should it shock me?"

"Well, you being older and all..."

Ouch! She made me sound like I had one foot in Little Old Lady Land. "I'm only forty-two. Besides, your generation didn't invent cohabitation."

"My father would disown me if he found out. Heck, he nearly disowned me when I moved out of the house and got my own apartment. He said nice girls live at home until they get married."

No wonder Erica made the proverbial dormouse look like the proverbial king of the jungle. The poor kid had grown up under the thumb of some domineering nineteenth-century Neanderthal. Then she had the misfortune to go to work for his twenty-first century Amazon counterpart. Talk about jumping from the wok into the inferno.

"Dicky's the first good thing that's ever happened to me," she said as if reading my thoughts.

Of that I had no doubt. I raised my coffee cup in a toast. "Here's to the first of many."

Her eyebrows knit together. "I don't want many boyfriends. I just want Dicky."

"Of many good things in your life."

She blushed. "Oh." Then she raised her coffee cup to meet mine.

Before we could click Styrofoam to Styrofoam, a knock sounded at the door. Batswin entered between my and Erica's simultaneous "Come" and "in," catching us with our cups in mid-toast.

"Celebrating something?"

Erica cringed at the sound of Batswin's voice. Her hand shook so hard, she nearly dropped her cup.

"In a manner of speaking," I said, "but it's personal. Nothing to do with your investigation."

Batswin walked over to the coffeepot and helped herself to a cup. "I'll be the judge of that," she said, her back turned to us.

I glanced at Erica. Her features froze into a tense mask, but I figured it was better to be truthful than to let Batswin assume we had something to hide from her. "Erica has a new boyfriend."

At the sound of *new*, the terror and tension melted from Erica's face, and she offered me a slight smile. Poor kid. She didn't want Batswin to think she was a loser, that she had never had a boyfriend before Dicky.

Batswin lowered herself into one of the remaining chairs, directly opposite me, her large form appearing less than comfortable squeezed into the cheap molded plastic seat. "Congratulations." She raised her cup toward Erica before taking a long sip.

"Thank you," mumbled Erica.

"Is there something we can help you with, Detective, or did you only come in for a hit of caffeine?" I asked.

Batswin lowered her cup to the table and held it between both her hands. She leveled her midnight eyes at me. I fought back the shiver that threatened to claim my body. Wheels were turning behind those sharp black orbs, and I wasn't sure they were necessarily the wheels of justice. At least not justice for me, no matter what she said about believing I didn't kill Marlys.

"I just spoke with the coroner," she said.

Erica sank deeper into her chair, as if trying to become invisible. I leaned forward, clutching my coffee cup. "You know who killed Marlys?"

"Not who. What."

"And?"

Batswin's stare grew darker, more pointed. "Marlys Vandenburg was killed with your glue gun, Mrs. Pollack, and the only prints on it are yours."

NINE

I COULDN'T WRAP MY mind around the preposterous idea of my trusty hot glue gun as a murder weapon. After all, a glue gun wasn't the weapon of choice for most murderers. Didn't killers tend to favor guns with bullets? You could get a pretty nasty burn from a hot glue gun if you weren't careful, but that was about all.

Unless … "Was she hit over the head with it?" I didn't remember seeing any lumps or bruises on Marlys, but I was too freaked at the time to take inventory.

"She was suffocated with the glue," said Batswin.

Suffocated? With a glue gun? I studied Batswin to see if she was trying to trick me in some way. Her features remained expressionless, a blank expanse between the two dream catchers swaying from her ear lobes.

I voiced my skepticism. "Are you sure the medical examiner didn't inhale one too many whiffs of formaldehyde, Detective?"

"Our coroner is quite competent, Mrs. Pollack. He found Fluni-trazepam in her system. Whoever killed Marlys Vandenburg first knocked her out with the drug, then sealed her mouth and nostrils with glue."

"Eeewwww!" Erica clapped her hands over her mouth and bent forward, making gagging noises.

I tamped down my own urge to gag. Squeezing my eyes shut, I tried to concentrate on my own breathing, but behind my closed lids I saw Marlys, glue strings streaming from her body like waxy spider webs. No matter how lousy an excuse for a human being, Marlys didn't deserve death by glue gun.

I took a final deep breath and opened my eyes. "What's Fluni-trazepam?" I asked Batswin.

"It's a benzodiazepine, a very potent tranquilizer similar to Valium, only many times stronger. You might know it better as Rohypnol or Roofies."

"The date rape drug?" asked Erica.

"Exactly," said Batswin. "You wouldn't happen to know how it got into your boss's Merlot, would you?"

Erica's eyes grew wide, her face filled with horror. "I didn't do it!"

"I'm not saying you did, Miss Milano."

"We don't keep alcohol in the office. It's against company policy."

"You always follow the rules?"

Erica cringed as if Batswin had slapped her. With her eyes averted, her voice timid and defensive, she answered, "Of course. I don't want to get fired."

"Not that rules ever stopped Marlys," I said. "She may have kept a bottle in her office."

Erica turned to look at me and shook her head. "I would have known."

I challenged Batswin, "Seems to me your killer is whoever shared a drink with Marlys last night, and that certainly wasn't me or Erica. Marlys wouldn't stoop to socializing with either of us."

"Mrs. Pollack, why do you keep handing me reasons to suspect you?"

I was beginning to wonder what the police academy taught in Basic Detecting 101. Maybe Batswin needed a refresher course. Or a copy of *The Dunderhead's Step-by-Step Guide to How to Catch a Killer*.

"Being dissed by a snob isn't grounds for murder, Detective. At least not as far as I'm concerned. Why are you wasting your time with me when you should be finding out who Marlys was with last night? By now the real killer is probably skinny-dipping in Aruba."

Detective Batswin leaned across the table. "Are you telling me how to do my job, Mrs. Pollack?"

"Heaven forbid, Detective. I have enough problems of my own."

"So you've mentioned."

That's when it hit me. Batswin wanted to wrap this case up as soon as possible. Whether she had the real killer or not. In her eyes I had motive, opportunity, and the murder weapon at my disposal. Why look any further?

I was getting the distinct impression that Batswin's latest theory involved Erica and me in cahoots to bump off Marlys. Erica drugged her. Then together we dragged her body into my office, where I went to work with my handy-dandy, trusty hot glue gun.

Tie a red satin bow around us and hand us over to the district attorney. Case closed.

I almost laughed at the absurdity except that Batswin sounded dead serious. Pun intended. With so little violent crime in Morris County, how many murders had she actually investigated, let alone solved?

I had no desire to spend the next thirty or forty years dressed in a neon orange jumpsuit as a guest of the state of New Jersey. If I wanted to save my tush, I needed to find the real killer. And fast. After all, I didn't have any money for a defense attorney.

Maybe *I* needed a copy of *The Dunderhead's Step-by-Step Guide to How to Catch a Killer*.

First, though, I needed a computer, and since Batswin and Robbins had locked mine up in the Morris County hoosegow, I borrowed Cloris's. In exchange, I caught her up on my latest interrogation by Batswin and Erica's bombshell of a boyfriend announcement.

"That's crazy," she said around a mouthful of angel food cake, one of the spares from her early morning wedding cake photo shoot for the June issue.

I eyed the cake sitting on the counter. My mouth watered. My Carb Junkie Gene shouted, "Feed me!" but I ignored its screams.

"What's crazy? Me bumping off Marlys with my trusty Smith and Wesson glue gun or Erica having a boyfriend?"

She shoveled another forkful of cake into her mouth. "Both, come to think of it. What would you have to gain by killing Marlys?"

"Money."

She nearly choked on her cake, reached for a cup of coffee, and raised one eyebrow high enough that it disappeared under her wispy gingerbread-colored bangs. "Want to explain that one?" she asked after washing the cake down with a gulp of java sludge.

Not really. I had hoped to keep Karl's financial infidelity a secret from my coworkers, but since Batswin and Robbins now knew about my money mess and Ricardo's fifty-thousand-dollars-or-else demand, I figured it wouldn't be long before word spread.

I gave Cloris the *Reader's Digest* condensed version.

"So the dynamic detective duo think you killed Marlys for the diamonds to pay off Ricardo?"

"Looks that way."

"Those diamonds were worth a hell of a lot more than fifty grand."

"Which would certainly get me out of the financial quagmire Karl created."

Cloris groaned. "You do have a problem." She placed her plate on the table and leaned over my shoulder as I scrolled down a page of book titles listed on barnesandnoble.com. "How can I help?"

I glanced over my shoulder. "Are you serious?"

"Of course, Sherlock." She stepped over to the counter and sliced herself another helping of wedding cake. "I know you didn't kill Marlys. Want some?"

"Thanks. For both the offer of help *and* the cake." I turned my attention back to the website. "Okay, Doctor Watson, now all we need to do is learn how to snare ourselves a murderer."

"On the Barnes and Noble website?"

"I'm looking for *The Dunderhead's Step-by-Step Guide to How to Catch a Killer.*"

"Is there such a book?"

I focused on the screen. "Apparently not. They've got everything else, including a completely illustrated, step-by-step guide to becoming a clairvoyant."

"That could work."

"I wish."

I exited the website, and grabbed the plate of wedding cake Cloris had cut for me. In the great diet game of life the score was Carb Junkie Genes one, Anastasia's Willpower zero.

"So now what?" asked Cloris.

"You bake me a cake with a file in it?"

"Let's hope it doesn't come to that."

"Let's hope what doesn't come to what?"

Cloris and I exchanged a quick glance and turned to find Naomi standing at the cubicle entrance. She wore a deep plum two-piece Dior suit and as usual, looked Grace-Kelly-elegant. But then again, Naomi was the kind of woman who'd look Grace-Kelly-elegant in Lucille's ratty chenille robe. No Carb Junkie Gene allowed in Naomi's family tree.

Behind her, Kim, her ever-present, ever-efficient assistant, clutched a stack of papers while talking on a portable phone she held in place with her shoulder. With her free hand she jotted notes on a legal pad.

Kim could juggle seventeen tasks at once and never break a sweat. Never show the slightest sign of frazzledom on that pert, freckled face of hers. I figured beside a combination of Chinese and Irish genes, she had to have a sprinkling of Speedy Gonzales in her blood line.

I also couldn't help but notice the serenity that emanated from Naomi this morning. I wondered if Grace Kelly had ever played a nun or a saint. If so, she would have looked exactly like Naomi looked at that moment.

Gone was the thick coil of tension that had snaked around her from the day Hugo brought Marlys aboard. Coincidence? Or something else?

I shook the thought of Naomi committing murder from my head and answered her with a lie I hoped she couldn't see through. "I'm having a bit of a problem getting my computer back from the police."

She turned to Kim. "See what you can do to expedite getting Anastasia's computer released."

Kim nodded as she continued to listen to the caller and take notes.

Naomi turned back to me. "How much of a problem do we have?"

"None as far as editorial. I have everything backed up on the server."

"Good. I'll get IT to hook up another computer for you. What time are you shooting today?"

"That's the problem." I grimaced as she raised one perfectly arched eyebrow. "I had to cancel the photo session. The police also took the models for the June spread. I had planned to finish the final pieces last night ..." I shrugged instead of finishing my sentence. Naomi knew all about last night.

"So now we have no models to shoot?"

"Exactly. Either we reschedule photography or pick up projects from an old issue."

I knew the latter was not an option. Neither rain, nor sleet, nor snow, nor wind, nor murder in the dead of night would cause

Naomi to run an old column or project. In the cut-throat world of women's magazine publishing, Rule Number One was: Never give your readers any reason to switch to a competitor's publication. And readers got really pissed when they plunked down three-fifty at the supermarket check-out counter only to get home to find the new issue contained repeats from past issues.

"Can you get new models made by the end of the day?" asked Naomi.

Not wanting to tarnish my miracle worker image—or jeopardize my job—I agreed. Even if I was at the same time kicking myself for being so accommodating.

"Fine. We'll shoot first thing tomorrow morning." She turned to Kim. "Take care of rescheduling."

Kim continued to listen and jot as she once again nodded, her shoulder length hair sweeping back and forth like an auburn silk curtain.

"By the way," said Naomi, "I'm going to give Erica a shot at Marlys's job."

Cloris and I exchanged glances.

Naomi cocked her head, waiting for some comment from either of us, but we were both speechless. "Either of you see a problem with that?"

"Not me," said Cloris.

"I suppose it makes sense," I said. "Erica always did most of Marlys's work anyway."

"But?"

Cloris wrinkled her nose. "But behind the scenes. She's a glaring *Fashion Don't*."

"With zero self-esteem," I added. "There's no way she'd survive the vultures of Seventh Avenue. And what about Fashion Week?"

"The press and tabloids will use her for target practice," said Cloris.

"But instead of arrows, they'll pierce her heart with a volley of Manolo Blahnik stilettos," I said.

"Right," said Cloris. "Don't get us wrong, Naomi. We all like Erica, but she's not exactly anyone's idea of a *fashionista*."

Naomi offered up one of her serene Grace Kelly smiles. "She will be."

"What do you mean?"

"Have faith." Naomi turned and headed down the hall, waving her Movado clad wrist in the air, Kim scurrying behind her. "*Ciao*, ladies. Let's get back to work."

I groaned.

"What?" asked Cloris. "You worried about Erica?"

"Right now I'm more worried about myself. I was hoping Naomi would cave for once and let me pull a wedding spread from an old issue. I didn't get to bed until nearly three last night."

And now besides crafting several pairs of bridal tennies, I'd have to remake three dozen birdseed roses before tomorrow morning.

Since I couldn't work at the office until Kim bailed my supplies and models out of the brig, I headed home, stopping along the way to pick up replacement materials for both projects.

I had planned to spend the evening cleaning out the apartment above the garage for the new tenant, but that would have to wait. At least I still had three more days before he moved in, as long as no new disasters hit between now and then. Too bad I couldn't appropriate a few of Kim's Speedy Gonzales genes.

———

Between the commuting time and a stop at A.C. Moore for supplies, I didn't arrive home until nearly two o'clock. Two police cruisers were parked in front of my house.

A million possibilities raced through my brain. None of them good. All of them somehow or other connected to the recurring theme of what-else-had-Karl-done?

TEN

I COULDN'T BLAME THIS additional dose of Bad Luckitis on my dearly departed husband, though. In a classic case of Murphy's Law, some entrepreneurial burglar had decided to do a little post-Christmas shopping and chose the Pollack homestead over bucking the traffic at the local mall.

"He did a real number on your place," said a lumbering uniformed officer who met me at the door. His name badge read *Fogarty*. He ushered me around a puddle of orange and white glop that covered my foyer floor and led me into my ransacked living room.

"Lucky me."

"Huh?"

"Forgive my sarcasm," I said. "I'm having a really bad week."

Avoiding eye contact, he shuffled his oversized black Oxfords on my hardwood floor. "Uhm … right. Your mother mentioned your recent loss."

I turned my attention to Mama. She sat on the sofa, her clasped hands shaking in her lap. A second officer, an older man whose name badge read *Harley*, sat beside her, his pencil stub poised over a small notebook. I guess even in the wealthier suburbs pencil stubs and small, lined notepads were standard issue. Made me wonder just what my local taxes paid for.

I crossed the room and knelt beside my mother. "Mama, are you all right?"

"Oh, Anastasia, it was awful. Simply awful."

"You were here?"

"I was coming back from visiting that dear, sweet Bernadette McPhearson down the street. Her brother recently lost his wife, you know."

"You saw him?"

"Her brother? No dear. He lives way up in Moosehead, Maine. Or was it New Hampshire? I'm so rattled, now I forget what Bernadette said."

"Not her brother, Mama. The burglar."

"The burglar? Of course I saw *him*. He nearly trampled me on his way out! Knocked Bernadette's Ambrosia Surprise right out of my hands. And after she went to all that trouble to make it for you and the boys."

That explained the mysterious orange and white glop on the floor.

"At least I prevented him from stealing anything," said Mama. "He ran out empty-handed."

"Did he hurt you?"

She shook her head. "Scared the bejeebers out of me at first, but I think I scared him more."

"From the way he tossed the place," said Officer Fogarty, "it appears he was searching for something specific."

"What do you mean?"

"Either that or he was more interested in vandalizing than stealing. I don't see any evidence of missing electronics equipment. All the computers, stereos, and TVs are still plugged in. You'll have to check to see if he grabbed any of your jewelry or any cash you have around the house. And check out the stuff you keep in the garage and the apartment above it. Looks like he ransacked those before he hit the house. But again, from what I could see, nothing's missing."

Ralph squawked from his perch on top of an emptied bookcase. I could have sworn I placed him in the laundry room and closed the door before I left the house. "*Something is rotten in the state of Denmark,*" he editorialized in-between squawks. "*Hamlet.* Act One, Scene Four."

The officers stared up at Ralph. "That's one damn smart bird," said the officer sitting next to Mama.

I nodded as I viewed the mess surrounding me. Every book was toppled from the bookcases. Furniture was overturned, cushions slashed. Pieces of what used to be knickknacks littered the floor. In the time it had taken the burglar to trash my home, he could have carted off three computers, four televisions, two stereos, two DVD players, and the VCR. I couldn't disagree with Fogarty.

"Any idea what the thief was after, Mrs. Pollack?"

Not only did I have a pretty good idea what the thief was after, I also had a pretty good idea of the thief's identity. I thought about mentioning Ricardo's call but just as quickly dismissed the idea. "No. No idea."

If I told the Officers Fogarty and Harley about Ricardo, I'd have to tell them about Karl's secret life. We live in a small town where gossip spreads as quickly as bathroom mildew in August.

The last thing I needed was to have my dearly departed's affair with Roxie Roulette and its aftermath the topic of town gossip, not to mention emblazoned across the front page of the local paper. I might not be able to protect my kids from the financial disaster we had suffered, but I'd do my damnedest to keep their father's seamier extra-curricular activities from them as long as possible.

Besides, I had no proof that Ricardo—if that was even his real name—was connected to the break-in. The timing of his calls and the subsequent break-in were probably a coincidence. Murphy's Law throwing me a huge gotcha. I was experiencing a lot of those lately.

But if it had been Ricardo, maybe he'd now believe I didn't have his fifty thousand dollars and would leave me alone. The Fates could cut me that one small break after dumping so much tribulation on me, couldn't they?

One of those tribulations chose that moment to arrive home. Lucille, looking like some deranged fashion *faux pas* in a purple and chartreuse paisley polyester pantsuit, circa nineteen seventy, barged her way into the house. She swatted her cane at Fogarty as he tried to stop her.

"Manifesto!" she screeched at the top of her lungs.

"*What's in a name?*" asked Ralph. "*Romeo and Juliet*. Act Two, Scene Two."

The cops reached for their guns.

Mama screamed.

"Don't," I yelled. "She's my mother-in-law."

The officers eyed Lucille, keeping their hands poised on their guns but not drawing them.

Mephisto, the Devil Dog, lumbered in from the kitchen. Some watchdog! I'll bet a month of triple-shot lattes he'd buried himself under a mound of dirty laundry at the first sign of trouble.

Steadying herself with her cane, Lucille stooped and with one Schwarzenegger-like arm and a grunt, lifted the lump of dog. Cuddling him against her sagging breasts, she clucked and cooed as she checked him from head to tail. Doggy jowl to Lucille jowl, Devil Dog responded with a drooly slurp.

Satisfied that the ugly mutt wasn't harmed, Lucille turned her attention, her shrill voice, and her wildly waving cane toward the police. "What's going on here? Where's your search warrant? How dare you ransack the home of a law-abiding citizen!"

"We've had a break-in, Lucille."

She glanced around at the chaos. "A burglary? I don't believe it."

"*Flat burglary as ever was committed*," squawked Ralph. "*Much Ado About Nothing*. Act Four, Scene Two." He swooped off the bookcase and landed on my shoulder.

Ignoring me, Lucille proceeded to harangue the officers. "A police state, that's what this country has turned into, thanks to certain people, and don't pretend you don't know who I mean. Any excuse to stick your snooping noses where they don't belong. Well, I won't stand for it."

She waved her cane at an upturned end table and broken lamp. "How do I know this isn't all your doing? You people engage in conspiracies and covert operations all the time. I know how you work. I have my sources."

Fogarty bristled. "Lady, back off, or I'll charge you with ob-structing an investigation."

"You lay one hand on me, young man, and I'll have your badge."

"Ignore her," I advised him.

"Does she ..." He cast a sideways glance at Lucille and cupped his mouth with his hand, "you know ... have Alzheimer's Disease?"

Lucille thumped her cane on the carpet. "Don't you dare whis-per about me in the third person. I'm saner than any of you."

Officer Fogarty's expression mirrored his skepticism.

"She's a communist," I said.

He nodded in understanding, as if Alzheimer's and commu-nism were one and the same. Maybe to him they were.

Lucille lowered Mephisto to the floor, then hobbled off down the hall. The dog followed at her heels. They reminded me of the villainous relative with the Siamese cats in *Lady and the Tramp*, except for the fact that Mephisto was a dog and not a cat. I guess I should be glad he didn't have a twin. Or that my mother-in-law wasn't versed in cloning.

Fogarty started to call her back.

"Leave her," I said. "Trust me. There's nothing in her room a thief would want."

He looked to Harley for guidance. The older officer watched Lu-cille disappear down the hall, then he turned to me and shrugged his oversized shoulders. "It's your house, Mrs. Pollack."

At least for today, I thought, righting an upturned chair. As I inspected the damage to the seat cushion, the phone rang.

I excused myself to the kitchen.

The display on the phone read *Out of Area*. Probably a telemarketer, but even a telemarketer would be a welcome reprieve at the moment. "Hello?"

"Where'd you stash the dough?"

At least now I knew who had broken into my house, but under the circumstances, I would have preferred your garden variety burglar.

"You trashed my house!" I wondered how long it took to set up a phone tap. Was Batswin or one of her cohorts listening in at this very moment?

"Smart lady. Now get this: Next time I'll do a lot more than toss the place."

Scared as I was, his veiled threat sent a surge of defiant anger pumping through my veins. I gritted my teeth to keep from yelling into the phone. "I told you, I don't have your money. That should have been evident after the strip search you conducted on my home."

Ricardo made that noise that sounded halfway between a *tsk* and a kiss. "And I told you I know otherwise. Now you know I mean business. I want that money by Friday."

"You said I had a week."

"I changed my mind."

"That's not fair!"

"Fair?" He snorted. "Fuck fair. Life ain't fair, bitch. Friday. Or else." With that the phone went dead.

I shuddered to think what Ricardo might do if Batswin and Robbins botched their end and he discovered I'd set him up, especially if their suspicions about him being Mafia were correct. And given that this was New Jersey, how could their suspicions not be correct?

As much as I loved my house, my neighborhood, and my town, living in New Jersey definitely had its downside. I'd learned to accept the sky-high taxes. At least we got great schools and decent public transportation in return, even if the cops didn't have smart phones. I just never expected the seamier side of the state's reputation to enter my life. I doubt there's much organized crime in North Sandwich, New Hampshire, or Cat Creek, Montana.

I glanced around the kitchen. So much for assigning cleaning tasks to Mama and Lucille. Dirty dishes teetered in precarious piles in the sink. More soiled plates and glasses were scattered across the kitchen table.

No one had bothered to put away any of the breakfast food, not even the perishables. I grabbed the nearly full gallon of skim milk and sniffed. Sour milk assaulted my nasal passages with a one-two punch.

"God damn it!" I screamed, pouring nearly five dollars worth of skim down the drain.

Based on the state of the kitchen, I knew I'd find wet towels on the bathroom floors. Laundry spilling out of the hamper. A layer of cat and dog hair covering every upholstered piece of furniture and all the carpets. And now on top of all that I had to contend with Ricardo's handiwork.

Between Mama the Scatterbrained and Lucille the *Prima Donna* Commie, I now had four children instead of two. Nick and Alex were more reliable and considerate than either of their grandmothers.

Feeling way too much like Cinderella before her fairy god-mother dropped in and bibbidi-bobbidi-booed her into a happily-ever-after, I put away the food, loaded the dishwasher, and wiped the English muffin crumbs off the counter.

"There's never a fairy godmother around when you need one," I muttered as I headed back into the living room to find Mama batting her eyelashes at the cops.

ELEVEN

"I HAVE WORK TO do," I told Mama after Fogarty and Harley left. "I'll be in my studio."

"What about this mess?"

"It's not going anywhere."

"Really, Anastasia. I brought you up better than that."

"Mama, I have work to do. Work that can't wait. This can." I glanced at the foyer and the ambrosia glop staining my hardwood floors a garish shade of Halloween orange. "Although it would be great if you could clean up that," I said. "You'll find the Murphy's Oil Soap, a bucket, and a sponge in the basement."

She didn't look thrilled, but she didn't argue with me as I grabbed my bags of supplies and headed for the back door.

Now more than ever, I couldn't afford to lose my job, but the last thing in the world I wanted to do at that moment was work on crafts projects. Especially bridal crafts, considering the recent less-than-happily-ever-after ending of my own trip down the aisle.

Someone should definitely update all those male-penned fairy tales.

The modern version had better warn Cinderella that Prince Charming might have a secret, serious gambling addiction that could leave her and the little princelings up a moat without a paddle. Forget about the ball. Maybe instead of turning a pumpkin into a coach, her fairy godmother should change the huge veggie into a trust fund that the prince can't get his hands on. Just in case happily ever after isn't.

Which it certainly wasn't for me. Thanks to Karl, I now had to find some way to earn more money. Even if Batswin and Robbins were successful in nabbing Ricardo, I still needed to pay off all that credit card debt, the past-due bills, and the home equity loan.

And then there was college for the boys.

I unlocked the studio door, dumped my bags of newly purchased materials on the counter, and pulled out a pad of paper and a pencil. The bridal crafts could wait. Starring as the celebrity whiner of my own pity party wasn't going to get me out of the mess Karl had plunged me into. Short of winning the lottery—not that I had an extra George Washington to waste on such a long-shot solution—I needed to come up with a creative way out of my financial quagmire.

I began jotting down a list of possible moonlighting jobs that would pay more than minimum wage and didn't require me to paste on a phony, perky smile and ask, "Do you want fries with that?"

Within a few minutes, I had listed several possibilities. I knew people who knew people. I could call in a few favors and maybe get hired as a crafts expert on one of the local morning programs.

I doubted Trimedia would object. Publicity whores that they were, they'd love the exposure—especially if it didn't cost them anything.

I could put together a proposal for a series of crafts books. The advance would knock a story or two off the Leaning Tower of Debt, and the royalties would help with college tuitions.

I scowled at the next item on my list. If neither the TV nor book deals panned out, I could always teach in the evenings and on the weekends. Bernadette McPhearson served on the board of the Methodist Home, and one of my other neighbors managed the local A.C. Moore. Both women were constantly after me to teach classes.

Been there, done that. After ten years of captivity in a junior high school art room, I had sworn I would never teach again. But that was before Karl's clandestine affair with Lady Un-Lucky. Teaching was definitely preferable to the only other idea on my list.

I glanced down at the remaining item on the page and wrinkled my nose. If I *really* got desperate, I could mass produce my own crafts and sell them to gift shops and at bazaars and fairs. The thought literally made me queasy. I enjoyed designing projects and making them once, not the mindlessness of assembly line crafting.

Which was probably why I was sitting making lists instead of tackling those three dozen birdseed roses—for the second time— thanks to Batswin and Robbins.

Of course, all of these money-making enterprises hinged on me not being charged with murder, which necessitated compiling another list. I tore off the first sheet of paper and set it aside. No way could I quietly sit back and leave my destiny in the hands of that undynamic detective duo. I labeled the top of the page *Who Killed Marlys?* and listed the three most likely candidates:

Vittorio Versailles?

Hugo Reynolds-Alsopp?

Naomi Dreyfus?

Not that I thought either Naomi or Hugo were killers. My money was on Vittorio.

Or Emil Pachette?

Marlys had a date with him Monday night. Had he met her at the office instead of her meeting him in the city? I added his name to the list.

Or maybe none of my suspects had glue gunned Marlys to death. Maybe her killer was one of the many other people she had stepped on, dissed, or screwed in her quest to conquer the celebrity world of New York fashion.

Someone from her distant past, even. Was the killer an old acquaintance who had held a grudge for years, perhaps going as far back as high school, his or her hate simmering just below the boiling point until the perfect opportunity presented itself?

Placing that thought on hold, I started another sheet: *Who Do the Police Think Killed Marlys?* My name topped the list. Followed by Erica's.

If I couldn't find the killer, I'd have to find some way to keep the police from charging either of us. Erica had an alibi and a witness, but what did I have? Just my word that I didn't kill Marlys. Meanwhile, I suspected Batswin and Robbins were in the process of building enough of a case against me to prove otherwise.

All of this supposition was producing nothing more than a whopper of a headache. I tossed the pad and pencil aside, closed my eyes, and massaged my temples. Enough procrastinating. My birdseed roses wouldn't sprout by themselves, and since I lacked the necessary magic wand, I couldn't bibbidi-bobbidi-boo them into existence, either.

I tried to focus my attention where it belonged—at least for the next few hours. I couldn't let go of my problems, though. As I snipped, sewed, and glued satin roses and rhinestone tennies, I continued to ruminate over money and murder.

THE BRIDE WORE TENNIES

Oh, those aching tootsies! Most brides, if given the choice, would opt for a foot massage rather than the honeymoon suite at the Plaza once the reception ends. Just ask any of your married friends. But why suffer the blisters in the first place? After posing for the wedding photos, remove those torturous stilettos and slip into a pair of handmade bridal tennies to boogie the night away.

And if you want a unique gift for your bridesmaids, have tennies dyed to match their gowns. Trim with coordinating or matching colored laces and trims.

Materials: one pair of white canvas tennis shoes; an assortment of lace appliqués; pearl, sequin, and rhinestone trims; satin ribbon roses; 2½ yds. 1¾-inch-wide lace; white craft gem glue; scissors.

Directions: Remove shoelaces from tennis shoes. Arrange appliqués and trims on front and sides of shoes as desired, with one shoe being the mirror image of the other. Glue appliqués and trims in place. Allow glue to dry thoroughly. Cut lace in half. Thread a piece of lace through eyelets of each shoe.

BIRDSEED ROSES

Rice is out; birdseed is in when it comes to showering the bride and groom in an environmentally friendly way. Use elegant satin roses to store the showering seed, and your guests will have a beautiful memento of the day to take home with them.

Materials: satin fabric in white or to match the wedding colors (one yard of 45-inch-wide fabric will make 77 roses); matching sewing thread; 6-inch lengths of 18-gauge stem wire; green floral tape; silk rose leaves, one or more per flower; pinking shears; sewing machine

Directions: Using the pinking shears, cut a 4 x 5-inch piece of satin for each rose. With right sides together, machine baste 4-inch sides of satin together with ¼-inch seam allowance. Turn right side out. Hand gather lower edge of tube, wrapping thread ends tightly around gathers to form the base of rose. Insert stem wire through bottom, bending the end inside the rose into a loop to keep it from slipping out. Wrap the base and stem of the rose with floral tape, adding leaves as you wrap. Fill each rose with a teaspoon of birdseed. Tuck in the top edge of satin about 1½ inches to keep the birdseed contained. A flick of the wrist will release the birdseed to shower the bride and groom.

I was just finishing up the first pair of tennies when I heard Mama clomping up the outside stairs.

"You never told me why you came home so early," she said as she opened the door and entered.

"Long story." I grabbed two matching lace appliqués and positioned them over the toes of the second pair of tennies, adjusting the angle first in one direction, then the other. "I had a lot of work to do and decided I'd be more productive at home. Less interruptions. Of course, I had no idea I'd walk into Chaos Central."

"Well, I'm glad you're home early." She shrugged out of her coat and tossed it on a chair.

Her cheeks glowed from the cold; her eyes twinkled with excitement. "I had the most marvelous inspiration this morning as I showered. You know how I always get my best ideas in the shower, don't you?"

"Hmm?" I glanced up to find her waving a handful of colorful, glossy brochures in the air between us. I stifled a groan but couldn't manage to hide my frown. Mama's ideas never came cheap.

"Don't pout, Anastasia. Trust me. You're going to love this."

"Love what?"

"A cruise. Just the two of us. A week basking in the Caribbean. Mother and daughter healing time."

I stopped work on the second pair of tennies. "Sounds lovely, Mama, but I can't afford it."

"Nonsense. Cruises are quite affordable."

"Peanut butter and jelly sandwiches are no longer affordable."

"What are you talking about? Surely Karl left you with plenty."

It was time to spring the bad news on her. "Karl left me with plenty, all right. Plenty of debt."

Her brows pinched together. "I don't understand."

No way would Mama be satisfied with the *Reader's Digest* condensed version. She'd insist on the entire epic, warts and all.

I sighed. "Sit down, Mama."

TWELVE

LIKE EVERYONE ELSE, MAMA loved Karl. At least, she had up until a moment ago. Mama always admired the way Karl had broken free of Lucille's communist stranglehold and created the American dream for his wife and kids. Only her version of that dream—along with mine—hadn't involved an affair gone bad with Lady Not-So-Lucky.

She reacted to the news in much the same way as Lucille had, except instead of blaming me, she turned her wrath on my mother-in-law. "This is all *her* fault."

"That's pretty convoluted reasoning. I don't think you can blame Lucille for her son's gambling addiction."

"She raised him, didn't she?"

"If you can call it that." Lucille had ignored Karl from the time he was old enough to fend for himself. Her political agenda came first, last, and always before her son.

"Precisely my point. And what kind of mother names her son after Karl Marx, for God's sake?" Her voice rose three octaves.

"Karl Marx Pollack. To saddle a child with a name like that! Nothing short of child abuse, as far as I'm concerned. Between that and all her other shenanigans—"

"Shenanigans?"

"Of course." She flailed her arms in true drama queen style as her voice climbed another octave. Never let it be said that Mama didn't love her soapbox. "If she'd spent more time with her son and less time trying to overthrow our government—"

"Let's not go there. It won't change the past, and it certainly won't erase the debt hanging over my head."

Worry swept away the defiance in her posture and settled over her face. "How bad is it?"

I quoted her a sum.

Mama blanched. "Before or after you collect on the life insurance?"

A bitter laugh rumbled up through my throat and escaped past my lips. "Karl borrowed against his life insurance policy. There is no insurance. And no savings. Just a Mt. Everest of debt and a Dead Sea of red ink."

"Red." With a glower, Mama cocked her head in the direction of the house. "Like her."

"Mama, please. Not now."

She rose from the chair, swept across the room, and enveloped me in a breast-squishing hug. "I'm sorry. I wish I could help."

"So do I." But most of what Mama had counted on for retirement had disappeared thanks to corporate bamboozling. She lived from spendthrift husband to spendthrift husband. You'd think at least one of her many husbands could have left her with a sizable estate, but Mama had always been attracted to epicurean men who lived like there was no tomorrow. Ironically enough, for them, there hadn't been a tomorrow.

"I have a few thousand tucked away for emergencies," she said. "It's yours if it will help. Not that it will make much of a dent in *that* figure."

I kissed her cheek. "Thanks, but you may need it. I'll manage."

"How?"

I grabbed my list off the table and waved it at her. "I've got a few ideas."

Mama reached for the paper and began to read. "*Who Do the Police Think Killed Marlys?*"

I snatched the paper from her hand. "Wrong list."

She stared at me, her eyes widening nearly to the size of her gaping mouth. She whispered, as if afraid that the very utterance of her question would convict me. "Who's Marlys, and why do the police think you killed her?"

This was not the way I planned to spend my afternoon. I had work to do. Besides, I hadn't wanted to worry Mama with my problems. Now I'd have to dump Marlys's murder—and my involvement in it—on her.

"What are you going to do?" she asked after I filled her in on all the sordid details.

"What can I do? I'm going to find out who really killed Marlys."

"Don't you think you should leave that to the police? I don't want you snooping after a killer. You could get hurt. Or worse."

"I'll be careful. Besides, if I don't find out who killed Marlys, you'll have to use that nest egg of yours to hire a lawyer to defend me on murder charges."

"You really think the police want to pin her murder on you? That's ridiculous."

"Of course it is, but from what I've seen so far, these detectives don't have much experience investigating murders. And that scares the freckles right off my nose. They leave me no choice. I've got to find the killer in order to save my tush."

Mama opened her mouth to say something, but she was interrupted by the sound of Nick and Alex, bounding up the stairs. "Mom?" called Alex.

"You up there?" added Nick.

"Not a word about any of this," I warned my mother before the boys opened the door. "I haven't told them about their father yet."

She pulled an imaginary zipper across her mouth as Nick and Alex tumbled through the door. Knowing Mama, that zipper would stay firmly closed for maybe an hour.

"Holy shit, Mom!" said Alex. "What the heck happened in the house?"

"More like holy double shit," added Nick. "And what's all that sticky stuff on the floor in the foyer?"

I scowled at Mama.

"I cleaned it up the best I could, dear. What did you expect me to do, get down on my hands and knees?"

That's exactly what I'd expected. Silly me. "Don't worry," I assured the boys. "It's really not as bad as it looks."

———

I arrived at work the next morning with three dozen satin birdseed roses, four pairs of wedding tennies, and a sore back from another night spent on the den sofa. I also sported a Texas-sized bruise on my thigh thanks to Mama's nocturnal gymnastics prior to exiling myself to the sofa.

Tonight Mama slept with Lucille, no matter how much she protested. On my way home from work I planned to buy a box of those anti-snore nose strips. If I had to, I'd even slap one across Mephisto's muzzle. I wanted my bed back, and I wasn't about to cave to any excuse or sob story.

Lost in lack-of-sleep grump mode, I smiled a voiceless greeting to an unfamiliar woman who offered me a wide smile as our paths crossed in the hall outside my office. A moment later, my brain caught up with my eyes. I stopped dead in my tracks and spun around. "Erica?"

She laughed. "I was wondering how long it would take you. I think Cloris is still scratching her head, trying to figure out who I am."

I stared at her perfectly made-up face. Her Donna Karan burgundy raw silk pantsuit, cut perfectly to mask her excess poundage and various love bulges but accentuate her double D-cup breasts.

My mouth moved, but no words came out. Now I understood Naomi's cryptic comment of yesterday. She had seen the potential hidden behind the sackcloth and sent Erica for a radical makeover.

With Marlys's demise, Naomi was not only rid of her arch nemesis, but she had transformed Marlys's ugly duckling workhorse assistant into a plus-size swan who wouldn't embarrass Trimedia.

Was Erica's metamorphosis all part of a well-organized plan that had begun with Naomi killing Marlys? Or had Naomi merely seized the opportunity presented by Marlys's death? I still couldn't accept Naomi as a cold-blooded killer.

Then again, my track record in the Character Judging Department was less than stellar, considering how blinded I was for eighteen years by my very own knight in not-so-shining armor.

"Well, what do you think?" Anticipation hung on Erica's question; a need for approval colored her features. She raised herself up on her toes. I glanced down. Erica had traded her standard knee socks and clunky Doc Martens for a pair of whisper sheer hose and strappy burgundy suede shoes that looked suspiciously similar to the Jimmy Choos we'd featured in last month's issue.

With one hand sweeping across a body no longer hidden beneath a shapeless jumper, the other brushing back the kicky bangs of her freshly styled and streaked hair, Erica executed a graceful pirouette. Coming to a stop inches away from me, she held her breath, awaiting my critique.

"I'm flabbergasted."

The corners of her perfectly painted mouth dipped. Her eyes clouded with doubt. "You don't like it?"

"Are you kidding?" I laughed. "As Billy Crystal would say, 'You look *maaavelous!*'"

Erica exhaled like a kid blowing out all the birthday candles at once. Her face burst into a mega-watt smile. She giggled. "I do, don't I?"

"Absolutely. So, tell me. What did Dicky say when he saw you?"

A deep blush traveled up her neck and suffused her cheeks. "I think he's a little worried."

"Why?"

She giggled nervously. "He said I was always beautiful to him, but now he might have to break a few legs if guys start hitting on me."

"I hope he means that metaphorically."

"Of course! Dicky's a big pussycat."

"The construction workers of the world will be happy to hear that."

"Huh?"

"All those wolf whistles you'll get walking down the street."

"Oh." She blushed again. "You think?"

Poor Erica. Improved packaging aside, she still needed a major overhaul to her self-esteem. I patted her shoulder. "Bet on it."

She studied me for a moment, worrying away the color on her lower lip as she seemed to debate whether to say something further.

I prodded her into action. "You look like a woman with a question."

She lowered her gaze to the floor. "Could I ask a big favor?"

"Of course."

"Naomi set up an appointment for me with Vittorio Versailles later this afternoon. Sort of a kiss and make-up interview."

"Or a baptism by fire. Hell of a way to start out on your first full day as fashion editor."

"She wants me to make it clear to him that Marlys alone was responsible for the editorial attack on him. That Trimedia respects him as a unique and creative designer and that he has our complete support."

"Unique and creative?" I couldn't contain my laughter. "How diplomatic."

As editorial director, Naomi was ultimately responsible for everything between the covers of *American Woman*. A consummate perfectionist, she scoured every word of copy in each issue. I couldn't help but wonder if she'd deliberately ignored the slice-and-dice hatchet job of Vittorio to set Marlys up for a fall.

"So you get to play Blame the Dead Woman?"

"I suppose. I was wondering…" She twisted the hem of her suit jacket into a wrinkled ball. "That is…I…I was hoping maybe…"

Were the Karmic gods and goddesses finally cutting me a much needed break? I had tossed and turned most of last night trying to think up some way to get past Vittorio Versailles' phalanx of gay goons in order to question him about Marlys's murder.

I had come up blank. Vittorio Versailles didn't grant audiences to lowly crafts editors. My odds of winning Mega Millions were greater. Could getting in to see the *primo don* of the fashion world and Number One on my hit parade of suspects be this easy?

"You'd like me to go with you?" I asked, finishing her sentence for her.

"Would you?"

"Sure. I'm free as soon as the photo shoot is over this morning."

Her face lit up. She grabbed both of my hands and squeezed them together between her palms and pumped. "Thank you, thank you. I'm in your debt. Anything I can do in return, just name it. Anything. I mean that, Anastasia."

I thought about asking for a few hundred thousand dollars but bit back the urge. If Erica had a spare hundred thou or so, she wouldn't be slaving away as a Trimedia drudge.

Besides, Cloris had promised to keep my financial fiasco a secret, but how many people would Batswin and Robbins leak the info to in their quest to ferret out Marlys's killer?

Several hours later I found myself in a purple-walled, peacock feather-festooned Seventh Avenue loft in midtown Manhattan. The showroom resembled a jungle designed by a colorblind decorator. Groupings of towering palms in bright citrus and fuchsia glazed pots reached nearly to the twelve-foot ceilings. Magenta, navy, and sapphire striped balloon valances hung from the tops of the floor-to-ceiling windows. A bubbling azure blue and cadmium yellow mosaic fountain filled one corner of the room.

Leopard upholstered lounging chaises lined the walls. On each reclined a mannequin dressed in one of Vittorio's latest creations. Small assemblages of House of Versailles costumed mannequins stood interspersed between the chaises.

The designer himself, wearing what could best be described as a wet-look black leather Spiderman outfit, complete with head-hugging hood, held court in the center of the room on a zebra print sofa with leopard throw pillows. His eight-man goon squad hovered in the background. Today they were dressed in chartreuse and avocado striped velvet jumpsuits, accessorized with matching striped velvet fedoras. They looked like anorexic watermelons.

Erica and I sat off to the side on gilt-edged Louis XVI chairs, patiently and silently waiting until the staff stylist had finished primping Vittorio and our photographer had captured enough shots.

After the photographer and stylist departed, Vittorio turned to Erica. He waved his hand in a gesture reminiscent of those old movies where Bette Davis played Queen Elizabeth. "You may apologize now," he said.

Without batting an eye, Erica plunged into her pre-rehearsed Blame-Marlys-for-Everything grovel speech. "As the new fashion editor at *American Woman*," she concluded several minutes later, "I want to assure you that you and your work will be treated with the utmost esteem and regard in future issues, Mr. Versailles."

Vittorio glanced over at his goon squad. "This one I like," he said. "She shows the proper respect."

They nodded like a row of bobble-head dolls.

Vittorio turned back to Erica and offered her a benevolent smile. "You may call me Vittorio."

Erica beamed. "Thank you, sir.

"Vittorio."

"Vittorio." Her cheeks grew crimson, but her body relaxed. She had successfully handled her first assignment.

I had kept quiet up to that point. Now I jumped in. "Vittorio, are you aware that Marlys Vandenburg was murdered several hours after you threatened her on Monday?"

He turned his attention to me, as if seeing me for the first time. "And you are?"

"Anastasia Pollack."

"Why are you here, Anastasia Pollack?"

"I came with Erica."

"To do what? Accuse me of murder?" He waved his hand dismissively. "You, I don't like. You may not call me Vittorio." He snapped his fingers. "Show her out."

THIRTEEN

VITTORIO'S GOON SQUAD APPROACHED like a chartreuse and avocado tidal wave. So much for my interrogation skills. Maybe I should have watched some old episodes of *Murder She Wrote* before tackling this amateur sleuthing stuff.

I rewound the tape in my brain and began again. "I'm sorry. I didn't mean to accuse you of anything. I wasn't sure you had heard about Marlys. That's all."

Vittorio held his hand up to stop the advance of the phalanx. "Why would I stoop to murder when the revenge of bringing Marlys to her knees would be so much more satisfying? And profitable."

I blinked. "Profitable?"

Vittorio stroked his leather sleeve as though he were making love to his arm. "As I told the police yesterday, my dear Anastasia Pollack, I had already contacted my attorneys about instituting libel lawsuits against both Marlys and Trimedia. Twenty-five million dollars will go a long way toward pacifying my hurt feelings and salvaging my tarnished reputation, don't you agree?"

"You're suing Trimedia?" Erica's jaw dropped. Her face paled under her Bobbi Brown make-up.

"Of course, I've dropped the suit against Marlys," he said. "After a bit of investigating, my legal team discovered she left virtually no estate. And since you can't get money from a corpse ..." His lips curled into a catbird smile. "Why pay the lawyers?"

"Does Trimedia know about this lawsuit?" I asked.

Vittorio glanced at his diamond encrusted platinum Rolex. "They do now."

I suppose that ruled Vittorio out as my prime suspect. There was no profit in murder—at least not Marlys's murder. Why dirty his hands committing a crime when he could both destroy Marlys's career and score millions through the legal system? Vittorio Versailles might be a god-awful designer, but he was a financially savvy, god-awful designer.

And as it also turned out, a financially savvy, god-awful designer with an iron-clad alibi for Monday night. While Marlys was getting glued to death in my cubicle, Vittorio was being feted in midtown Manhattan at a dinner sponsored by the Italian-American Fashion Collective. Several hundred witnesses could attest to his whereabouts at the time of the murder.

As apparently Batswin and Robbins already knew. Maybe the Dynamic Duo wasn't as incompetent as they led me to believe. I wondered what other suspects they had already ruled out. What clues had they uncovered?

———

"You really thought Vittorio killed Marlys, didn't you?" asked Erica on the train ride back to the office.

"I was hoping. He certainly had a good motive after the way Marlys skewered him in our latest issue."

"And we all heard him threaten her."

"Too good to be true. Nothing is ever that easy. I suppose anyone devious enough to kill Marlys would be smart enough not to make his identity so obvious."

"Too bad he's got an alibi." She shifted position to face me. Worry clouded her face. Her lower lip trembled. "Those detectives scare me, Anastasia. They think I had something to do with it."

I patted her clenched fists. "They suspect both of us. Which is why I need to find out who really killed Marlys. I can't sit back and leave my fate in the hands of Batswin and Robbins."

"Neither can I. What would Dicky think if I were arrested?"

"If we're arrested for murder, Dicky will be the least of your worries."

"True."

"However, even if Batswin and Robbins find the real killer tomorrow, we now have another problem."

"What?"

"Vittorio's lawsuit."

"How does that affect us?"

"If Vittorio is successful, he'll bankrupt Trimedia. No Trimedia, no *American Woman*."

"We'd lose our jobs!"

"Exactly. And I can't afford to lose mine."

"Just when everything was starting to go right in my life. I've worked so hard. He can't do this to me!"

"Not much you or I or anyone else can do about it. The lawyers will fight it out. The shark with the most ferocious bite will win."

Erica pounded her fist on the seat. "I feel so helpless. All these people controlling my fate. There's got to be something we can do."

"First, we need to clear ourselves of any involvement in Marlys's murder. If we're locked up as killers, our jobs won't matter." I mulled over our options. Next on my list of suspects was Marlys's Monday night date.

In her new position as fashion editor, Erica had entrée to fashion's newest rising star. And if Emil Pachette were anything like his many counterparts on Seventh Avenue, he'd grovel and drool for exposure. *American Woman* might be a second-rate supermarket monthly, but it was a second-rate supermarket monthly read by millions of women.

Erica sat silently for a moment, as if debating with herself. Finally, she asked, "Is there something I can ... uhm ... do to ... you know ... help?"

"Absolutely. When we arrive back at the office, you need to set up an interview with Emil Pachette. The sooner the better. I'll come along as your assistant."

"But don't you think the police have already questioned him?"

"Probably. But if he is the killer, he would have been expecting the police and prepared for their questioning. Maybe we can catch him off guard."

Erica rifled around in her purse and pulled out an iPhone. She waved it in the air like a kid who had just found the surprise in a box of Cracker Jacks. "Why wait until we get back to the office? I'll phone him now."

"You have Emil Pachette's phone number programmed into your iPhone?"

She smiled a guilty smile and patted the phone. "A gift from Dicky. I have Marlys's entire Rolodex and half her computer files programmed into this baby. Made playing slave a lot easier when information was this handy. Especially when she'd call me in the evenings or on weekends."

Poor Erica. Yet another indication of her jellyfish backbone. Marlys demanded she jump, and Erica hoisted herself onto a trampoline, no matter the day or hour.

Instead of commenting, though, I simply said, "Smart woman."

Her face broke out in a self-satisfied grin. "And finally getting the credit for it. Dicky was right."

"About what?"

"He said all I needed was the chance to prove myself. It really made him mad that I was doing all of Marlys's work, and she was taking all the credit."

"We all felt that way."

"Did you?"

"You didn't realize that?"

Erica shook her head as she tapped her finger against the screen, then raised the cell to her cheek. "I guess I was too wrapped up in being angry and feeling sorry for myself to notice."

After a moment, she spoke into the phone. "Hi, Gina. This is Erica. Is Emil available ... Oh? ... I see." Her brow furrowed. "When do you expect him back? ... Really? ... Yes, please leave him a message. I'd like to set up an interview ... Thank you."

Erica disconnected the call. "You're not going to believe this. Emil Pachette didn't shown up for work today. Or yesterday. No one's seen or heard from him since before lunch on Monday."

FOURTEEN

"Angela Lansbury made it look so easy on television," I told Cloris upon returning to the office. After a quick search, I had found her camped out in the test kitchen. "It took Jessica Fletcher all of an hour to catch the killer each Sunday night."

"Less if you factor in the commercials," she said around a mouthful of mango macadamia muffin. "Like everything else, reality takes a bit longer."

"And reality just got a lot more complicated."

"What do you mean?"

I told her about Vittorio's lawsuit, as well as Emil's disappearance.

"Shit. I can't afford to lose my job. I've still got a kid in college."

"And I can?" Leaning against the counter, I pulled apart a still warm muffin and popped a piece into my mouth. Once again I had missed lunch, having gone straight into the city with Erica after the photo shoot. Besides, stress made me crave sweets.

"Hmm." I closed my eyes, hoping the combination of sweet and tangy flavors would expunge the thought of impending unemployment. "You're a spawn of the devil, tempting me like this."

"Thanks. I think. I'm experimenting for an article on exotic combinations. If we have a magazine left to run such an article." She reached for another platter. "Here. Tell me what you think of these."

"What are they?"

"White chocolate and plum brownies."

I hesitated. "How many calories per bite?"

"What the hell are another thousand calories or so in the greater scheme of life?"

Easy for her to say with her mach ten metabolism. I had a sneaking suspicion that Cloris exhaled calories and fat grams instead of carbon dioxide. On me, the calories and fat moved directly from my mouth to my hips, bypassing the entire digestive process.

But that didn't stop me from caving in and grabbing a brownie. My willpower never stands a chance against my salivating taste buds. Besides, chocolate releases endorphins, and right now I needed all the endorphins my brain was capable of delivering into my blood stream.

"I suppose if I spread those thousand calories out over the course of seventy or eighty years, you've got a point. Besides, who's going to notice the added poundage under one of those neon orange prison jumpsuit?" I took a bite and moaned around the mouthful.

"Good?"

"Are you kidding? Let's just say, white chocolate and plum put mango and macadamia to shame. If only I could catch a killer as easily as you kill my willpower."

Cloris finished her muffin and helped herself to a brownie. "I'd think you'd be excited over Emil's disappearance. Doesn't this make him the prime suspect? You and Erica are off the hook."

"And I'm so relieved," said Erica, strolling into the test kitchen. She pulled out a stool and sat down at the end of the counter that also served as a table. "No more looking over my shoulder, worrying that those detectives are lurking in the shadows waiting for me to slip up."

Both Cloris and I stared at her, Cloris's expression mirroring the "uh-oh" feeling churning in my stomach.

"Slip up about what?" I asked.

Erica helped herself to a brownie and studied it, as if debating whether or not it was worth the calories and fat grams now that she had exchanged her shapeless jumpers for designer duds. "Nothing," she said, speaking to the brownie instead of me.

She nibbled a corner and mumbled around the bite. "You know what I mean. Just having them snooping around and thinking I killed Marlys makes me feel guilty."

She glanced up at me, then at Cloris. "Not that I have anything to feel guilty about but ... "

"Don't try to explain," I said. "You're not the only one those two detectives make nervous. But I don't see how Emil's disappearance gets either of us scratched off the suspects list."

"People don't vanish without a trace unless they have something to hide, do they?"

"And don't forget the diamonds," added Cloris. "All that ice could buy a brand new identity in a country where the police don't ask too many questions."

Anything was possible, but I couldn't buy into the theory. I mulled over another possibility. What if someone wanted Emil out of the way because he knew too much or had seen something? "I don't think Emil took off because he killed Marlys. Maybe he's hiding because he's scared. Or maybe the killer is actually someone who was jealous of the publicity Marlys was going to give Emil."

"There's another possibility," said Cloris.

"What's that?" asked Erica.

"We could be going about this backwards. What if Emil Pachette was the intended victim and Marlys got in the killer's way?"

"So you're thinking that Marlys may have met Emil as planned?"

"Who knows?"

"One flaw in that theory," I said. "Why would the killer bring Marlys back here to kill her?"

"Right. Why wouldn't he have killed her where he killed Emil?" asked Erica.

"Maybe he couldn't for some reason," said Cloris.

"Doesn't make sense," I said. "Marlys's car was parked in the lot when I arrived back at Trimedia."

Cloris reached for the coffeepot and poured three cups. "Maybe the killer followed her back here." She added a generous amount of half-and-half to her cup before taking a sip. "If the killer set things up to look like someone at Trimedia had killed her—"

I finished her thought. "He'd divert suspicion from himself."

"Why not? I'm just trying to look at this from all angles."

Only as far as I could see, this particular angle was pockmarked with holes of flawed logic. "If Marlys saw someone kill Emil, why would she come back to the office? Why wouldn't she call the police?"

Erica blew into her coffee. "With Vittorio eliminated as a suspect, my money's on Emil."

"Marlys was about to give Emil tons of free publicity that would send his career soaring," I said. "Why would he kill her?"

Cloris exhaled a frustration-laced sigh. "We're going around in circles, getting nowhere fast."

"What if we search Emil's office and apartment," said Erica. "Maybe we could find some clues."

"Good one," said Cloris. "Ever hear of breaking and entering?"

Erica ignored the question as she pulled out her iPhone.

An hour and a half later the three of us were bucking the tide of rush hour crowds as we fought our way up the steps from the subway. Once on the street, I glanced at my watch.

"What time is it?" asked Cloris.

"Nearly five."

"We're probably too late. We should have waited until tomorrow morning."

"Gina promised to wait for us," said Erica. "She'll be there."

"Even if some stud with tight buns asks her out for drinks?" asked Cloris.

Erica shook her head as the three of us jogged across the street, skirting slower pedestrians and dodging cabs turning in front of us. "Gina doesn't drink," she said.

"Everyone in New York drinks," said Cloris. "It's practically a residency requirement. How else do you think they cope with all this." With a sneer, she swept her arm in front of her.

Cloris despised the city. She was thrilled by our relocation to a meadow in Morris County. I was surprised when she'd volunteered to accompany us on our late afternoon field trip, but curiosity and an innate love of snooping had won out over hordes of humanity, bumper-to-bumper snarling SUVs, mind-numbing noise, and sidewalks filled with putrefied piles of trash.

"Gina has very strong feelings about alcohol," said Erica. "Her father's a drunk. Besides, all the guys who work for Emil are gay."

"Including Emil?" asked Cloris. "Maybe he killed Marlys because she called him a fag."

"Except Emil," she said.

Cloris and I stopped short and stared at her. "And you know this because ...?" I asked.

Erica's cheeks, bright pink from the stinging cold wind whipping down the street, deepened to crimson. "Gina has a huge crush on him."

"Another suspect," I said. "Gina could have killed Marlys."

"You think she saw Marlys coming on to Emil and decided to eliminate her competition?" asked Cloris.

"Possibly."

"No," said Erica, her voice firm and defiant as she led us to a dilapidated tenement sandwiched between two high-rises. "Gina did not kill Emil."

"How do you know so much about Emil Pachette's secretary?" I asked as we entered the miniscule lobby.

Erica pushed the button for the elevator. "She's not his secretary. She's his assistant."

"That still doesn't explain how you know so much about her," said Cloris.

"She's my cousin."

"The plot thickens," said Cloris.

After a groan and a creak, the elevator doors opened, and the three of us stepped inside. "That doesn't mean she's not a killer," I said.

Erica stabbed the button for the fifth floor. The elevator shuddered to life, jerking and rattling its way skyward. With mounting trepidation, I eyed the tiny graffiti-covered confines of the compartment.

"Gina agreed to help us," said Erica, her voice now petulant. "That proves she didn't have anything to do with Marlys's death."

"Maybe Emil was about to ditch Gina for Marlys," said Cloris. "You know what they say about hell having no fury like a woman scorned."

The elevator lurched to a halt. My stomach caught up with the rest of me several seconds later, but it took an additional ten or fifteen seconds before the doors stuttered open. I glanced down. The elevator had come to a stop at least eight inches below the cracked and dirt-caked vinyl flooring.

"We walk down," I said.

"No complaint here," said Cloris.

After we hoisted ourselves out of the elevator, Erica led us down the grimy, dimly lit hall to a frosted glass door at the end of the corridor. Half-hidden under a fine layer of soot, swirling black-rimmed gold letters spelled out *House of Pachette*.

"I think we can rule Emil Pachette out as the murderer," I said.

"How so?" asked Cloris.

"If you worked in this dive, would you kill the goose offering you a platinum egg?"

"Shh," said Erica, her hand poised on the doorknob. "Gina's very upset about Emil's disappearance. She thinks we're here to help her figure out what happened to him, not find evidence to convict him of murder."

Cloris saluted her. "Lead on, Macduff."

We entered into a cramped workroom overflowing with industrial sewing machines, steamers, mannequins in various states of dress and undress, dozens of bolts of fabric, and bins brimming with notions. An enormous cutting table took up most of the center of the room. Squeezed into one corner was a battered metal filing cabinet and an equally battered oak desk with a mismatched chair.

A frazzled-looking, pudgy young woman with red-rimmed eyes rose from behind the desk. She stared at us for a moment, puzzlement settling across her face. Then with a gasp, she ran into Erica's arms. "Omigod! Erica, I almost didn't recognize you."

Erica laughed. "You're not the only one. I look in the mirror and see a stranger."

Gina stepped back. Holding Erica's hands in hers, she studied her cousin from head to toe. "But a drop-dead gorgeous stranger."

She pulled one of her hands free and tucked a clump of straggly dishwater brown hair behind her ear. "I must look like something the cat wouldn't bother dragging in, but I'm so glad you're here. I can't stop crying."

With that she collapsed sobbing into Erica's arms and wailed, "I don't know what to do. It's like he's vanished off the face of the earth. No one's seen or heard from him since late Monday morning."

FIFTEEN

"Where was Emil headed when he left?" I asked Gina after her sobbing had subsided to an occasional hiccup.

She lifted her head from Erica's shoulder. Swiping at her cheek with her shoulder, she sniffed back her tears and directed a wary, watery brown gaze toward me. "Who are you?"

Erica stepped out of Gina's embrace but kept her arm wrapped around her cousin's shoulders as she made introductions. "These are the friends from work I told you about. Anastasia and Cloris. They're here to help."

Gina's expression remained cautious as her gaze darted between Cloris and me. "Emil had a meeting downtown."

"With whom?"

She fiddled with a button on her work smock. "He didn't tell me."

"Nothing written in his appointment book?"

"He doesn't keep one."

Or keeps it from her. "So you don't know if he ever made it to his meeting?"

She answered with a shake of her head, accompanied by a mournful sigh.

"Do you know anything about his date with Marlys Vandenburg Monday night?"

Gina's features hardened. Her body stiffened under her billowy cobalt blue work smock. "It was a business meeting, not a date."

"But you knew he was supposed to meet her?"

She tugged on both ends of the yellow tape measure slung around her neck and scowled at a pair of scuffed black boots that peaked out beneath a frayed pair of stonewashed denim jeans. "I knew."

Cloris cleared her throat. "You don't sound very happy about it."

"Why would I? Marlys Vandenburg strutted around like she was Queen of the Fashion District, even though she only worked for some third-rate monthly."

When Cloris arched her eyebrow, Gina quickly added, "No offense."

"We prefer to think of ourselves as second-rate," I said, "but go on."

Gina paced between the cutting table and the bank of sewing machines that lined the far wall of the room. Her fingers fidgeted with the ends of the tape measure. "Emil couldn't stand Marlys, the way she used and abused people. He used to mock her behind her back. But when she took an interest in his new line, he decided to milk her for as much publicity as he could get. Better to suck up, he figured, than wind up another victim of her poison pen."

She stopped pacing and spun around to confront me. "Believe me, no way was he looking forward to spending Monday night with her." She gulped back a sob. "And now he's missing."

Why did I get the feeling I was watching a scene from a Grade-B soap opera? Believe her? Gina's body language announced in ninety-six point extra-bold type that she was either laying on a whopper or holding back a huge chunk of truth. "Have you filed a missing persons report with the police?"

She hesitated, darting a quick glance toward Erica. "Sort of."

"*Sort of*?" asked Cloris.

Gina paced over to the windows and slumped into one of the sewing machine chairs. She clenched her fists in her lap and lowered her head. "The police came looking for Emil yesterday. Said they wanted to ask him some questions. I figured it was about Marlys's murder. I got scared."

"You didn't tell them he's missing?" I asked.

"I said he was out of town, that he hadn't said where he was going, and I didn't know when he'd be back. I'm not sure they believed me."

Since Gina's acting abilities were on a par with the late Anna Nicole Smith's, I'm sure they didn't. "Do you mind if we look through the computer and his files?" I asked.

"I've already gone through everything several times, but be my guest. Maybe you'll discover something I missed."

But after an hour of looking through dozens of cyber and paper files, prying into every nook and cranny of the workshop, sifting on hands and knees through every drawer and bin, not a clue to Emil Pachette's whereabouts turned up. "What about his apartment?" I asked.

Once again Gina hesitated, glancing at Erica before she answered. "He's not there. I checked."

"You have a key?" asked Cloris.

"Emil keeps a spare set locked in the filing cabinet. When he didn't show up for work yesterday and didn't answer his phone or cell, I decided to check for myself. I thought he might be ill."

"Did you look for any clues as to where he might have gone?" I asked.

Her chin shot up. Her cheeks flushed to near purple. She backed up until her rump banged into the corner of the sewing machine cabinet, spilling a plastic container of straight pins onto the hardwood floor. "I didn't snoop through his things," she cried.

In my mind I heard Ralph squawking, "*The lady doth protest too much, methinks. Hamlet.* Act Three, Scene Two."

"We're not accusing you of snooping," snapped Cloris.

"We're here to help," added Erica. She crossed the room and placed a hand on her cousin's forearm. "Why don't we all go over to Emil's apartment and take a look? Maybe we'll find a clue."

Gina mulled the idea over for a moment before agreeing. "Maybe that's a good idea," she said as she shrugged out of her work smock and tossed it on the cutting table. She crossed the room to the desk and removed a worn leather shoulder bag from the bottom drawer. After fishing around in her purse for a set of keys, she grabbed a navy pea coat hanging from a clothes tree near the entrance, then flipped off the lights and opened the door.

"Aren't you forgetting something?" I asked.

She glanced around the room. "I don't think so."

"What about the keys to Emil's apartment?"

Gina's cheeks once again flamed as red as a neon bar sign. The girl blushed as much as a heroine in a Barbara Cartland romance novel. Her fist tightened around the ring of keys in her hand. "I have them."

"On your key ring?" asked Cloris.

Gina threw back her shoulders and jutted out her chin. "I forgot to put them back in the filing cabinet. Is that a crime?"

With Gina focused on Cloris, I shot Cloris a back-off-I-need-her-cooperation-to-clear-me look.

"Of course not," I said in my best reassuring tone. "I'll bet you've been totally distracted with worry. I know I would be."

She offered me a shy smile that I suspected was meant to throw off my suspicions. I smiled back, letting her think I bought into her act. Gina definitely knew more than she was divulging.

———

Fifteen minutes later, the four of us stood inside Emil Pachette's cramped third-floor walk-up in Hell's Kitchen. A quick perusal of the studio apartment revealed someone had left in a hurry. Half-emptied dresser drawers were pulled open, clothes strewn across the bed and on the floor. An open box of Frosted Flakes lay on the table. Dirty dishes filled the sink.

I turned to Gina. "Did the apartment look like this yesterday?"

"Yes."

"No toothbrush," said Cloris, peaking out from the closet-sized bathroom.

I walked over to the desk and rifled through the mail. "Bills. Utilities. Cable. Phone." I lifted the pages of the phone bill and scanned the list of long-distance calls. "Where is Emil from originally?" I asked Gina.

"Paris."

I studied the bill further. "You sure?"

"Of course, I'm sure. Most of his family still live there."

"Have you ever met any of them?"

"No. Emil's parents are afraid to fly. Especially after September 11th. They don't even want him flying home to visit them."

"So he speaks with them regularly?"

Gina sat down on the edge of a slightly tattered nubby cocoa and tan herringbone loveseat. She picked up a saffron-and-celery-colored toss pillow laying to her left and wove the fringe through her fingers as she spoke. "Quite often. He calls his parents at least once a week."

"From the office?"

"No." She continued to fidget the fringe, pouting at the pillow as she spoke. "Emil never makes personal calls from the office phone."

"Then how do you know he speaks with his parents?" asked Cloris.

Gina tossed the pillow aside and glared at Cloris. "Because he tells me."

———

"So what do you think?" asked Cloris after we left Emil's apartment. We had forced ourselves into an already over-packed subway car headed back to Penn Station. There are few experiences in life equal to full body contact with total strangers on a New York subway, but if we didn't catch the last rush hour train to Morris County, we'd have an hour's wait for the next one.

"I think Emil has Gina and everyone else bamboozled," I said as the train came to a halt and we fell out onto the platform.

Now that my arms were no longer pinned to my sides, I glanced at my watch. We had less than five minutes to race through the underground maze connecting the subway system to New Jersey Transit.

"What do you mean?" asked Erica, trying to keep up with the jogging pace Cloris and I set. I slowed a tad. Poor Erica probably wished she could wave a magic wand and transform those strappy burgundy suede Jimmy Choos into her broken-in Doc Martens.

"If that man's from France, I'm from Venus."

"Want to explain?" asked Cloris.

Ahead of us, I saw the *Now Boarding* sign flashing above the steps to our platform. I waited to answer until we had raced down the steps and onto the train.

"According to his phone bill," I said, collapsing into the first available three-person bench seat, "Emil Pachette didn't call Paris once last month."

Erica's eyes widened as she gulped in a few deep breaths. "But Gina said he calls his parents at least once a week. Why would he lie to her about that?"

"He didn't."

"But you just said—"

"I said he didn't call Paris, but he did phone Horse Thief Falls, Minnesota, nine times. I think Emil Pachette is a big phony."

"So?" said Cloris. She unbuttoned her coat and fanned herself with the beret she had pulled off her head. "Lots of people create new personas for themselves in order to advance their careers. It might be unethical, but it's not necessarily illegal. Or a motive for murder."

"Maybe. Maybe not," I said, unbuttoning my own coat. New Jersey Transit had two temperature settings on their trains—Hell and Siberia. Thanks to my participation in the subway marathon, Hell had graduated to hotter-than-Hell.

"What are you getting at?" she asked.

"Think about it. We're all assuming Marlys had adopted Emil as her next pet project."

"She practically announced it at the staff meeting Monday morning," said Erica.

"We all know Marlys never did anything that didn't benefit Marlys first and foremost. What would she get out of promoting a questionable fashion talent like Emil Pachette?"

Having seen his work, I had little doubt the mediocre designer would eventually wind up as an assistant buyer for moderately priced women's wear at Macy's. "What if that was a ruse to cover up her true intentions?"

"Of course!" cried Cloris.

"What?" asked Erica, glancing first toward Cloris, then shifting her attention to me.

Jessica Fletcher, move over. It may have taken me a bit longer than an hour, but I had figured out whodunit. "Somehow, Marlys discovered Emil's true identity. Marlys being Marlys, she decided to blackmail him, but she got more than she bargained for."

It all made perfect sense. "Knowing he had little choice," I explained, "Emil agreed to the blackmail. He then probably came up with some pretext to get Marlys back to the office Monday night. Once there, he pulled out a bottle of Merlot. When Marlys wasn't looking, he doctored her glass. And the rest, as they say, is *Murder She Wrote*—or in this case, *Murder He Glued*."

———

On the way home from the office, my cell phone rang. I glanced at the display. This time I recognized the number. Zachary Barnes.

What could he want? My brain zeroed in on the obvious. He'd had second thoughts about leaving Manhattan and was pulling out of the rental agreement.

Wasn't there some law that allowed for reneging from a signed contract within two or three days? Shit and double-shit. I'd already spent his deposit check on some of my own bills. Now what?

I answered the phone, expecting to hear the worst. "Hello?"

"Hi, it's Zack Barnes. I'm back from New Mexico and was wondering if I could drop by sometime tonight to do a bit of measuring."

I couldn't help myself; I let loose with a huge laugh of relief.

"Something funny?"

"Just one very over-active imagination," I said. "I was worried you were calling to pull out."

"Never. That apartment is perfect for me. So do you mind?"

"I had a late day at the office. I'm on my way home now. Come whenever it's convenient for you."

"Great. And by the way, Anastasia ... "

"Yes."

"You'll find I'm a man of my word. I don't go around screwing people."

Sure, I once thought the same of Karl. What was that old saying? *Fool me once, shame on you; fool me twice, shame on me*? From now on my skepticism ran deep.

I arrived home after nine, tired and hungry, but relieved that I no longer had to worry about Batswin and Robbins pinning a murder rap on me—or Zachary Barnes pulling out of the rental. My newly elevated comfort level lasted only until I pulled into the driveway and my headlights spotlighted the broken basement window.

SIXTEEN

My heart raced as I grabbed my cell phone and called the house. One ring. Two rings. I had no idea if the intruder was still inside. Three rings.

"Hello?"

"Nick, is everything okay?"

He laughed. "Kind of depends on your definition of okay, doesn't it, Mom?"

Was this a hint of a problem? "What do you mean?"

"Well, the Grandmas are accusing each other of plotting the world's destruction, as usual. Mephisto and Catherine the Great are circling each other like two cocks about to spar, as usual. And Ralph is squawking play-by-play, as usual. So I guess nothing's really okay, but it's pretty much normal for here, right?"

"Right."

"Where are you?" he asked.

"In the driveway."

"Huh?"

"I'll explain in a minute." After placing a call to the Westfield police, I shut off the engine and headed for the back door.

As much as I had hoped the broken window was the result of a stray baseball, the evidence proved otherwise. Someone had definitely broken into my house. Again. Large, muddy footprints led from the top of the washing machine, which sat directly under the cellar window, across the laundry room, through the basement, and up the stairs.

Of course neither the boys nor their grandmothers had noticed—let alone cleaned up—the dirt that was tracked across the kitchen floor and ground into the dining room and living room carpets.

"Anything missing?" asked Fogarty when he and Harley arrived five minutes later.

"Not that I can see," I said.

Unlike the previous break-in, the house hadn't been trashed. Otherwise, I would have immediately suspected Ricardo. However, like last time, the intruder had left undisturbed both the few pieces of good jewelry I owned, and the electronics and computer equipment.

This made two break-ins in twenty-four hours with nothing taken. And that sent a sub-zero wind chill coursing up my spine and through my veins. Was the burglar looking for something very specific, or were we dealing with some creep playing a perverted game? Did all of this have something to do with Karl's secret life? Were there more unsavory things I had yet to learn about my husband? More unsavory associates of his waiting to pounce on me and my family?

"And no one saw or heard anything?" asked Harley, his stub of a pencil poised over his spiral-bound pocket notepad.

"*Heard you of nothing strange about the streets? Antony and Cleopatra.* Act Four, Scene Three."

Harley jumped at the sound of Ralph squawking his two cents worth of Shakespeare, then forced a chuckle to mask his embarrassment. "Forgot about him," he muttered, shaking his head.

"That's one damn smart bird," said Fogarty. "Ever think of putting him in show business?"

"He only speaks when the mood strikes him," I said, watching Ralph swoop from one lampshade across the room to another, where he had a better bead on Catherine the Great. The haughty feline paused from grooming her privates to bestow a disdainful glare on Ralph.

"Too bad he can't tell us what he saw." Harley turned his attention to the boys. "How about you guys? See or hear anything?"

Nick and Alex shook their heads. "We didn't get home until after five," said Alex. "I was at the library."

"I had basketball practice," said Nick.

Fogarty turned to Mama and Lucille. "What about you ladies?"

Lucille, clutching a growling Mephisto to her chest, glowered at Fogarty as if he had just accused her of voting for Ronald Reagan. Twice. "I was out all day. And I have plenty of witnesses."

Fogarty and Harley exchanged odd glances but neither commented. Fogarty backed away a step or two but kept a leery eye on Mephisto.

Harley continued his questioning. "And you, ma'am?" he asked Mama.

She tossed her head back and finger-fluffed a lock of newly cut and colored hair with her freshly polished French manicure. "Not while I was home," she said in a perfect imitation of Liz Taylor's seductive little girl voice, "but I did spend several hours at that day spa on Elm this afternoon." Then she batted her mascara-coated eyelashes at him.

Poor Seamus O'Keefe was still warm in his coffin, but that didn't stop Mama, the quintessential flirt, in her quest for Husband Number Six—even if Officer Harley was nearly young enough to be her son.

I stole a quick glance at the third finger of his pudgy left hand. No wedding band, but that didn't necessarily mean anything.

I thought about warning him, but if Mama hooked him as a Seamus replacement, I'd have one less headache—not to mention bruiseless legs. So I kept quiet. Every woman to herself. Besides, all's fair in love and war, and Officer Harley looked quite capable of taking care of himself.

Harley scrubbed at his jaw, apparently immune or unaware of Mama's seductive charms. "That's when the perp must've struck. Maybe he heard you come home and high-tailed it out before he could grab anything or do any damage."

He turned to me. "This may or may not be the same guy as last time. We've had a rash of burglaries in the area over the past few days and not much in the way of clues."

"Similar to mine where the house is trashed but nothing taken?"

"No, that's the odd part of this. All the other homes reported items missing."

"And none of them were tossed the way yours was yesterday," said Fogarty. "We've beefed up patrols in the neighborhood, but if I were you, Mrs. Pollack, I'd think about getting an alarm system installed."

Sure, with the one hundred thirty-seven dollars and fifty-three cents left in my checking account. "I'll consider it," I said as I walked Fogarty and Harley to the door.

"The cops in this town are a waste of taxpayer money," muttered Lucille after I closed the door behind the officers. "Those two are no different from all the rest. Only interested in harassing honest, hard-working people."

I suspected her comment had something to do with the jaywalking ticket she'd received the day before. You'd think after nearly getting herself killed jaywalking across Queens Boulevard several months ago, my mother-in-law would have learned her lesson. Not Lucille. She expected the world and all its traffic to stop whenever she stepped off a curb. Intersection or no intersection. Green light or red.

Mephisto bared his teeth and growled in agreement of her assessment of Westfield's finest.

That did it. I was tired, hungry, cranky, and pre-menstrual, and that poor excuse for a dog was a convenient target.

I spun around, baring my own pearly whites. "Some watchdog you are. If you want your daily dose of kibble, you'd better start pulling your weight around here. I can't afford you *and* an alarm system."

He answered me with a king-of-the-jungle snarl. Too bad he acted like the Cowardly Lion. Instead of behaving like other members of his species and chewing the intruder's tibialis and gastrocnemius into mincemeat, the yellow-bellied chicken of a dog had probably hidden under a bed at the first sound of breaking glass.

Lucille's face hardened. Her eyes narrowed. The purple veins on both sides of her forehead throbbed to attention. "He's not a watchdog," she said, "and now you've gone and upset him!"

With one arm still clutching Mephisto to her bosom, she shuffled down the hall, her cane echoing her anger as she pounded it on the hardwood.

I refrained from growling back at both of them.

I'd spent all of last night cleaning up from the last break-in with little help from the rest of my family. Everyone had had a handy excuse. Lucille cited her recent injuries, Mama managed to come down with a convenient migraine, and both boys had tests to study for and homework assignments due the next day.

Tonight I was accepting no excuses. After handing Mama the carpet cleaner and ordering the boys to wash the kitchen floor, stairs, cellar floor, and top of the washing machine, I grabbed my keys and coat to head for Home Depot.

"What about Grandmother Lucille?" asked Nick.

"Yeah, how come she doesn't have to help?" asked Alex.

"Because if she got down on her hands and knees to scrub— not that she would—it would take the four of us to haul her back up. Besides, between her poor eyesight and rotten attitude, we'd only have to redo whatever she did."

I left to the sound of grumbling complaints. You'd think I'd asked them to clean the floors of Grand Central Station with a toothbrush. Maybe it was time I came clean to my sons and told them the bitter truth of our situation.

I'd totally forgotten about Zachary Barnes until I arrived home to find him sitting at my kitchen table with Mama, Alex, and Nick. For two smart kids, mine sure act like a couple of nincompoops sometimes. As for Mama, her common sense disappeared sometime between her Periwinkle and Ramirez stints and hasn't been seen or heard from since.

"Sorry I wasn't here when you arrived," I told him, "but I guess it really didn't matter, did it?" I said this last part as I glared at my sons.

"What did we do?" asked Nick.

"You tell me. We've had two break-ins in two days, and you let a total stranger into the house? What's wrong with this picture?"

"What stranger?" asked Alex. "He's our new tenant."

"And exactly how did you know that?"

"Because he said so."

"Well, then, my apologies. *He said so.* And with that every safety lesson ever drummed into the two of you flies out the window."

"Jeez, Mom. Chill."

"Chill, Nick? You let a stranger into our home, and *you're* telling *me* to *chill?*"

"You told us his name," said Alex, coming to his brother's defense.

"Did you ask to see ID?"

Of course not. I could tell by their expressions.

"Did it ever occur to you to pick up that handy gadget Mr. Alexander Graham Bell invented and *call your mother* before opening the door *to a total stranger*?"

They both mumbled something I couldn't make out.

"Is my life not complicated enough lately, guys? Do I have to worry that you two have been abducted by aliens and returned minus your Common Sense Genes?"

"Honestly, Anastasia, I think you're over-reacting just a little bit, don't you?" said Mama. She flashed one of her Flora-on-the-prowl-for-a-new-husband smiles at Zack. "After all, how could anyone with such an honest face not be who he says he is?"

"I give up!" I turned to Zack, "Mama says you have an honest face, so *mi casa es su casa*."

"Sorry," he said. "It never occurred to me that I'd be igniting a world war, but you're right. Your sons shouldn't have let me in, not without first asking to see ID. I guess I figured if you had to go out, you would've mentioned I'd be coming."

"Frankly, I forgot you were coming," I said. "It's been a little crazy around here since I got home."

"So I hear. *Two* break-ins?"

Here it comes. A perfect excuse to pull out. With all his expensive camera equipment, I'm sure the last thing he wanted was an apartment in a burgeoning crime zone. "That's right. Two break-ins. In two days. So I guess you've changed your mind and now want out of our agreement?"

"Did I say that?"

He hadn't, but I figured it was only a matter of moments until he did.

"What kind of security precautions are you taking?" he asked.

"Two-by-fours across the basement windows."

He laughed. The man actually laughed at me. "Two-by-fours? You've got to be kidding. That's not going to stop someone bent on getting in."

"It's all I can afford. I plan to bolt them to the walls, not nail them. That should do the trick."

"Mom, Zack said he could install spy cameras for us," said Nick.

"Mr. Barnes," I corrected. "I guess along with sucking the common sense out of you, the aliens also made off with your manners."

"He said we could call him Zack."

I turned to the hunk in question.

"As long as you don't mind," he said.

"Fine. If you don't mind, I don't mind." I had bigger battles to fight. "Did you finish your homework?" I asked my sons.

"Sort of," said Nick.

"Almost," said Alex. "Zack said he's got all sorts of cool equipment, Mom."

"*Very* cool equipment," said Mama, back in Elizabeth Taylor mode and letting her gaze drink in Mr. Perfection.

"Mama!"

Zack had the decency to blush. Knowing Mama, the conversation would only get more X-rated from here. I turned to Alex and Nick. "Homework."

"Just when we're about to get to the good stuff," complained Nick.

I pointed toward their bedroom. "Now."

As they reluctantly headed down the hall, Mama continued her full frontal assault. "Can I assume the apartment is for you and you alone, Zack, dear?"

"Told you so," grumbled Nick. "We never get to stick around for the good stuff."

"Just me," Zack answered, trying to keep from laughing. It didn't take a PhD in psychology to realize he was enjoying this farce way too much.

Mama batted her lashes. I wondered if any of the local amateur theaters were casting a senior citizen version of *A Streetcar Named Desire*. Mama would make a perfect sexagenarian Blanche DuBois. "No wife?" she said. "How is that possible, a good-looking man like you?"

Good Lord, couldn't she at least wait until Seamus had turned into a worm banquet before casting her husband-catching net upon the available waters? The woman had absolutely no shame.

Or maybe she was just scared to be alone and without a man in her life. As embarrassed as my mother made me at times, I did feel sorry for what was turning into an endless streak of bad luck for her. Ever since my father had died, whenever Mama gave away her heart, fate threw her a curve ball.

"I was married once," said the overly-accommodating available man in question. "It didn't work out."

"And no significant other?" continued the Cross Examiner from Hell.

"Not at the present."

"No children?"

"Wasn't married long enough."

It was time for me to step in as the adult in this situation. "You don't have to humor her," I told Zack. "And as for you, Mama, enough with the Flora Inquisition."

Then I turned back to Zack and in my mind, the more pressing issue. "You're welcome to install whatever you want for the apartment. At your own expense."

"I intend to, but I'd be happy to fix you up with some equipment, too. We could catch this guy red-handed if he returns."

"So you still want to move in?"

"Why are you finding that so hard to believe?"

"You'll have to forgive my daughter," said Mama. "She's not into men."

"Mama!"

"Hey, whatever floats your boat," said Zack. "I don't pass judgments."

But was that a flicker of disappointment I saw streak across his face or just my own imagination shifting into overdrive?

"I'm not a lesbian!" I said.

"Well, honestly, Anastasia! Whatever would make you say such a thing?"

"You just implied—"

"I implied no such thing."

"But it's good to know," said Zachary Barnes. He winked. *Winked!* What was that all about? "Want some help putting up those two-by-fours before I leave?"

Did I ever! But declining seemed a more appropriate response at the moment.

Unfortunately, Mama beat me to the punch. "We'd love your help, wouldn't we, dear?

"Oh, and by the way, speaking of lesbians—"

"We weren't speaking of lesbians, Mama."

"Of course we were, dear. You brought the subject up. Don't you remember?"

"I give up!"

Mama turned back to Zack. "As I was saying, speaking of lesbians, you're not gay, are you, Zack dear? That's not why your marriage ended, was it? Not that I have anything against gays, mind you. Anastasia's cousin-by-marriage Lawrence Goldberg is gay, and he's a lovely young man, isn't he, Anastasia?"

"Sure, Mama. Larry's the salt of the earth, but Zachary's sex life is none of your business. Can it."

"I was only making conversation, dear. No need to get all huffy. I still say you need a vacation. This stress is getting to you."

What was I going to do with her?

Was Flora Sudberry Periwinkle Ramirez Scoffield Goldberg O'Keefe setting her sights on becoming Flora Sudberry Periwinkle Ramirez Scoffield Goldberg O'Keefe Barnes? Or was she trolling for a new son-in-law? I'd have to read my mother the Riot Act before she went to bed tonight. Meanwhile, I guess I was getting some help with those studs—from a stud.

———

"You realize this is a safety hazard, don't you?" asked Zack. Using Karl's electric drill, he fastened a bolt through one end of the two-by-four I held, securing it to the concrete wall alongside one of the six basement windows. "It may even be a building code violation."

"How so?"

"What if there were a fire and you were trapped in the basement. You'd have no way to get out."

"If the fire were upstairs, I'd have time to grab the drill and free up one of the windows."

"What if the fire started from the furnace exploding?" he asked.

I glanced across the room and frowned at the furnace. "I didn't think of that."

He gave me one of those looks men reserve for women whom they think aren't as smart as they are. I really, really hate that look.

I thought for a moment, then shrugged. "If the furnace exploded, I'd either be severely injured or dead, so it wouldn't matter. Either way, I'd be in no condition to climb out a window, bolted or not."

He moved to the other end of the two-by-four and set about attaching the second bolt. "Now that's a pleasant thought. Do you always look at the glass half empty?"

"Actually, up until last week I always assumed it was half full."

"What changed your mind?"

"My husband died and left me with a parting surprise—not a dime to my name and a secret mountain of debt."

He stopped drilling and turned to face me. "Jeez, I didn't know. For some reason I just assumed you'd been divorced for a few years. And here I've been—"

Dare I say it? "Flirting?"

He gave me one of those little-boy-caught-with-his-hand-in-the-cookie-jar looks. "Human nature for a red-blooded male. I'm sorry."

"No need to apologize," I told him. "I'm flattered. And my ego thanks you for the much needed stroking. It's not every day a slightly overweight, middle-aged working mom receives attention from someone who's been in *People* magazine."

"Those were nothing but photo ops instigated by a money hungry publicist and a well-positioned photographer on his payroll."

"Hey, I could strip down to my undies and strum a guitar in Times Square. I doubt I'd make it into *People* magazine."

He eyed me head to toe, and I felt the heat rushing to my cheeks. "You never know."

"You're still doing it," I said, but I couldn't keep from chuckling. Zachary Barnes had a way of making me forget the shit swirling around me, even though we were talking about that very shit.

"I figured your ego wouldn't mind. But you're right. I'm a jerk."

I shrugged. "Forget it. Shit happens. I just never expected it to happen to me."

"These break-ins certainly haven't helped," he said. "You've sure had your share of bad luck lately."

"You have no idea." No way was I going to tell him about Ricardo and Marlys. I'd probably said more than I should already, but something about Zack Barnes made me feel safe in opening up to him. To a point.

We moved to the next window. "By the way," I said. "I'd appreciate it if you didn't mention the debt thing to my kids. I haven't told them yet. I wanted to give them time to deal with their father's death first."

"No problem. I'm good at keeping secrets."

"So while you were waiting for me to come home, my sons and mother didn't tell you every single detail of my life, down to the color of my toothbrush and whether I have an innie or an outie?"

Or that I found a dead body in my office Monday night and the police think I killed her?

He grinned. "Nothing about a toothbrush, but there was some mention of an innie."

"You're doing it again."

"But you haven't whacked me with one of those two-by-fours yet, so I figure your ego still needs some attention."

"That's totally not fair, you know."

He screwed in another bolt. "How so?"

"Because thanks to my bigmouthed sons and mother, you now know so much about me—"

"And you think it's only fair to have an even playing field?"

"Exactly."

"You're right. Equality among the sexes." He moved to the other side of the window and secured the second bolt. "I guess I should admit that I, too, have an innie."

"Great. I feel so much better knowing that about you, Zachary Barnes."

"Okay," he said as we moved to the third window. "I'll tell you a couple of other things."

"They don't have anything to do with unexposed body parts, do they? Because if so, I'll pass."

"No body parts, exposed or otherwise."

"And nothing that will embarrass me?"

"That I can't guarantee. But I don't think so."

"Oh, you're good. Tease me just enough that I have to know. So what are these two things?"

He fastened another bolt before speaking. "I think your kids are pretty cool, Anastasia Pollack. And your mother's a hoot." He turned to look at me. "Was she really coming on to me?"

I laughed. "Can't get anything past you."

"You'll find I'm a very observant person."

"Mama somehow managed to be born without the Subtle Gene. She's on the prowl for her next husband. Take that as a friendly warning."

"As flattered as I am, I'm afraid I'll have to disappoint her."

"How surprising."

"Think she'll be heartbroken?"

"For at least forty-eight hours. That's about as long as it should take her to set her sights on my next potential future stepfather."

SEVENTEEN

AFTER ZACK LEFT I headed for Alex and Nick's room. The time had come for the family talk I'd put off since learning of Karl's deceit. Both Lucille and Mama already knew what Karl had done. Sooner or later one of them was bound to let something slip.

Better the boys heard the truth from me. Minus the Ricardo chapter. I figured one member of the family scared out of her wits was already one too many. Alex and Nick were still trying to come to terms with their father's death. Dumping abject poverty on them was enough of an added whammy without them having to worry about some threat-hurling low-life scum stalking us.

"How could Dad do this to us?" asked Nick. He pounded his fist so hard on his desk that his wireless keyboard went flying. Luckily, it landed on the bed.

"Sorry," he mumbled.

"Try to control yourself. We can't afford any repair bills right now. Or new computer equipment."

I placed my hand on his shoulder. His most recent growth spurt had added another two inches to his lanky frame, which now hovered just shy of the magic six-foot mark. Both boys had inherited their father's good looks, but Nick, still suffering from the gawkiness of adolescence, had yet to grow into his.

At first the boys greeted my pronouncement of destitution with stunned silence. It took awhile for the news to sink in. Then their silence transformed to anger, and Nick had taken his out with his fist.

"What about college?" asked Alex.

Time for me to harness a Scarlett O'Hara moment: *As God is my witness, I'll scrub floors if I have to.* But floor scrubbers don't make enough to pay Harvard tuition and neither do editors of second-rate women's magazines. My salary would cover monthly bills, but there would be little left to dig us out of the debt Karl had plunged us into, let alone pay for college.

Still, I couldn't leave my kids without hope, no matter how slim. "Scholarships. Loans. Part-time jobs."

Who was I kidding? Harvard was over forty grand a year. Even the reasonably priced local community college now loomed out of reach, but somehow we'd manage. I just needed to figure out a game plan.

"Goddamn fucking asshole!" yelled Alex. "That selfish bastard's ruined my life!"

I didn't blame him for the outburst, and now was not the time to reprimand him about his language. I knew he loved his father, but he felt betrayed. He'd worked hard to achieve his dream. His grades proved that, but his parents hadn't held up their end of the bargain.

He turned his anger on me. "Damn it, Mom, how could you let this happen?"

My eyes welled up with tears that I fought back with a loud snuffle. "I don't know. I'm sorry."

The damning truth was, I should have known. I'd been kicking myself twenty-four/seven since learning of Karl's deception.

With a full-time job, two kids' schedules to juggle, and a mental block when it came to anything remotely mathematical, I had gratefully accepted Karl's offer to handle the family finances. Hell, I never even bothered to glance at our 1040s each year, just blindly signed my name to the bottom of the first page of the tax form and handed it back to him.

Karl had handled our finances, all right. Manhandled them into non-existence. Now we were all suffering because of my lame-brain idea that a wife should be able to trust her husband. What was I thinking?

"Are we going to lose the house?" asked Nick in almost a whisper.

"I don't know. I hope not."

"How bad is it, really?" asked Alex.

"Really bad."

"Fuck!"

"But I have a few ideas. We'll make it through this. Somehow. I promise."

Alex wrapped his arm around my shoulders. The hostility drained from his face. "Okay. I suppose this is one of those spilled milk times, right? Nothing's going to change what's been done, so we need to make the best of it and move on, yada-yada-yada?" He didn't sound like he was all that convinced.

"Trust me, if crying could solve our problems, we wouldn't be having this conversation."

"So what can we do to help?"

"Yeah, just say the word," added Nick. "We'll pitch in any way we can."

That's what I'd been hoping to hear. I'd expected angry outbursts, blame placing, and sullenness that would last weeks, if not months, before they finally accepted this additional cataclysmic shift in our lives. Their maturity in light of the situation swelled my heart.

"Will we have to give up cable?" asked Nick.

So much for maturity. Maybe the reality hadn't completely sunk in yet. "Definitely."

He frowned, then shrugged. "I suppose I can live without ESPN." He cast a sideways glance at me, his eyes hopeful. "If I *really* have to."

Poor kid. A fate worse than death for a teenager who lived sports round the clock. "You *really* have to. The Internet connection goes, too." Between the two, I'd save over a hundred and fifty dollars a month.

"Mom!" They both jumped on me at once.

"I'll get a paper route. A job at McDonald's," said Nick. "I *need* the Internet."

"And when will you have time for school, homework, and sports?" I paused for a moment and eyed him. Nick spent far too much time online as it was, and he knew that I knew it. Maybe doing without some things wasn't such a bad thing, at least not from this parent's perspective.

He tried another tack. "We need the Internet for homework."

"You can use the computers at school and the library when you have to go online."

"But, Mom—"

"No buts. Desperate times call for desperate measures. I got through school without an Internet connection in my home, and you can, too."

"They didn't have Internet in the Stone Age," he said.

"And I survived in spite of it."

"I suppose this means no car, huh?" asked Alex.

Karl had promised him one for his seventeenth birthday. Karl's company car was reclaimed from the airport parking garage the day after his death. We had one car and would have only one car for a very long time to come.

"Definitely out of the question." I didn't add that he'd have to postpone getting his license because we couldn't even afford the additional auto insurance. *One whammy at a time* was my new mantra.

"What about Grandmother Lucille?" asked Nick.

"What about her?"

Nick scrunched up his face. "Does this mean she's going to live with us forever?" He glanced at his brother. "No offense, bro, but sharing a room with you really sucks."

"You're the slob," said Alex, jabbing his brother in the shoulder.

"You snore," retaliated Nick.

"She's the only family we have," I said, "and she has nowhere else to go."

"There's no old age home for crotchety commies?" asked Alex.

"Not that I know of."

"So we're stuck with her?" asked Nick.

"We're stuck with her."

Both boys groaned. Of all the ugly truths of our new situation I'd just hit them with, I think that was the one hardest for them to accept.

———

By eleven o'clock the next morning, I was on my fourth cup of coffee. Once again I had gotten far less than my suggested daily requirement of Zs, thanks to Mama's nocturnal aerobics and my eventual flight to the den sofa.

It's not that I didn't have the courage of my convictions. I fully intended to lay down the law and make Lucille and Mama share Nick's bedroom last night. However, Lucille threw a monkey wrench into my plans when she locked herself and Mephisto in—and Mama out—of the bedroom after Harley and Fogarty left.

While we were all gone yesterday, that conniving commie hadn't been "out all day" as she'd claimed to Fogarty. For part of the day she'd been home having a lock installed on Nick's bedroom door. No wonder she got all defensive when Fogarty questioned her about her whereabouts.

Anyway, repeated poundings on the door last night refused to budge the stubborn, sulking pinko. I figured she'd at least have to open up to let Mephisto do his doggy business at some point, but no such luck. The dog must have a bladder the size of Texas because neither Lucille nor Mephisto made an appearance until early this morning.

As I headed for the break room and Caffeine Fix Number Five, I added one more item to my to-do list. As soon as I returned home this evening, I planned to remove the lock from Nick's door. One more night on the den sofa and I'd wind up a crippled zombie.

I groaned as I entered the break room. Some inconsiderate bozo—most likely one of the chauvinists in sales who looked on coffee-making as woman's work—had finished the pot and hadn't started a fresh one.

It's a good thing I didn't know who it was because I refuse to accept responsibility for my actions when I'm dealing with PMS as well as sleep and caffeine deprivation. I started the coffee and waited impatiently until it had finished brewing.

"Mrs. Pollack."

At the unwelcome sound of Detective Batswin's voice, I froze mid-pour. Pasting a smile on my face and still holding the coffeepot, I spun around to find the dynamic detecting duo hovering in the break room doorway. Dressed head-to-toe in black, except for the splotches of yellow and red on the Dick Tracy tie knotted around Robbins' neck, both looked as grim as twin Reapers.

"Detectives. Making any headway in finding Marlys's killer?"

"Possibly," said Batswin. "We'd like to take a look in your office if you don't mind."

"Most of my office now resides at your headquarters," I reminded her as I finished pouring my caffeine fix, "but be my guest."

A quick mental inventory of the contents of my cubicle revealed nothing that could be of interest to Batswin and Robbins. The police already had my computer and files. And my tools and supplies. Even my chair, since Marlys had been glued to it.

Yesterday while I gallivanted around Manhattan, playing Jessica Fletcher, someone at Trimedia had removed the crime scene tape from the entrance to my cubicle, cleaned up the fingerprint powder, and installed a replacement computer and chair. The only other items in my cubicle were my coat and purse, a few family photos, a shelf of books, a spare sweater, and an umbrella.

All the same, I had to force my hands not to tremble. I couldn't shake the feeling that these two were out to get me.

Masking my nervousness with hospitality, I raised the pot toward them. "Java?"

"Don't mind if I do," said Robbins. He turned to Batswin. "Fred?"

Did I hear him correctly? "*Fred*?"

"Short for Winifred," she said, her lips thinning to a tight line. "I'll take a cup."

I poured two additional cups, passed them to the detectives, and waited while Robbins added two packets of sugar to his and Batswin lightened hers with a drop of half-and-half.

After they had both taken a sip, I waved my hand for them to precede me into the hall. "After you."

When we arrived back at my cubicle, Batswin reached for a framed photograph of Karl and the boys. She studied it for a moment. "I knew I'd seen him before." She passed the photo to Robbins.

Robbins took one look at the photo and agreed. "That's him, all right."

Batswin turned to me. "Mrs. Pollack, would you mind explaining why you failed to mention your husband was having an affair with Marlys Vandenburg?"

EIGHTEEN

AND TO THINK, ONLY last night I'd wondered if there were more unsavory details I had yet to learn about my husband. Extramarital affairs had not been one of them. In the bedroom and out of it, Karl had given every indication that after eighteen years I continued to light his fire. Even if I did fake my own conflagration more often than not.

Karl and Marlys? Even if he were cheating on me, the very notion of him with Marlys bordered on the absurd. Marlys wouldn't give the time of day to a slightly overweight, middle-aged, folliclely challenged auto parts salesman. Even if he did bear a striking resemblance to a balding Harrison Ford.

Come to think of it, given her track record, Marlys had probably spread her legs for the real Harrison Ford at some point. Or at least extended the offer.

I laughed. "You're kidding, right?"

The dead-serious expressions on the detectives' faces stated otherwise. "We don't kid when it comes to murder," said Batswin.

"This morning we received an anonymous tip," said Robbins. "The caller asked if we'd bothered to check out the photos in Ms. Vandenburg's apartment."

"She had quite a collection of herself with all sorts of celebrities," said Batswin.

"Hanging on every wall and covering just about every horizontal surface," added Robbins.

"So? Marlys was a publicity junkie."

"Yeah, that's what we figured at first," he said. "We really didn't pay much attention to them when we searched the place for clues Tuesday. Figured they were all press shots from fashion shows and premiers and stuff."

"So we went back this morning and took a closer look," said Batswin. She pulled a framed photograph out of her briefcase and passed it to me. "And we discovered this on her night table."

My legs turned to overcooked rigatoni. I collapsed into my new chair and stared at the photograph. Karl and Marlys. Looking for all the world like lovers as they snuggled together for the camera. A row of slot machines and a neon casino sign filled the background.

Every synapse in my brain backfired and sputtered to a halt at the sight of my husband making goo-goo eyes at Marlys Vandenburg.

"You might want to consider hiring a lawyer, Mrs. Pollack," said Robbins.

My head shot up. "Are you arresting me?"

"Not yet," said Batswin.

"I didn't kill Marlys," I said. "I had no idea she and my husband even knew each other."

Batswin cocked an eyebrow.

"I mean, they met once or twice at our annual office Christmas party, but they never said more than two words to each other. Karl wasn't Marlys's type. She dated minor celebrities and players. Guys who came with big bucks and business managers and publicists."

For all I knew, she'd even dated Zachary Barnes. Maybe I should ask him.

"Marlys wouldn't recognize Karl if they passed on the street."

"Looks to me like they knew each other real well," said Robbins.

At the thought of looming arrest, my brain kicked back into action. Enough whining. I took a deep breath and challenged Batswin and Robbins. "This photo doesn't prove Karl and Marlys were having an affair, and it certainly doesn't prove I killed Marlys. If it did, you'd arrest me now."

Batswin tapped her index finger on the glass covering the photo. "We've already established you had the means and opportunity, Mrs. Pollack. Now we have the motive. We know your husband left you swimming in debt and at the mercy of a loan shark. Here's why. He was living the high life with his mistress."

"You found out about the affair after his untimely death," said Robbins, "and killed Marlys for the diamonds to get yourself out of hock."

The Dynamic Duo had me scared shitless, but they also had me angry, and I wasn't going to let them railroad me. I thrust the photograph back at Batswin and jumped to my feet. "That's a Swiss cheese theory. Full of holes and I think you both know it."

"Really?"

166

"Really." I raised my own index finger and waved it under Batswin's nose. "First, if I killed Marlys for the diamonds, which I didn't, why—as I've pointed out to you from the very beginning—would I bother to inform you of their existence? You're forgetting that *I'm* the one who gave you the killer's probable motive. If I planned to pawn the diamonds, don't you think I'd have enough intelligence to keep my mouth shut about them?"

She said nothing. Neither did Robbins. Then I thought of something else. I plunged forward. "How tall are you, Detective Batswin?"

"What does that have to do with anything?"

"Humor me."

"A tad shy of six feet," she said.

"And your weight?"

"About one sixty."

I eyed her from head to toe. "Marlys Vandenburg was near your height but probably thirty-five or forty pounds lighter. I'm all of five feet, two inches."

I pushed up my sweater sleeve and jiggled the flab under my upper arm. "As you can see, I don't work out. Do you seriously think I have the strength to lug six feet and a hundred twenty pounds of dead weight from Marlys's office to mine, let alone haul her up into my desk chair?"

"We're thinking you probably had an accomplice," suggested Robbins.

"Have you found any evidence of an accomplice? Were there rug burns or carpet fibers imbedded in her skin from this ficti-tious co-conspirator and me dragging her halfway across the building?"

When they glanced at each other, I knew I'd struck a nerve. Marlys hadn't been dragged from her office, down the hall to my cubicle.

I continued. "Or are you proposing that we carried her that distance? I've read my share of murder mysteries and watched enough cop shows to know you should have some evidence to indicate how she was moved, and I'm willing to bet she was carried by one person."

"Maybe your accomplice was a man," said Robbins. "Someone capable of hoisting Marlys over his shoulder."

These two had already tried and convicted me in their minds. They were too lazy to bother looking beyond the obvious, yet improbable. "Rein in the bait and tackle, Detective. You're on a fishing expedition."

"Is that so?"

"Yeah, and meanwhile, the real killer skipped town. Instead of trying to entrap me, you should be tracking down Emil Pachette. Are you aware that no one's seen or heard from him since Monday afternoon?"

"We have a nationwide APB out for Emil Pachette," said Batswin.

"Then get off my back, Detective. He's your killer. Not me."

"We're exploring all leads, Mrs. Pollack. And we're thoroughly investigating all suspects. Including you," said Robbins.

At that moment my cell phone rang. I fished it out of my purse and glanced at the display. *Private Call.* Every nerve in my body froze. *Private Call* had come up on Karl's cell phone when it rang Monday morning. I took a deep breath. "This could be Ricardo."

"Answer it," said Batswin.

I pushed a button. "Hello?"

"You got the money, Sweet Cheeks?"

"I have the money."

I didn't bother to ask how he got my cell phone number. He'd already unearthed my direct office line, my e-mail address, and my unlisted home phone number. Chances were he even had my social security number and bank account numbers by now. Not that they'd do him any good, considering both my savings and checking accounts had balances hovering just shy of zero.

Hell, he'd probably dug up my report cards going all the way back to elementary school. Ricardo was nothing if not resourceful. He'd be a real asset to the FBI and CIA if he wasn't such a sleaze-ball crook. Then again, for all I knew, he moonlighted as a CI for both.

He snorted. "So, you had it all along, huh? I figured as much. Safe deposit box, right? A little advice, Sweet Cheeks—don't try to con a con. You're over your head and way out of your league."

"No. I ... uhm ... I borrowed the money."

"Not that I believe you, but I don't care if you had to kill for it. Just so's I get what's mine. Now listen carefully. You take a ride up to the Short Hills Mall. At exactly five o'clock tomorrow night you walk into Burberry and buy one of those oversized tote things they sell. The one that goes over the shoulder."

"Burberry?" I couldn't afford Walmart, let alone Burberry.

"Yeah. The plaid crap."

"Why Burberry?"

"Cause my girl wants one."

"So buy her one with the fifty thousand dollars I'm giving you. I can't afford a Burberry tote."

169

His voice lowered to an ominous growl. "You can't *not* afford it, Sweet Cheeks. So you better do exactly like I say. *Capisce*?

I shuddered. "Fine. Burberry."

Maybe Batswin and Robbins could swing some additional cash for this sting operation of theirs. I certainly didn't have an extra four hundred dollars up my sleeve. Not after what I spent last night at Home Depot on my do-it-yourself home burglar-proofing kit.

"Then what do I do?"

"You go into the little girls' room on the first level. Last stall on the left. Place the fifty G's in the bag."

"And?"

"You wait for my call. And remember, Sweet Cheeks, you tell *no one*." He hung up.

Ignoring his warning, I disconnected on my end and conveyed the conversation to Batswin and Robbins.

"We'll bring the money here tomorrow afternoon," said Batswin. "Meanwhile, we'll check the LUDS on your phone. Although, I'm betting this guy uses pre-paid, disposable phones."

She placed the photo of Karl and Marlys back in her briefcase and turned to Robbins. "Let's go."

As soon as they left, I collapsed into my chair and buried my head in my hands.

"What did those two want?" asked Cloris.

I raised my head to find her standing in the entrance to my cubicle. Erica hovered behind her. "Just bringing more doom and gloom. But I don't buy it. Even with everything Karl hid from me, there's no way he could have been having an affair with Marlys."

"What?" Cloris's eyes nearly popped out of her head. She and Erica crowded around me.

"What do you mean?" asked Erica. "What did Karl hide from you?"

Shit! Nothing like stress and sleep deprivation to induce diarrhea of the mouth. I had wanted to keep that unsavory chapter of my widowhood out of the office gossip mill. I looked to Cloris for help.

"Cat's out of the bag now," she said. "You might as well tell her."

So I did. Reluctantly. And only after swearing Erica to secrecy.

"I promise," she said.

I omitted all the gory details. "After my husband died, I discovered he had a gambling problem. He left behind quite a bit of debt."

"That's terrible," she said. "I'm so sorry, Anastasia. I wish I could help."

"You can help by keeping your mouth shut about it," said Cloris.

Erica cringed as if Cloris had slapped her. "I already promised Anastasia I wouldn't say anything."

"Just don't forget." Cloris turned back to me. "Now what's all this about Marlys and Karl?"

"Batswin and Robbins found a photo of the two of them." I went on to explain the detectives' new theory. "Maybe Karl was cheating on me," I said. "He certainly deceived me about everything else. But not with Marlys. What would she see in him?"

"It's not like he could help advance her career," said Erica.

"And we all know that's the only reason Marlys put out for anyone," added Cloris. "Have you considered the possibility that the photo was doctored?"

I had. "I suppose anyone with a little knowledge of Photoshop could have switched Karl for whomever was originally photographed with Marlys."

"But where would that person get a photo of Karl?" she asked.

The strobe light in my head flashed on, forcing my brain into overdrive. "He took it when he broke into my house last night."

I slapped my hand on the table. "Batswin and Robbins didn't notice the photograph on Tuesday because whoever is trying to frame me didn't plant it in Marlys's apartment until sometime yesterday."

"So who's trying to frame you?" asked Cloris. "Emil Pachette?"

"Maybe."

"Or someone trying to protect Emil Pachette." She stared pointedly at Erica.

"You can't mean Gina!" Erica glared back at Cloris. "Gina wouldn't do something like that."

"She was hiding something," said Cloris. "It doesn't take a rocket scientist to have figured that out yesterday."

"No, you've got her all wrong," said Erica. "She's just worried about Emil. Gina would never harm anyone."

"Not even to protect the man she loves?" asked Cloris.

I held up my hands to stop them before they came to blows. "If Gina broke into my house and stole a photo of Karl, she did it before we spoke with her yesterday. It doesn't add up. She first met me last night."

"But she knew about you," said Cloris. She turned to Erica. "Didn't she?"

Erica stared at the floor. She twisted her fingers into pretzel knots and mumbled, "I did tell her about the murder and Anastasia finding Marlys's body glued to her chair." She lifted her head and turned puppy dog eyes to me. "I've known Gina all my life. She wouldn't do this to you. To anyone. It's got to be someone else."

I wasn't so sure. Some women would do anything for love, and Gina struck me as so head-over-heels gone when it came to Emil Pachette that she might be capable of anything. Even an accessory to murder. I decided to have another chat with Gina, but without Erica or Cloris.

NINETEEN

On the way to Emil's studio, I called Zachary Barnes. "Sorry to disturb you," I said after introducing myself over the phone.

"Calling to make sure I'm still not backing out of the apartment?"

"I'm usually not such a worry-wart. As you now know, life kind of flew off into Bizarro Land lately."

"More so than you let on last night?"

"Exactly what else besides belly buttons did my family tell you last night?"

"Something about a dead body."

As much as I'd wanted to keep the boys from hearing about Marlys's death and my involvement in it, our forefathers had written in that annoying Article in the Bill of Rights about freedom of the press. Marlys's murder had made both the New Jersey and New York papers. I'd been mentioned as having discovered the corpse. Overnight my kids became school celebrities because their mother had stumbled across a dead body in her office. It's amazing what will boost a teenager up the ladder of popularity.

Only time would tell whether I'd be listed among Westfield's famous or infamous residents. We had them both—cartoonist Charles Addams of Addams Family fame and John List, a man who'd brutally murdered his family in the early seventies and eluded capture for nearly twenty years.

"Hey, don't worry," said Zack. "I believe in innocent until proven guilty."

Which meant last night Mama had probably said something about me being a suspect. "Good to know."

"Is that why you called?"

"In a way. I was wondering if you'd ever dated Marlys Vandenburg."

"Running out of suspects?"

"How did you—?"

"You left your *Who Killed Marlys* list on the table in the apartment. I saw it when I was jotting down measurements last night."

Since I was now certain between my bigmouthed sons and my bigmouthed mother, Zachary Barnes knew plenty already, I filled in the few blanks left, including about the photo the cops had found. At this point, what did I have to lose?

"I don't know what to believe about Karl anymore," I said, "but I find it hard to believe he was having an affair with Marlys Vandenburg."

"You think someone's framing you?"

"Exactly."

"And how do I fit into this?"

"I thought if you had dated Marlys, you might be able to give me some insights to help me clear myself. Or find the real killer."

"Wish I could. Never met the woman. I photograph wildlife, not the wild life."

"What about your night life?"

"What about it?"

"According to the gossip columns, you frequented the same clubs."

"Didn't your mother ever teach you not to believe everything you read, Anastasia Pollack?"

"But—"

"I did tell you those were all staged photo ops, didn't I?"

"Right. I just thought maybe—"

"I'm not the club type. Unless it's a golf club. Or a club sandwich. Believe it or not, I never dated any of those women I was photographed with. None of them are my type."

"Oh."

"Sorry to disappoint you."

Okay, so part of me had hoped that Zachary Barnes would pull a name out of his hat and hand me a killer. However, another part of me was glad he'd never fallen under Marlys's spell. But I chalked that feeling up to pre-menstrual scrambled hormones and lack of REM sleep. And a sorely battered ego that still needed a bit of stroking.

If it wasn't, I didn't want to know what it was because there was also the tiniest part of me smiling over the fact that Zachary Barnes didn't date *those women*.

And where the hell had *that* come from?

Two hours later I stood in the hall outside Emil's studio. Throughout the train ride into Manhattan I had pondered how I'd approach Gina, but I still had no idea what to say to her or how to say it without causing either her suspicions or hackles to rise. I'd have to wing it.

Ratcheting up my courage, I reached for the doorknob and opened the door.

Gina jumped up from her desk chair and greeted me with an ear-to-ear grin. "Anastasia! Look who's back." She turned to a *GQ*-esque stud with spiked black hair and a fine layer of fashion stubble covering his jaw.

Dressed head-to-toe in black jeans and a black turtleneck, he sat in what looked like a trash-picked folding chair alongside the battered desk. A pair of black framed glasses perched on the tip of his nose. He sized me up in the way that men who know they're God's gift to the double-X chromosome eye women.

"I'm so relieved," said Gina. She grabbed one of his hands in both of hers and graced him with a smile of unabashed adoration. His lips thinned into a tight line as he pulled his hand out from under hers.

"Emil Pachette?" I asked.

He rose. "*Oui*, and you are?"

Gina introduced me. "This is Anastasia Pollack. She works with my cousin Erica. You know? Marlys's assistant? Erica and Anastasia helped try to find you yesterday."

"I told you I wasn't lost, *ma chère*." He spoke in an affected French accent that could only fool Gina or someone from a galaxy far, far away.

Gina flushed; her voice rose into a high pitched whine. "But I didn't know that, Emil. Not then. What was I supposed to think? You didn't call, didn't answer your phone." She shuddered and gulped back a sob. "You could have been dead. Like Marlys."

"Do you know the police have an APB out on you, Mr. Pachette?"

He waved his hand as if shooing away a dust mote. "No more."

"You've spoken with them?"

"*Oui.*"

"It was all a huge mix-up," said Gina. "Emil didn't even know Marlys was dead until earlier today."

Emil rose from his chair and sauntered over to a second folding chair sitting beside the cutting table. He dragged the chair over to the desk and indicated I sit on it.

"You look like a woman with a million questions on the tip of your tongue, *ma chère*."

Only a million? My mind swirled. "So where were you since Monday afternoon? Minnesota, perhaps?"

He spun around and glared at Gina.

"I didn't tell her! I swear!"

"She didn't," I assured him. "But how about dropping the *faux* French accent and coming clean?"

He sighed. "First," he said, "you must promise not to divulge my secret to anyone."

"Is this secret illegal?"

His jaw dropped, his eyes grew wide in mock horror. "*Mais, non!*"

Gina jumped in to defend her love. "Emil wouldn't do anything illegal."

His glare pierced her with a warning expression that told me Gina's ardor for her boss fell far short of being reciprocated.

"Well?" he asked me.

I slipped out of my coat and sat down. "As long as it's nothing illegal, you have my word."

"I can assure you I've broken no laws." He took his seat and crossed one leg over the other. "My real name is Edwin Peepers."

"Why the deception?"

"Would you spend three thousand dollars for a designer gown from *The House of Peepers*?"

"I see your point." Although from what I had spied of Emil's— or Edwin's—couture, I wouldn't shell out three *dollars* for one of his dubious creations.

He raised his arm and waved it in an overly dramatic flourish, like some minor prince casting a crumb of information to a knowledge-starved dolt of a peasant. "Emil Pachette is my fashion *nom de plume.*"

"Along with the phony accent by way of Horse Thief Falls, Minnesota?"

His arm and his jaw dropped simultaneously. Along with his phony accent. "How did you—?"

I didn't bother to explain. "I'm betting you've never even been to France."

He sighed and shook his head. "Only in my dreams."

"So what happened?"

In upper Midwestese, he continued. "Late Monday morning while I stood on line at the corner deli, waiting for a sandwich, I received a call that my parents were involved in a head-on collision. The call from the hospital said they were both in the Critical Care Unit and not expected to live. I rushed home to pack a bag, then grabbed the next flight out of La Guardia."

"And didn't bother to tell anyone?"

His features hardened. "Business was the last thing on my mind."

"So Marlys didn't know not to expect you to show up for your date with her?"

"Meeting," muttered Gina.

He shot her a glance but continued to speak to me. "If your parents were close to death, would you remember to cancel a dinner date?"

So why was he now back here so soon after the accident? I would have thought he'd be busy making funeral arrangements, dealing with lawyers. "Did your parents pull through? Are they all right?"

He laughed. "Oh, they're fine. Never better, as a matter of fact."

"I don't understand."

"Neither do I. Except that some creep has a sick sense of humor. He not only scared the shit out of me, he sent me on a wild goose chase through the worst blizzard to hit northern Minnesota in over a decade."

He stood and paced across the cramped room. "My plane was the last to touch down in Duluth before the airport closed. I rented a car and drove six hours through a blinding snowstorm. When I finally arrived at the hospital, guess what I discovered?"

"What?"

He spun around, his arms akimbo. "They'd never heard of my folks!"

"Were they at another hospital?"

"There are no other hospitals within a hundred-mile radius. I tried calling them at home, but by then all the phone lines were down."

"What about cell phones? Don't they have one?"

"Cell phones?" He spit out a wry snicker. "Horse Thief Falls isn't exactly the Manhattan of Minnesota. The entire county is a dead cell area. It took me another hour to drive what should have taken ten minutes to get to their house. I found them snuggled under quilts, roasting marshmallows in front of the fireplace."

"There was no accident," said Gina.

"Obviously," sneered Emil/Edwin. "Anyway, the roads finally got plowed late yesterday, but the power didn't come back on until this morning. The phone lines are still down. I was stuck in that godforsaken middle of nowhere, freezing my butt off, all that time. No phone. No cable. No Internet. And stuck with two doddering old fools who thought it was all a grand adventure."

Emil/Edwin, the devoted son, had learned he was a wanted man when the Duluth police pulled him aside as he tried to board a pre-dawn flight back to New York earlier today. Two hours of interrogation later, his steel-clad alibi removed him from the list of suspects.

"When I learned of Marlys's murder, I figured someone wanted me out of the way Monday night," he added, almost as an after-thought.

But who? My list of suspects had dwindled down to a precious few. All I had left were Naomi and Hugo, neither of whom I believed capable of murder.

Or Gina?

I studied her as she gazed longingly at Emil/Edwin. Was it possible Gina had sent him off to the hinterlands in order to rid herself of the competition in his absence? His reactions to her led me to discount her version of his relationship with Marlys.

I'd bet my last nickel—and that's about all I had left in the way of available funds at this point—that Emil Pachette/Edwin Peepers, like many before him, had fallen hard and heavy for Marlys.

A quick glance at the muscle defined by his form-fitting garb, revealed all too clearly what Marlys had seen in Emil/Edwin. And it wasn't his talent as a designer.

I wondered if Gina had known that her sophisticated Parisian boss really hailed from the rural Midwest. Yesterday she'd been so adamant about his French connection. "You knew, didn't you?" I asked her.

"About what?"

"Emil's true identity."

Her body grew rigid, her voice defensive. "So?"

"So why did you lie to us?"

"To protect Emil's reputation."

"I see." I stood to leave. "Well, I'm glad you're safe and sound," I said to Emil. "Nice meeting you."

"You *will* keep my secret." He said it more as a threat than a need for assurance.

"I have no desire to ruin your reputation." I figured his lack of talent would do that soon enough. He didn't need my help.

Gina stopped me as I approached the door. "Anastasia, why did you come?"

I pasted an innocent smile on my lips, placed a comforting hand on her arm, and lied through my teeth. "You seemed so upset yesterday. I was worried, and since I was in the neighborhood, I thought I'd stop in to check on you."

Luckily, Gina was too fixated on Emil/Edwin to pick up on my lack of talent as a fiction fabricator.

I glanced toward the equally unaware Emil/Edwin. "But I can see there's nothing to worry about."

Gina smiled back. "Yes, everything is going to be fine now."

"So you think Gina glue gunned Marlys to death?" asked Cloris.

I had made it back to the office by two o'clock. My stomach roaring from neglect, I ducked into Cloris's cubicle to see what culinary delights she had hidden away. Apologizing for the slim pickings, she handed me a half-empty bag of slightly stale gourmet potato chips.

"She's far gone enough over Emil," I said stuffing a handful of chips into my mouth. As soon as I swallowed, I felt an additional layer of fat globules taking up residence on my hips, but I was too hungry to care.

"Gina takes puppy love to new heights. Or maybe it's new depths. Frankly, I don't see what she sees in that pompous, no-talent phony." I thought for a moment, then smirked. "No. Scratch that. I did see what she sees in him. And what Marlys saw in him."

"Nice packaging?"

"Right off the pages of *GQ*. Nothing but hot air and arrogance inside, though. He treats Gina with such ill-concealed disdain that I wanted to grab her by the shoulders and shake some sense into her."

"Kind of the way we felt about Erica and Marlys," said Cloris.

I reached into the bag for another handful of chips. "Must be genetic."

"People who let other people walk all over them sometimes reach a point where they go postal. Did you get the impression that Gina was so blinded by love that she'd go to any lengths to eliminate her competition?"

I had mulled that question over throughout the train ride back to New Jersey. "I don't know that she's got the smarts, and I doubt she's got the strength."

"Unless she had an accomplice."

TWENTY

With a handful of chips poised to enter my gaping mouth, I stared at Cloris. "So how well do we really know Gina?"

"Only what Erica told us about Gina and what we observed ourselves yesterday."

"Plus what I saw today."

I scanned the instant replays of Gina as they darted through my mind. My perceptions of her didn't match Erica's vociferous defense of her cousin. "As much as I hate to admit it, I suppose we have to question Erica's credibility, considering her staunch devotion to Gina."

Cloris reached for the bag and shoveled a handful of chips into her mouth. "Exactly my point," she said around the mouthful.

"If Gina did kill Marlys, she would have needed help moving the comatose body to my office."

"Emil?"

"Impossible. He can prove he was fighting a blizzard in Minnesota while Marlys was getting herself killed in New Jersey."

I felt no guilt over having divulged the Emil/Edwin connection to Cloris. Telling Cloris would have no adverse effect on *The House of Pachette*. Had someone told her Jacques Pépin was actually John Peterson of Prairieville, Kansas, she'd be shouting, "Holy exposé! Stop the presses." But being into food, not fashion, Cloris could care less about Emil's true identity.

"Besides," I continued, "you're forgetting that Emil doesn't return Gina's affection, at least not from what I observed of them together. Emil is arrogant and ambitious. Marlys held the means to hoist him a little closer to the twenty-four-carat gold ring of fashion stardom. He had no motive for killing her."

"Someone had to help her. How else would Gina have gotten into the office after hours?"

The thought hit us both at once. I clapped a chip-greasy hand over my mouth. "Omigod! You don't think—?"

"Anything's possible," said Cloris. "They both had enough motive."

"Erica isn't that devious."

"I wonder." Cloris tapped her nails on her desk. "Sometimes I find it hard to believe that anyone could be as naïve and innocent as Erica leads everyone to believe she is. After all, the kid grew up in the Bronx, not Mayberry."

"You don't like Erica much, do you?"

Cloris hesitated before speaking. "Let's just say the jury hasn't reached a verdict yet."

"I know she's grating at times, but all other factors aside, Erica's no actress. If she was involved in Marlys's murder, she'd have caved the moment Batswin and Robbins first started questioning her."

"I suppose you're right. But now what?"

"Now I get some work done, or Naomi will have my tush in a sling. I'll have to think about Gina later."

"Don't wait too long," warned Cloris. "I get the feeling Batswin and Robbins want to wrap up this investigation as soon as possible."

Even if they arrest the wrong person. That ominous thought settled in my stomach like a grease-soaked, fifty-pound gourmet potato chip.

Back in my own cubicle across the hall, I stared at the flickering cursor ticking off the seconds on my computer screen. Or was each pulse a countdown to impending doom? In a matter of days, my life's story had segued from normal to insane, from working mom to widowed murder suspect. Not to mention Chump of the Decade, given how blind I'd been to Karl's deceit and secret life.

For all I knew, he did have an affair with Marlys. Maybe she'd been systematically working her way through each colleague's husband just for kicks. And only because she knew she could, knew the power she wielded whenever she set her sights on any man. I glanced down at my cellulite-dimpled, pear-shaped body and wondered what having such domination over the male species must feel like.

Tears welled up behind my eyes. What a mess! I was a prime candidate for a Lifetime Channel movie-of-the-week. Under the circumstances, concentrating on Fourth of July craft projects proved next to impossible.

However, since I couldn't run the risk of losing my job, I forced myself to leave the pity party and get back to work. Snuffling the tears into submission, I turned my attention to a no-brainer task, tackling the stack of reader mail that had accumulated over the past several weeks.

Once caught up on my paperwork, my mind had clicked sufficiently into work mode to concentrate on the July issue. I cobbled together a three-project proposal and attached an assortment of fabric and color swatches to it. Jeanie Sims, our decorating editor, had left me a memo about having found pre-made bandana toss pillows to incorporate with the denim furniture she planned to feature, so I concentrated on patio crafts.

Naomi insisted on two criteria for all the craft projects that appeared in *American Woman*: quick and easy. Our readers weren't die-hard crafters. I needed to come up with ideas where even the novice, most-all-thumbs reader would feel like Martha Stewart when she gazed at her finished project.

Naomi also liked a variety of mediums in each issue, so for the Fourth of July spread, I included ideas that incorporated sewing, painting, and scrap crafts.

RECYCLED JEANS PLACEMATS

Stop! Before assigning those favorite but now threadbare jeans to the rag heap, carefully cut out the back pockets for these nearly no-sew, perfect-for-a-picnic placemats.

Materials: denim fabric (1 yard will make 6 placemats); one jeans back pocket per placemat; red bandana fabric (1⅓ yards will make 6 napkins); red and blue sewing thread; basic sewing supplies; fabric glue.

Directions: Pre-shrink denim and bandana fabric. For each placemat, cut denim to 15 x 18-inch rectangles. Machine stitch around perimeter of denim, 1 inch from cut edges. Fringe all four sides of placemat to stitching. Position pocket at lower left of placemat. Glue in place around sides and bottom edges.

For each napkin, cut bandana fabric to 16 x 16 inches. Machine hem all four edges. Fold napkin and insert into pocket. Place silverware in pocket over napkin.

NOTE: For an even quicker project, use store-purchased napkins instead of bandana fabric.

FOURTH OF JULY CLAY POT CANDLES

Party the night away by the light of these easy-to-make patriotic candles.

Materials: 4-inch diameter clay pot and matching saucer; white primer spray paint; red, white, and blue acrylic paints; satin spray varnish; paint brushes; 1-inch square compressed craft sponge; tacky glue; pencil; scissors; 3-inch red pillar candle.

Directions: (NOTE: Allow paint to dry thoroughly between steps.) Spray paint cup and saucer with primer. Paint inside and outside of saucer red. Paint inside of pot and outer rim in red. Paint remainder of outside of pot blue. Paint white vertical stripes around pot rim.

Draw a star on a compressed (dry) sponge. Cut out. Wet sponge to expand. Using white paint, sponge paint stars randomly around blue portion of pot.

Glue pot to saucer. Apply several coats of varnish. Insert candle.

DECOUPAGED FLAG TRAY

In just a few easy steps you can turn fabric scraps and an unfinished wooden tray into a red, white, and blue patriotic masterpiece.

Materials: unfinished rectangular wooden tray (available in craft and hobby stores); white primer spray paint; blue spray paint; clear acrylic varnish; scrap of red bandana fabric large enough to cover inside of tray; scraps of blue print fabric and white fabric measuring one-quarter the size of tray; pencil; scrap of cardboard one-quarter the size of tray; scissors; decoupage medium; brush.

Directions: (NOTE: Allow paint to dry thoroughly between steps.) Wash fabric to remove sizing. Spray paint tray with primer, then two coats of paint.

Using the tray bottom as a template, cut a piece of bandana fabric to size. Place inside tray. If necessary, trim fabric slightly until it fits within tray without puckering.

Make a star template with the cardboard and trace the shape on the white fabric. Cut out star. Position blue fabric in upper left corner of tray. Center the star over the blue fabric. Adjust dimensions of blue fabric and star until satisfied. Remove fabric from tray.

Brush the inside of the tray with decoupage medium. Position bandana fabric, right side up, inside tray. Brush right side of fabric with more decoupage medium. Repeat for blue fabric and star, applying decoupage medium over entire fabric surfaces each time. Allow to dry. Apply two coats of clear acrylic varnish to entire tray.

By the time I finished the proposal, everyone else had gone for the night, including the cleaning staff. My jaunt into the city to question Gina had resulted in another late evening at the office. I grabbed my purse and coat and headed down the hall to Naomi's office to drop the proposal in her IN basket before I headed home.

With any luck, the fickle Goddess of Working Moms was on duty tonight and had intervened on my behalf, persuading Mama or one of the boys to fix dinner. No matter how hard I prayed, though, the Goddess of Working Moms had no influence over Comrade Lucille. However, having tasted some of Lucille's culinary *messterpieces* in the past, perhaps that was a good thing, and in her own way, the Goddess of Working Moms was looking out for me and my kids.

As I rounded the corner, I realized I wasn't the last to leave the office, after all. Angry voices rose from behind Naomi's closed door.

"Damn it! If your brain hadn't been dangling between your legs—"

"Don't go there." Hugo's voice, normally soft and fatherly, took on an ominous edge.

Creeping closer to the door, I morphed into full Jane Bond mode. Normally, I would have respected Naomi's and Hugo's privacy, but these were not normal times. A murderer was still on the loose, and in the eyes of Batswin and Robbins, I was still *Suspect Numero Uno*.

A girl's gotta do what a girl's gotta do to save her tush, even if it means turning into a full-fledged, ear-pressed-to-the-door snoop.

"Why not?" yelled Naomi. "It's all your fault."

"I'm warning you—"

"Or what? You'll kill me?"

"Don't be stupid. Everything will work out. I made a mistake. There. I admit it. Satisfied?"

"A mistake?" Naomi's shrill decibels reverberated through the closed door and into my eardrum.

"Yes, a mistake. Nothing more. It's over. Forget about it."

"Over? We're smack in the middle of a gargantuan dung heap."

"Not if we play our hand right."

"What are you suggesting?"

"That you let me handle things. Okay?"

Naomi mumbled something I couldn't make out.

"Listen," continued Hugo in a pleading tone, "we have a chance to set things back on track."

"Not with this new situation."

"A minor wrinkle. Trust me."

Once again I couldn't make out Naomi's reply.

"Grab your coat," said Hugo. "Let's get out of here."

I froze.

Even if I morphed into Marion Jones, I'd never be able to sprint back to my cubicle in time. Naomi and Hugo would see me as they rounded the corner.

I also nixed the idea of ducking into one of the surrounding empty offices. They'd notice my car in the parking lot and realize I may have overheard their incriminating shoutfest. I had but one option.

I waited until I heard Hugo approach the door. Pasting a smile of innocence on my face and forcing a sing-song lilt into my voice, I raised my fist and rapped twice. "Naomi?"

The door flew open.

Panic covered Hugo's face, but I pretended not to notice. I spoke over his shoulder to an equally panic-stricken-looking Naomi. "Hi. I thought I'd drop off the July spread proposals before I left."

"Oh, Anastasia. Uhm ... fine. Thank you." She pointed to a wire tray on her desk.

I forced myself not to stare at her shaking hand and ignored the guilt-riddled glances she exchanged with Hugo, but being fib-challenged, I was at a genetic disadvantage. My defective Prevarication Gene caused me to break out into an involuntary smirk whenever I lied. If I could pull off this act straight-faced, I was a shoo-in for an Oscar.

"I'll go over it first thing tomorrow," said Naomi.

Hugo stepped back to open the door wider. Projecting what I hoped appeared as naïve innocence, I bounced into the office, deposited the folder in the tray, and waved as I retraced my steps. "See you tomorrow."

As I crossed the threshold, Hugo reached for my arm. "We're on our way out, as well. After what happened the other night, I don't feel comfortable with you walking alone to your car."

He turned to Naomi. "Ready?"

She swung her Fendi purse over her shoulder and fiddled with the strap for a moment. "Coming."

The three of us walked in silence to the elevator, with me smack in the middle of a triple-decker, high-anxiety sandwich. Part of me wanted to make small talk to dispel any indication that I may have overheard something incriminating. The other part of me feared saying something that might indict me. All of me wanted to believe there was some other explanation for their damning words. I didn't want to believe Naomi and Hugo were involved in Marlys's murder, but how could I not suspect them after what I had heard?

The elevator opened seconds after Hugo pressed the button. "After you, ladies." He swept his arm to indicate we precede him. I ordered my leaden feet to comply.

As the elevator made the short descent, Hugo placed his hand on my shoulder and cleared his throat. "I'm not sure I conveyed how sorry I was to hear of your recent loss, Anastasia."

I inhaled a deep, shaky breath, relieved he had presented me with an opportunity to direct my emotional turmoil to an appropriate topic. At the same time, though, I couldn't help but wonder how calculated his concern was. Why now? Hugo had had plenty of opportunity to offer his condolences over the last few days.

I offered him a sad smile. "Thank you, Hugo. The flowers you sent to the funeral were lovely. I appreciated the gesture."

He slid his hand down to my forearm. "I'm sorry I wasn't able to come in person. I'm sure it hasn't been easy for you. If there's anything Naomi and I can do … anything … please don't hesitate to ask." He glanced at Naomi for confirmation.

"Of course," she said, her lips curling into a benevolent smile. "Anything at all."

Hugo and Naomi walked me to my car. They waited until I had locked myself in and started the engine. Then they proceeded to Hugo's Mercedes, the only other car in the parking lot. That in itself raised my eyebrows—along with my curiosity.

Not to mention my suspicions.

I could only think of one reason for Naomi and Hugo to be traveling together, and it had nothing to do with carpooling to save on fuel.

The big questions, though, were when had Naomi and Hugo gotten back together? And what connection did it have to Marlys's murder?

TWENTY-ONE

THE NEXT DAY CLORIS was off interviewing Donna the Donut Diva. She arrived back at the office, her arms brimming with bakery boxes, shortly before three o'clock. "We need to talk," I told her.

"Sure." She dumped the boxes on her counter, opened one, and passed me a glazed donut the size of Rhode Island. "Here. Try this. Maple sugar with blueberry filling."

How could I, the willpower-challenged Queen of Cellulite, refuse such an offer? I accepted the donut and took a bite. And another. And yet another. After practically inhaling half the donut, I told Cloris about the argument I'd overheard the previous night.

She chewed on both my words and a sugar-sprinkled cruller. "The plot continues to thicken."

I polished off the remainder of my donut, washing it down with a gulp of coffee. "I feel like I've been sucked up into an Alfred Hitchcock vortex. Conspiracy to the left of me, conspiracy to the right of me. I don't want to believe Naomi is involved in Marlys's murder. I like her too much. But I also know I didn't kill Marlys."

"Me, too. But you've ruled out most of the other suspects."

I started work on a second donut, raspberry glaze with vanilla cream cheese filling, speaking around the fat and calories. "Except Gina."

"With Erica as her accomplice?"

"Highly unlikely." I dropped into the spare chair in Cloris's cramped cubicle and licked the sugar off my fingers. "But then, so is the idea of Naomi and Hugo as killers."

"At this point anything's possible. *Someone* killed Marlys."

"True. She obviously didn't drug herself and commit suicide by glue gun."

Cloris opened a second bakery box and held it out. "Ginger orange spice. What are you going to do?"

I waved the box away. One more donut and I'd start looking like a Sumo wrestler. "I don't know."

Ratting out Naomi and Hugo might get Batswin and Robbins off my back, but a huge part of me still doubted their involvement, no matter what I'd heard to the contrary. "Neither one of them admitted killing Marlys. They could have been arguing about something else."

"Like what?"

That question had kept me awake most of last night. "Something. Anything. I don't know. But it's not fair to use them to exonerate myself unless I have more proof."

"If you don't report the fight, is it withholding evidence?"

I hadn't thought of that. Ralph's squawks echoed in my brain. *Double, double toil and trouble. Macbeth.* Act Four, Scene One.

Keeping new evidence from Batswin and Robbins could land me in a cauldron of bubbling trouble. One more black mark against me might be all the proof they needed to haul my tush off to the county jail. "But is what I heard evidence or hearsay?" I asked Cloris.

She opened a third box and popped a boysenberry donut hole into her mouth. "Don't look at me, Sherlock. I'm no walking, talking legal library."

"I think there's a difference between refusing to answer a question and not volunteering information."

"Yeah, it's called dancing on the head of a pin."

With two left feet, I thought.

Before we could speculate further, Daphne arrived, summoning me to the conference room. "Those detectives are back snooping around," she said. "They want to speak with you again."

"Thanks," I said.

She hugged her middle. "Those two give me the creeps. Especially the guy. Like I half expect him to whip off one of those cartoon ties he wears and use it to strangle a confession out of me. You know what I mean?"

Cloris and I exchanged glances. "Is there something you haven't told us?" I asked.

Daphne's eyes bugged out as she stepped away from me. "No! I didn't … I mean … that's not what I …"

Cloris doubled over with laughter. "She's pulling your leg."

Our shared assistant eyed me. "For real?"

"For real. I thought you could use a laugh, but it was a bad joke. Tell them I'll be right there, would you?"

"Uhm … okay. Sure." She nearly tripped over her feet as she jogged down the hall toward the conference room.

"Looks like I won't solve my financial problems by moonlighting as a stand-up comic."

"I don't think Whoopi Goldberg has to worry about you breathing down her neck any time soon," said Cloris.

I started to leave, but she grabbed my arm. "Seriously, before you go in there, think about this: if the situation were reversed, would Naomi and Hugo protect you?"

———

Probably not.

Batswin and Robbins hadn't come to ask more questions, though. They had come to deliver the sting money. "Nervous?" asked Batswin.

"I'm used to playing with craft materials, not playing Mata Hari." I stared into the navy canvas duffel she handed me and gulped.

"Something wrong?" asked Batswin.

"I've never seen this much money before."

"Don't get any ideas," said Robbins. "The bills are marked."

My head shot up. "Contrary to whatever erroneous opinion you have of me, Detective, I'm a law-abiding citizen. I've never stolen anything in my life, and I don't plan to start now."

He puffed out his chest and glared back as if in challenge, but his tightly pursed lips didn't move.

Batswin handed me a white business envelope. "The only bag at Burberry that comes close to what you said Ricardo described is four hundred dollars. This contains four hundred twenty-eight dollars. Get a receipt."

"Of course." Accountants rule the world, no matter what your line of business.

I was glad that Batswin had thought to calculate the tax and add it to her catch-an-extortionist request from petty cash. The tax had slipped my mind. I knew I didn't have an extra twenty-eight dollars in my wallet. Twelve or thirteen maybe. Definitely not more. Imagine the fiasco at the Burberry counter had I come up short.

"We're working in conjunction with the Essex County police," said Robbins.

I turned my attention back to him and for the first time noticed the dark red stain on his Green Hornet tie. Spaghetti sauce? Or blood from another murder case?

"Officers will be positioned throughout the mall, in the store, and in the restroom," he continued.

Batswin took over. "When Ricardo calls to give you instructions for the drop, repeat what he says."

"So the officer in the restroom will hear me?"

"Exactly."

"Will someone follow me to the mall?"

"Several unmarked cars will tail you," said Robbins. "Why?"

Was I the only one among us who watched television? "In case all this cloak and dagger is Ricardo's way of foiling a possible sting."

They both stared at me, their faces impassive. I spelled it out for them. "I don't know what this guy looks like. What kind of car he drives. Neither do you. For all we know, he's lurking in the parking lot at this very moment. Maybe his real plan is to force me off the road somewhere between here and the mall."

That triggered a more ominous thought, which launched a lump of dread pinballing around my insides. Woods and fields hugged many of the roads that connected Trimedia to the mall. Woods and fields perfect for body dumping.

"Even if I get to the mall without a hitch, who knows what wild goose chase he's concocted for me after I buy the Burberry bag? His ultimate plan could involve grabbing the money, then ridding himself of the only witness to his extortion." I thumbed my chest. "Me."

"We've covered all contingencies," said Batswin.

Instead of assuring me, her laid-back, monotone voice only increased my anxiety. "I have my kids to think of. If something goes wrong—"

"Follow directions, and nothing will go wrong," said Robbins.

His gruff, irritable tone ratcheted my apprehension up beyond the stratosphere, but I had no choice other than to go along with the detectives' strategy. Refusing to help them catch Ricardo would add credence to their original theory—that I killed Marlys for the diamonds in order to pay off Ricardo—even if that theory had more holes in it than my kitchen colander. But that didn't seem to matter to Batswin and Robbins.

Dangerous as their scheme seemed, at least if it worked, I'd shake a two-thousand-pound gorilla off my back and have one less Karl-created debacle sucking me into the La Brea tar pit of debt. I zipped the canvas duffel and hoisted it onto my shoulder.

"I'm ready," I told Batswin and Robbins.

As the detectives followed me out of the conference room, an image of Karl floated across my mind. Had my darling, deceased husband ever given us a thought as he gambled away our security and his sons' futures?

And how many other Ricardos had he left in his wake, waiting to pounce on me?

Leaving Batswin and Robbins cooling their heels at the elevator, my anxieties and I headed back to my cubicle to retrieve my coat and purse. On the way, I bumped into Naomi and Erica. They both eyed the weighty bag dragging down my shoulder.

"Weekend getaway?" asked Naomi.

"I wish."

She returned her attention to the sheaf of papers in her hand, but Erica's brows knit together as she continued to stare at the duffel. "I swear I saw Detective Robbins carry that same bag into the conference room earlier. Why do you have it now? What's in it?"

Naomi shifted her attention back to the duffel. She and Erica followed me into my cubicle.

I worried the duffel strap as I wracked my brain for a plausible explanation. When I was seven years old, Mama had told me she knew when I lied because my face contorted into a smirk. I didn't believe her until years later when I discovered I had passed along that same defective Fib Gene to Alex. Nick had inherited Karl's Look-You-in-the-Eye-and-Lie-With-a-Straight-Face Gene.

Turning my back to Naomi and Erica, I placed the duffel on my chair and answered while slipping into my coat. "Just some of my supplies the police confiscated during the murder investigation. Since they don't need them for evidence, they released them back to me."

With the lie out of my mouth and the smirk hopefully gone from my face, I heaved the duffel back onto my shoulder, grabbed my purse, and turned back to them. "I have a meeting with a yarn manufacturer. See you both Monday."

Naomi and Erica filled the doorway, blocking my exit. Neither made any effort to step aside.

"Aren't you forgetting something?" asked Erica.

I glanced around the small space. I had my coat. My purse. I patted my pocket and heard my keys jingle. "I don't think so."

Erica pointed to the duffel. "Why are you taking your supplies with you?"

Think fast, Anastasia! "I … uhm … since I've been out of the office so much lately, I thought I'd get caught up on some work over the weekend."

Erica's face grew more puzzled. I glanced at Naomi. Her *haute couture* composure had slipped a notch. Turmoil swam behind her normally focused eyes.

Erica continued her questioning. "I don't understand. I thought you had a studio at home. Why do you need to lug supplies back and forth?"

Her questioning began to feel more like an interrogation than idle curiosity. Flippancy being the better part of cowardice, I chose to throw her bloodhound pursuit off the scent with a quip. "The dog ate them?"

Before she had a chance to ask another question, I nudged her to the side, scooted around her, and headed for the elevator.

TWENTY-TWO

IN THE END, NEITHER murder nor mayhem descended on me as I traveled the twenty miles to the mall. Not that my overactive imagination didn't conjure up one dreadful scenario after another the entire length of the drive. But as it turned out, my biggest dilemma involved the Hyundai's temperamental windshield defroster, not some behemoth SUV running me into a ditch.

When I finally pulled into a parking spot in one of the covered garages, I loosened my death grip on the steering wheel. Although my nerves would never be the same, the first leg of this hare-brained escapade had ended without physical trauma—blunt or otherwise—to my slightly overweight, middle-aged body.

Maybe my worries were groundless. Batswin and Robbins would nab Ricardo as planned, and I'd be home in time for another night of mac and cheese. I tried to convince both myself and my queasy stomach of that possibility as I entered the mall and headed for the Burberry store.

The main difference between the Short Hills Mall and the Upper East Side of New York is a roof. The same upscale, pricey boutiques and shops that line either side of Madison and Fifth Avenues occupy two polished marble floors under a skylight in Short Hills, New Jersey. Five of the finest department stores in the country act as anchors and add to the sophisticated ambiance.

Up until recently, I had enjoyed window-shopping at the mall on rainy weekends. Sometimes I even succumbed to an impulse splurge—if it was on sale. Now the sight of all these chi-chi shops only reminded me of my recent fall from Middle-classdom.

My glance darted around the concourse as I made my way toward Burberry. Hand-in-hand couples, women pushing baby carriages, and matrons laden with packages strolled or rushed from shop to shop. Here and there a single man loitered outside one of the stores.

A bored husband waiting for his wife?

An undercover cop?

Ricardo?

Afraid to know one way or the other, I avoided eye contact with all of them, clutched the duffel tighter, and picked up my pace.

Two other customers, both men, were in Burberry. One contemplated a rack of lined raincoats; the other fingered the fringe on a selection of scarves arranged on the counter in front of him. Salesmen hovered near each. As I made my way over to the display of totes, I felt all four men's eyes tracking my every move.

A woman wearing a *café au lait* Chanel suit, over which she had draped a signature Burberry scarf, stepped from the back room. She had pinned the scarf in place below her left shoulder with a gold initial pin. Opposite the pin, above her right breast, she wore a nameplate, identifying her as Nanette. From her perfectly coifed platinum pageboy down to her matching Burberry plaid pumps, Nanette looked more like a society matron than a sales-clerk.

Her sad smile made me wonder if we belonged to the same Wronged Wives Club. Had her husband died and left her wallowing in debt? Or had he dumped her for a trophy wife? Nanette certainly didn't look like she'd spent her life in retail. More likely she now had to supplement her monthly Social Security check by working where she had once shopped.

Or maybe she was a damn good undercover cop.

"May I help you?" she asked.

"I'd like one of these totes," I said, pointing to the appropriate bag.

"Certainly." She left the tote in the display and headed back toward the stock room. As I waited, I glanced across the room. The two shoppers and their salesmen quickly averted their eyes. I hoped they were all cops and not Ricardo with a posse of henchmen.

A minute later Nanette returned with a box. "Anything else?"

Did I look like I was rolling in money? I shook my head. "No, that'll be all."

"Cash or charge?"

"Cash." I opened my purse, removed the envelope, and counted out the four one hundred dollar bills, one twenty, a five, and three singles.

"Would you like me to gift-wrap this for you?" she asked after I had paid for the tote and placed the receipt back in the envelope.

"No, thank you."

Nanette placed the box in a shopping bag, thanked me for shopping at Burberry, then offered me the standard end-of-sale retail mantra, "Have a nice day."

The entire transaction had taken less than five minutes. The four men watched me leave, but none of them followed as I exited the store and headed across the concourse to the ladies' room.

The mall restroom suite looked more like those found in five-star hotels. A large black and white marble lounge with mirrored walls and oversized black leather chairs branched out into a ladies' room at one end and a men's room at the other. Stalls in the ladies' room were the size of department store dressing rooms.

Three other adults occupied the lounge. One woman primped in front of the mirror at the far end of the room. Another sat in one of the chairs and nursed an infant, while a man, presumably her husband, tried to cajole an extremely fussy toddler.

I entered the ladies' room and glanced around. Three women, all of them chatting about the sale at Bloomingdale's, washed their hands at the sink. Seven women stood in line, waiting for stalls to free up. I took my place behind them. One-by-one toilets flushed, women exited stalls, and I crept forward.

Eventually I secured the stall Ricardo had indicated, locked the door, and settled my bags on the pull-down baby-changing table. I had yet to hear from Ricardo. Before transferring the money from the duffel to the tote, I checked my phone to make sure the battery hadn't died. The indicator showed I had plenty of juice left.

The ladies' room felt like a sauna. Warm air blasted down from a vent in the ceiling. I removed my stadium coat and draped it over the hook on the door.

In the stall directly across the aisle, a woman cajoled a recalcitrant child to go potty. To my right, another woman multi-tasked. While doing her business, she gossiped on her cell phone in a voice loud enough to be heard in the parking garage. As I withdrew bound stacks of hundred dollar bills from the duffel and placed them in the tote, I learned more than I cared to about someone named Eileen, her bladder, her intestines, and her philandering husband.

Eventually, both my neighbors left and others took their place, but Ricardo still hadn't called. I pushed up the sleeves of my sweater, swiped the perspiration from my forehead, and fanned myself with the folded shopping bag.

More women came, flushed, and left. I glanced at my watch. Nearly an hour had passed since I first entered the ladies' room. How long was I supposed to wait?

After another ten minutes I grabbed my packages and coat and headed for the sink to splash cold water on my face, neck, and arms. Then I walked out to the lounge.

Another woman, dressed in a pink and purple running suit and white Reeboks, exited the ladies' room behind me. She scanned the room before taking up a position several feet away from me.

The couple with the baby and toddler were gone, but the primper remained in front of the mirror, a good indication that she was the designated lounge cop. She wore a pair of black jeans, a gray Columbia University sweatshirt, and a pair of black Nikes. For someone who had spent the last hour in front of a mirror, her face was decidedly devoid of make-up, and her hair was pulled back into a no-nonsense ponytail. Definitely a cop.

I watched her watch me as I deposited my bags and coat on one of the overstuffed chairs and settled into the one beside it. Uncertainty played across her face. I had revised the script, and I suppose she wasn't sure how to proceed. Too bad. Unless Ricardo was a fly on the wall, he wouldn't know the difference. Besides, I couldn't deliver his money if I fell victim to an overdose of blast furnace heat.

The primping policewoman took a seat as far away from me as possible but positioned herself in such a way that she had a bird's-eye view of me, along with everyone who entered and exited the lounge. She and the purple-clad woman exchanged glances.

I pulled out my cell phone and stared at the blank display. *Ring, dammit!* But will as I might, the frigging phone failed to comply.

More people came and went. Some sat for a few minutes before leaving. They made phone calls or rearranged shopping bags of purchases or just rested from having shopped until they dropped. Others headed straight for the ladies' or men's rooms, then hurried back out into the mall. Several times the two shoppers from Burberry walked through the lounge to the men's room, then left as quickly as they'd come.

I continued to check my watch and the display on my phone. The minutes crept by in slow motion. By eight-fifteen I'd had enough. I waited until only the purple-clad woman and the primper remained in the lounge, then announced, "He's jerking me around."

They stared impassively at me.

"You can drop the surveillance mode," I told them. "We know why we're all here."

"You shouldn't be speaking to us," said the primper, glancing around as if she expected Ricardo to materialize from behind one of the potted plants.

I rose. "I'm not spending all night here. It's obvious he's not going to call, and even if he does, my cell phone travels with me."

"You can't leave," said the other woman.

"Watch me." I shoved my arms into my coat sleeves and picked up my purse, the empty duffel, and the money-laden Burberry tote, but I hesitated. I'd already sustained two break-ins at home. The last thing I wanted was fifty thousand dollars of police money sitting in my house all weekend.

I proffered the Burberry bag to the cop in the purple running suit. "You can give Batswin and Robbins back their money. I don't want to be responsible for it."

"I don't think that's a good idea," she said, refusing to accept the tote.

"I think it's an excellent idea."

"What if the perp comes to your home for it?" asked the primper.

"I'll tell him I brought it to the bank for safekeeping when he didn't call as planned."

"The banks are already closed for the night," said the purple-clad cop.

I dropped back into the chair and pulled out my phone and Batswin's business card. "I'm calling Batswin."

"Don't. I'll call for instructions." The primper pulled out a cell phone of her own and punched in a number. After apprising the person at the other end of the situation, she hung up and turned to me. "Take the money home with you, Mrs. Pollack. We'll have someone follow you and keep an eye on your house."

I didn't like the sound of that, but with both cops refusing to accept the money, I had no other choice. Leaving fifty thousand dollars sitting in a mall lounge wasn't a viable option.

I adjusted my purse, the tote, and the empty duffel over my shoulders. Clutching them tightly against my body, I turned to exit the lounge. The two women cops showed no signs of tagging along. "Aren't you going to escort me to my car?"

"Someone else will keep an eye on you," said the primper. "We don't want to tip our hand in case the perp is lurking somewhere in the mall."

In other words, my safety took a back seat to their completing a successful sting. Anger emanating from every pore of my body, I yanked open the lounge door and headed for the parking garage.

Several times I had the feeling someone was following me. I hoped it was one of the cops. A quick glance over my shoulder revealed no one paying any attention to me. I quickened my pace anyway.

Once in the garage, I heard footsteps behind me. Heavy footsteps. This time, instead of taking a look, I broke into a sprint for the last twenty yards.

After several shaky attempts, I managed to unlock the car. I threw the bags onto the passenger seat, slipped behind the wheel, and locked the door before starting the engine.

Taking the circular exit ramp as fast as I could without plowing into a concrete pylon, I peeled out of the mall and made the normally twenty-five-minute trip back to Westfield in under fifteen. If

Ricardo or the police were following me, they were sure taking their bloody sweet time about it.

———

I arrived home to a dark house. Totally dark. Not a single light casting a warm glow from any window. Every hair on my body jumped to attention. Even though the heater in the Hyundai refused to exhale anything above a piddling lukewarm whisper of heat, perspiration trickled down my cleavage-challenged chest.

As I parked the car, I tried to convince myself we'd had a power outage, but the well-lit homes of my neighbors belied that theory. Unless the main circuit breaker had tripped, and no one knew how to reset it. I held onto that glimmer of hope even though the logical half of my brain told me my resourceful kids knew how to reset the circuit breakers, and even if they had forgotten, they would have gone next door for help.

Grabbing the flashlight I kept in the glove compartment, I quietly eased out of the car, locked my purse and the fifty thousand dollars inside, and crept toward the back door. Along the way, I arced the light across the side of the house to check the basement windows. All appeared still boarded. At the back door I turned the knob and found it locked.

I decided to check the windows on the other side of the house before entering. Fifty-year-old azalea and rhododendron bushes, planted by the original owners, flanked the east side of the rancher. In order to check the windows, I had to squeeze between the dense shrubbery and the house.

By the time I had inspected both basement windows and fought my way out of the prickly bushes, I was covered with a wintry mix of icy twigs and dead leaves. I considered it a small price to pay for the satisfaction of knowing no one had broken through my make-shift Home Depot security system. But if someone hadn't broken in, why was the house dark? I headed for the front door to find out.

As I rounded the house, a blaze of searchlights blinded me. Someone yelled, "Police. Freeze! Hands above your head!"

TWENTY-THREE

"Where the hell were you guys a few minutes ago?" I yelled at them.

"Mrs. Pollack?"

I recognized Fogarty's voice. "Mind dousing the glare, Fogarty? You're blinding me."

"Kill the spot, Harley."

I blinked into the darkness and waited for my eyes to adjust.

"What were you doing prowling around your own house?" he asked, advancing toward me.

I told him.

"So you decided to play detective?"

"What would you have done? Blithely walk in on who-knows-what? The creep who's broken into my home twice could be holding my family hostage in there at this very minute. Meanwhile we're out here playing Twenty Questions."

"You should have stayed in your car and called 9-1-1 on your cell phone," he said.

"I was going to. As soon as I checked all the windows." Except my cell phone was in my purse, which was locked in my car, but I decided not to admit that mistake to Fogarty. Instead, I opted to go on the offensive. "What are you doing here?"

"We got a call to keep an eye on your place. Seems you're making quite a few enemies, Mrs. Pollack."

More and more, I was convinced I had only one sleazeball turning my life upside-down and inside-out, but now was not the time for a discussion on investigative theories. My kids and Mama could be in danger. And Lucille.

I waved toward my house. "What about my family? They could be bleeding to death in there."

He walked back to the cruiser to confer with Harley. A moment later both men approached, guns drawn. Harley carried a flashlight.

"Give me your house key," said Fogarty.

I placed the key in his outstretched palm.

"Stay here," Harley told me. "We'll check things out first."

Fat chance. I was right behind them as they unlocked the door and stepped into my foyer. My extremely frigid foyer. Without electricity, the furnace didn't kick on. The power must have gone out several hours ago for the house to have gotten this cold.

"The switch is to the left," I said, indicating the wall switch plate with the light from my flashlight, even though I knew it wouldn't work.

Harley spun around, shining his flashlight directly into my eyes. "I thought I told you to stay outside."

Ignoring him, I reached for the switch, clicking it up and down several times. No lights. "The electric panel is in the basement at the bottom of the stairs," I said, pointing the way with my own flashlight. "A few feet down the wall on the right."

"Wait here. Or I'll cuff you to the banister," said Harley as he headed for the basement.

"It's too quiet," I told Fogarty.

"Maybe they all went out to dinner or a movie."

"In twenty-degree weather without a car?"

"Someone could've picked them up."

I shined my flashlight into the living room, sweeping across each piece of furniture, paying particular attention to Ralph's favorite perches and the cushions where Catherine the Great liked to lounge. "Along with the dog, the cat, and the parrot?"

"Right," he admitted. "Odd."

"Wait," I said.

"What?"

"Did you hear that?" I could have sworn I heard a muffled groan.

"The wind's picking up," said Fogarty. We had left the front door open. He shut it.

"No. It wasn't wind." I held my breath and listened. "There it is again."

"It's coming from down the hall," he said. "I'll check it out."

"Not without me." I dogged his heels as he headed for the bathroom. The door was closed. "We always leave the bathroom door open when no one's using it."

"Get back," he said. "Over there." He waited until I stood where he indicated.

As if on cue, the power came on the moment Fogarty swung open the bathroom door. "Jeez!"

"What?" I ran up behind him and stood on tiptoe to see over his shoulder. "Omigod!" Alex, Nick, Mama, and Lucille were all trussed up with duct tape, their hands secured behind their backs, their legs bound together at their ankles, all wriggling and squirming and banging into each other as they grunted and groaned behind duct tape gags. Blindfolds covered their eyes.

Mama and Lucille were taped together back-to-back. All were shoehorned into the bathtub with Nick and Alex sprawled on top of their grandmothers.

Fogarty lifted the boys out of the tub and settled them on the floor. Then he ripped a strip of silver tape from Mama's mouth. She screamed.

"Sorry, ma'am." He removed the blindfold. "There's no gentle way to get this stuff off. Faster is better."

"Mama, what happened?"

"That awful man. He had a gun."

"Who, Mama?"

"How should I know his name? But I think he might have been the same nasty man who ran into me during the first robbery."

"Did he hurt you?"

"Every joint and muscle in my body is screaming. What time is it? I swear we've been in here for hours. Where've you been?"

"On a wild goose chase," I said as I worked free the tape around her body—a task made even more difficult because Lucille continued to squirm and jerk.

"Stop moving!" yelled Mama, shoving her butt backwards into Lucille.

Fogarty ripped the tape from Nick's and Alex's mouths. "Did either of you boys see anything?"

"The house was pitch black when I got home," said Nick. "He came up from behind me. Next thing I knew, I was in the tub with the grandmas."

"Same here," said Alex. "Except Nick was already in the tub when he dumped me in."

"When was that?" asked Fogarty.

"About six-thirty."

"Over two hours ago," said Fogarty.

"What!" shrieked Mama.

Lucille twisted, jerked, and growled. Fogarty tossed me a do-I-really-have-to? glance before ripping the tape from her mouth. "Where the hell have you been, Anastasia? If you came home from work at a decent hour instead of gallivanting all over creation—"

"I'd be stuck in the tub with the rest of you, and who would have rescued us?"

Harley poked his head into the bathroom. "Looks like he cleaned you out this time, Mrs. Pollack."

"What do you mean?"

"He got all the electronics equipment. Stereos. TVs. Computers."

"Shit! My term paper's on my computer," cried Alex. "All my research notes! The rough draft."

"Did you back up?" asked Mama.

Back up? Since when had Mama become computer literate?

"Not sure that's going to help," said Harley. "Unless you kept the disks hidden somewhere. Looks like he took anything that wasn't nailed down. The desk drawers were all upended. I didn't see any disks."

Alex groaned, and it wasn't from the tape Fogarty was ripping off his wrists.

"Your bedroom's been ransacked, too, Mrs. Pollack. Looks like he grabbed some jewelry."

Mama climbed out of the tub as soon as her limbs were freed. Poor Mama. Her joints creaked and cracked, but she didn't complain.

Too bad the same couldn't be said for Lucille. "Watch where you're putting those hands, young man," she yelled at Fogarty. "How dare you touch me there! I'll sue for sexual harassment."

Fogarty dropped his arms to his sides and stepped away from the tub. "Sorry, ma'am. I'm only trying to help you out. Maybe you'd like to do this on your own?" He spoke in a calm, civil voice, and I gave him credit for keeping his cool. A lesser man would have dumped her back on her rump and walked away.

"Just give me your hand," she demanded.

He stepped forward and held his hand out to her, but she couldn't hoist herself up. Eventually, she had to give in to the inevitable, and it took both Fogarty and Harley lifting her from under the armpits to hoist her up and over the rim of the soaker tub.

Alex had retrieved her cane and handed it to her. She waved it in my face. "If you had a normal bathtub, I wouldn't have had a problem."

Of course, it's always my fault. I'm surprised she didn't blame me for the break-in.

"Where's Manifesto?" she demanded.

I turned to Harley. "Did you see any animals? A dog? A cat? A parrot?"

"The dog's in the kitchen, but I—"

"Out of my way!" Lucille pushed Harley aside and hobbled out of the bathroom. "Manifesto? Where are you, my darling? Come to mother."

"Ma'am—" Harley reached for her arm, but she swatted him away and headed toward the kitchen.

"What is it?" I asked.

"The dog and cat are lying on the kitchen floor. The parrot's—"

"Manifesto!" Lucille's scream cut off the rest of his sentence.

The Devil Dog, Catherine the Great, and Ralph weren't dead, just drugged. The thief had apparently laced their food and water bowls with a sedative or something. Fogarty called headquarters to dispatch the animal control officer. Ten minutes later Mephisto the Devil Dog, Catherine the Great, and Ralph were on their way to the We Care Animal Clinic.

Lucille insisted on accompanying her dog, but Officer Fogarty refused to let her leave. "You're witness to a crime," he said. "Either you answer my questions here, or I cart you down to headquarters."

"You can't do that. I know my rights."

"Have it your way." Fogarty reached for the set of handcuffs attached to his belt.

Lucille's eyes widened. She stumbled backwards, steadying herself with her cane. "You wouldn't dare!"

Fogarty called her bluff. Or at least I think he was calling her bluff. "Wanna bet?"

With a grunt and a mutter, Lucille plopped onto the sofa, folding her arms across her chest. I swore I could see little puffs of steam emanating from the top of her closely cropped, utilitarian-styled head.

"Can you describe your assailant?" asked Harley, his ever-present stub of a pencil poised over his ever-present spiral notepad.

"He was tall," said Lucille. "Well over six feet. And fat. Maybe around three hundred pounds."

"He was not," said Mama, settling herself in the center of the sofa. "Don't listen to that crack-pot commie. He was five-nine. I remember because he was exactly the same height as my third husband."

"You can't even remember your third husband," said Lucille. "You don't keep them around long enough." She turned to Harley. "He was at least six-three, maybe six-four." She pointed to his notebook. "Write that down."

"How dare you!" cried Mama. "Are you going to believe this ... this *communist* or a law-abiding citizen and member of the Daughters of the American Revolution?"

She glared at Lucille. "At least *my* husbands have the misfortune to die. They don't run off on me and never come back."

"Isidore didn't leave me," said Lucille. "He was abducted."

Mama, the boys, and I exchanged baffled glances. This was news to us. Karl claimed his father had walked out on his mother.

"By aliens?" asked Nick.

"By J. Edgar Hoover and his battalion of right-wing cronies," said Lucille. "I have reason to believe they buried him under one of the goalposts in Giants Stadium."

Mama snorted. "That's Jimmy Hoffa, you pinko idiot. Besides, Giants Stadium wasn't even built when your husband walked out on you."

Way to go, Mama. I had no idea she had such a wealth of trivia hiding beneath those wavy strawberry blonde locks of hers. Maybe I should sign her up for the seniors' *Jeopardy* tournament.

"And for your information, I remember each and every one of my husbands, thank you very much. That man was exactly the same height as my dear departed Oscar Scoffield. And he *wasn't* fat." She turned to Harley. "He was very muscular. Like a body builder."

Fogarty rolled his eyes. "What about hair?"

"Black," said Mama.

"Light brown," said Lucille. "What was left of it. He had a large bald spot in the front."

"He had a full head of hair," said Mama. "Thick. Like my first husband's." She turned to me. "You remember what a gorgeous head of hair your father had, don't you, Anastasia dear?"

"Yes, Mama."

Fogarty and Harley shook their heads. Lucille and Mama exchanged looks that could kill if given half a chance. Nick and Alex tried to stifle their laughter. They weren't very successful.

"Why don't I make some coffee?" I suggested.

"I'm hungry," said Nick.

"Me, too," added Alex.

I headed back into the kitchen and opened the refrigerator. I flung open the freezer.

I ran across the room and yanked open the pantry.

"That bastard!" I screamed.

TWENTY-FOUR

ALEX, NICK, MAMA, FOGARTY, and Harley came running. The refrigerator and freezer doors stood open, bare bulbs illuminating their cavernous, totally *empty* interiors. The pantry was equally bare.

"He didn't leave us with so much as a lousy cornflake!" I said.

I wanted to throw myself on the linoleum and kick and scream like an overtired two year old, but I contained my tantrum to an adult-like two-fisted pummeling of the refrigerator door. In hindsight, considering the size of the dent I created, I should have gone with my first and baser instinct.

"He was here a long time," said Mama. "Surely one of the neighbors saw him carrying stuff out the front door and can give the police a description."

"Yeah, Mom," said Nick. "Batty Bentworth probably even wrote down his license plate number. You know what a busybody snoop she is."

Fogarty grimaced. "We know all about Mrs. Bentworth. She calls at least once a day to report alien sightings. No one at the station pays attention to her."

"Maybe you should this time," said Mama.

Fogarty shook his head. "We'll check it out, but most likely the perp pulled a truck around to the back before ringing the front doorbell. He wouldn't have been seen from the street, and you have high shrubbery masking the yard from your next door neighbors."

"He also may not have been here as long as you think," added Harley.

"But it had to take hours to empty the house," I said.

"He probably had help," said Fogarty. He turned to Mama and the boys. "Did it ever sound like more than one person was in the house? Did you hear him speaking to anyone?"

"I couldn't hear much of anything," said Nick.

"Me, neither," added Alex.

Mama scrunched up her face and shook her head. "Not with the way that woman was carrying on with her grunting and groaning."

"This guy is a real sicko," said Harley. "We'd better check the garage and apartment. He probably hit those, as well."

I turned to reach for the keys I kept on a hook by the phone. They weren't there.

Harley and Fogarty, their hands poised on their guns, headed out into the back yard.

"I'm starving," said Nick.

"What are we gonna eat?" asked Alex.

He and Nick began to open and inspect the contents of every cupboard and drawer, for what I couldn't imagine. It wasn't like I hid Hershey bars inside the crock-pot. Not that we still had a crock-pot. Ricardo—and at this point I had absolutely no doubt the burglar was Ricardo—had helped himself to all the small appliances as well. However, my normally reasonable and understanding sons reverted to whining babies when hungry. And like babies, they needed feeding every two to three hours or things got ugly.

Having checked every nook and cranny of the kitchen, the boys moved on to the mud room. "Jeez, Mom! He even took the dog and cat food."

"And Ralph's bird seed," added Alex.

I let loose a string of four-letter words that made Mama blush. "Anastasia!"

Too bad. Between the few dollars in my wallet and the forty left in my checking account, I might be able to feed three adults and two teenagers for a day or two. Tops.

Trimedia cut payroll checks every two weeks. I wouldn't see another dime until next Thursday. I'd never stretch fifty dollars or so until then. And that left nothing for the menagerie. Not to mention gas for the car.

And I didn't even want to think about the vet bill. Mama and Lucille were responsible for Catherine the Great and Devil Dog, but what would the vet charge for the care and feeding of a Prozac-riddled parrot?

Harley and Fogarty returned, shaking their heads. "Looks like he helped himself to anything of value," said Harley. "If I remember, you had a computer in the apartment, right?"

"Yes."

"It's gone. So's the lawn mower and snow thrower. I don't re-member what else you had in the garage in the way of garden giz-mos. If you had a leaf blower, he helped himself to that, too."

"We'll need a list of the missing items," said Fogarty. "So will the insurance company."

I wondered how long it took our homeowner's policy to pay out a claim on a robbery. I was still waiting for a check from the damage Ricardo inflicted Monday.

In all the years of owning the house, we'd never had to place ourselves in the insurance company's trademark good hands. Now, two claims in a week. I wondered how much that would increase my premium—assuming the good hands people didn't simply wipe their hands of me, since I was fast becoming an extremely poor risk.

We had to eat. I saw but one option. "Mama, I'm going to need to borrow some money."

"Don't worry, dear, I'll get my purse."

She headed for the bedroom.

The rest of us returned to the living room where Lucille waited impatiently, her arms still folded across her chest, her mouth set in its classic grimace. I explained the latest catastrophe, adding, "I'll need to borrow whatever you've got in the way of cash in order to buy food for all of us."

"Only if you promise to buy Manifesto's regular food, not that cheap dry crap you forced on him."

Unfortunately, I knew she was serious. Mephisto came before her grandchildren. "Be reasonable, Lucille. A can of that stuff costs as much as a quart of milk."

"He's having digestive problems, thanks to your selfishness!"

And I was getting a whopper of an ulcer thanks to her. "Look, Lucille—"

Before I could finish, Mama returned empty-handed from the bedroom. "My purse is missing," she said. "My wallet. My credit cards. My check book. My passport. All gone."

"And Lucille's purse?" I asked.

Mama shook her head.

"Now what do we do?" asked Nick.

"You can have whatever I've got, Mom. Alex reached into the back pocket of his jeans. His jaw dropped. "I don't believe it! That creep pinched my wallet."

Nick checked his pocket. "Mine, too."

That left me with no choice. I couldn't let my family starve to death. Not when I had fifty-thousand dollars in marked bills locked in my car. Batswin and Robbins would have to understand.

Fogarty and Harley waited for back-up to take their place watching the house, then left to file their report. As soon as they were gone, I scrawled an IOU on a scrap of paper and added it to the envelope with the Burberry receipt. Then I removed two crisp hundred dollar bills from one of the stacks and stuck the envelope in the tote with the money.

But the thought of continuing to ride around with fifty thousand dollars in a car without an alarm system creeped me out. So I decided to freeze the assets. Literally. After stuffing the money-laden tote in the empty freezer, I headed for the nearest twenty-four hour supermarket.

———

At ten-thirty on a Friday night, most people had better things to do than push a shopping cart up and down the aisles of ShopRite. Once upon a time when I led a predictably normal suburban, middle-class life, I was one of them. No more. I sailed up one aisle and down the next of the near-empty supermarket, filling my cart with low-priced store brands. Cheap was good. Cheap on sale was even better.

As I stood in front of the spaghetti aisle, studying the little shelf labels to figure out which brand was the best bargain per pound, my cell phone rang. I fished it out of my purse and looked at the display. *Private Call.* Not a good sign. I pushed the button. "Hello?"

"You set me up, bitch."

Even though I was prepared to hear it, I nearly dropped the phone at the sound of Ricardo's menacing voice. "No! I went to the mall. I did everything like you said. I waited. You never called."

"The mall was crawling with cops. I warned you not to tell anyone."

"I didn't!"

"So they just happened to be hanging around for the hell of it, huh?"

"I have your money."

"In marked bills, no doubt. I wasn't born yesterday, Sweet Cheeks. I've been keeping an eye on you. I know what you've been up to."

"You've got it all wrong."

"Oh yeah? How many other people in Westfield have their phones bugged and cops watching their houses?"

"How do you know that?"

"I told you. I've been keeping an eye on you. I even know where you are right now. No food in the house, huh?"

I gasped, spinning around to check up and down the aisle. I saw no one except a bored-looking teenage clerk stocking cans of tomato sauce, and he wasn't talking on a phone.

Even though I suspected Ricardo had broken into my house, assaulted my family, drugged the pets, and robbed us blind, hearing him confirm it was like getting flattened by a Hummer. I leaned against the shelf of spaghetti for support. "You've taken everything I have. There's nothing left. Leave me alone."

"What I took doesn't even make a dent in what Karl owed me. I want my money."

"I don't have it!"

"Look, Sweet Cheeks, I know Karl had the money. I helped him get it."

"What do you mean?"

"Your husband was one mean son of a bitch. I really admired him for that. Balls of steel. Lousy gambler, though. Too bad he had to die. I was racking up a nice piece of change from all those sucker bets he placed. The sap couldn't pick a winner if it sat on his head."

"What are you saying?"

"You know that accident his mother had? The hit-and-run on Queens Boulevard?"

"What about it?"

"That was no accident. It was a set-up to knock her off so Karl could get his hands on the money she had stashed in her apartment."

My brain went numb. A sickening feeling settled in my stomach. "Karl tried to kill his mother?"

"His idea but I drove. So's he wouldn't chicken out at the last minute. Amateurs. You never know if you can trust 'em or not.

"That broad's one tough bitch, though. And lucky. I woulda nailed her good except some SOB in a pick-up cut me off at the last minute. So's I only wound up winging her.

"Then Karl, he comes up with another plan. While she's in the hospital, he helps himself to the dough, then torches the place to cover up the theft."

"I don't believe you. Karl wouldn't do something like that. You're lying."

He snickered. "They always say the wife's the last to know."

My legs gave way, and I slumped to the floor. A wave of nausea swept over me. Eighteen years of marriage and no clues I'd shared a bed with a lying, cheating, murdering Dr. Jekyll and Mr. Hyde. "Three people died in that fire."

"We all gotta go sometime, Sweet Cheeks." He paused for a moment, then continued, "Some sooner than later, if you get my drift."

I got it all right. And it set my heart pounding into my throat.

"So's you see, I know Karl had the money."

"Why didn't he give it to you right away? Karl died weeks after that fire."

"The cops picked me up on some bogus warrant. Took a while to get sprung. Good for nothing shit lawyers. When I got out, I contacted Karl. We made arrangements for him to hand over the dough. Only he never showed."

No, instead Karl had hopped a plane to Las Vegas. I suppose all that money sitting around for weeks had been too much of a temptation for him. Then, after he gambled away Ricardo's money,

Karl dropped dead, leaving me to deal with Lucille, the debt, the bills, *and* Ricardo.

"Why are you telling me all this?"

"So's you know I mean business, Sweet Cheeks. You want to keep your kids healthy, you come up with the money."

"How? I'm broke. Karl left me destitute. There's no insurance money. He drained our bank accounts. Maxed out the credit cards."

"Not my problem, Sweet Cheeks. Sell the house if you have to."

"The bank will take the profit to pay off the home equity loan."

"There is another way," he said.

"What?"

"I have some friends you could go work for. Evenings. Weekends. Easy money." He sniggered. "They run a service-type business. Classy looking broad like you could work off that debt in no time."

I shuddered at the suggestion. "Tempting as the offer sounds, thanks but no thanks. I'll find some other way to raise the money."

"I ain't got forever, Sweet Cheeks, and I'm still not convinced you ain't got the dough stashed someplace. But hey, I got a soft spot for brunettes. Since you're new to all this, I'll cut you a break. You got one more week. But this time you keep your trap shut. I find you working with the cops again, and the deal's off. *Capisce?*"

He hung up before I could answer.

TWENTY-FIVE

DINNER THAT NIGHT CONSISTED of store-brand peanut butter and jelly sandwiches on day-old, half-priced bread. Carrot sticks on the side with a milk chaser. Quick, cheap, and covering all of the major food groups. So I didn't feel too guilty, especially since I'd bought whole wheat bread instead of white.

Something Ricardo had said kept niggling at the edges of my exhausted brain cells. As I munched on my sandwich, I replayed the conversation in my head. "He knew too much!" I said, slapping my hand on the table.

"Who knew too much?" asked Alex.

"Dad?" asked Nick.

Lucille leaned forward on her tree trunk arms and leveled one of her trademark narrow-eyed glowers at him. "Don't you dare blame my son for anything, young man. If your father were still alive—"

"He'd be making even more of a mess than the one he left behind." Mama rose from the table and carried her empty plate and

232

glass to the sink. "God forbid we blame the saintly Karl Marx Pollack for anything."

"Mama..."

She spun around. "Why pussyfoot around the subject, Anastasia? Karl hoodwinked you. But what can you expect, considering he was raised by a traitor?" She jabbed a finger toward Lucille. "No Christian values. Total disregard for the law. A lack of respect for this wonderful country of ours. Under the circumstances, the man didn't stand a chance of developing proper morals."

Lucille's face darkened to an extremely unbecoming shade of magenta. "Traitor? I'll have you know that as a communist, I fight for democracy!"

Alex and Nick traded uncomprehending glances. "That doesn't make sense," said Alex. "How can—?"

"Enough!" I jumped to my feet. "I wasn't talking about Karl."

Puzzlement settled over Mama's face. "Then who?"

"Never mind." I snatched my purse off the kitchen counter, fished inside for my cell phone and Batswin's card, then headed for the back door. "I have to make a call."

The furrows of bafflement on Mama's forehead deepened. "Outside?"

"Definitely outside." There were only two ways Ricardo could have known as much as he did. Either he'd planted a bug in my house, or he had inside help.

Under the yellow glow of the back porch light, I punched in Detective Batswin's number. "Not only did your great plan fail," I said when she answered, "but now I'm in worse shape financially than I was before I let you talk me into playing a bag lady."

"Calm down, Mrs. Pollack. There could be any number of reasons why he didn't show tonight," she said. "He'll contact you to set up another drop. We'll nab him then."

"He's on to you, Detective."

"What do you mean?"

I began to recount the evening's events from when I left the mall. "By the way, I had to borrow two hundred dollars from the money you gave me to buy food for my family."

She groaned. "Those were counterfeit bills."

"Counterfeit?" Angry cloud puffs of breath hung in the air as I shouted into the phone. "You told me they were marked! Even I know the difference."

"It wouldn't have made a difference if you'd followed orders."

"You're out to get me one way or the other, aren't you? If you can't pin Marlys's murder on me, you'll arrest me for passing bogus bills. What gives, Batswin? You down a few arrests on your monthly collaring quota? Bucking for a promotion?"

"This has nothing to do with me. The counterfeit bills were available."

"Available? You just happened to have fifty grand in counterfeit bills lying around the station?"

"It's evidence from another case. We borrowed it. It was quicker and easier than getting our hands on marked bills. You have any idea what kind of red tape that involves? Besides, you weren't supposed to spend any of that money."

"I had no choice! Ricardo stole every crumb of food in my house. Even the pet food."

"You don't know Ricardo was the thief. According to the Westfield police, there've been a rash of burglaries in your area lately."

"He called me."

"Ricardo?"

"No, Antonio Banderas."

"When? We didn't pick anything up on your phone."

"That's because he knows my phone is bugged."

"Impossible."

"Really? He called on my cell a little while ago. Bragged about knowing everything—including your sting. I'm lucky he only robbed me blind tonight instead of killing my kids and mother." I rubbed my arms and stamped my feet to ward off the cold from both the winter night and the sickening dread infiltrating my body.

Batswin grew defensive and accusatory, probably because she was now up to her eyeballs in shit with her job on the line. I didn't know much about police procedures, but I suspected "borrowing" evidence from one case to use in another was a humongous no-no.

"He couldn't have found out about the sting unless you mentioned it to someone," she said. "We warned you not to say anything."

"I didn't."

"Then how the hell did he find out?"

"You tell me, Detective. The way I see it, either he bugged the Trimedia conference room, or you've got a corrupt cop on the force."

When she didn't respond, I thought the connection had gone dead, but finally she said, "I'll have Trimedia swept for bugs and contact the Union County police to do a sweep of your property. If he's planted any sort of spying devices, we'll find them."

"And if there aren't any bugs?"

"We'll get to the source of this one way or another."

"Before or after he harms my family?"

"We won't let it come to that."

And she expected me to believe her? "You've got police in several jurisdictions working together, and Ricardo managed to outsmart all of you. What makes you think you'll even get another shot at nabbing him?"

"He's greedy. He wants his money, and he's made it clear he'll stop at nothing to get it."

"Oh, that makes me feel so much better. Good night, Detective. I'm off to have a nightmare or two or twelve." I hung up the phone and headed for bed, but sleep—nightmare-filled or otherwise—proved elusive.

———

At six-thirty the next morning, the doorbell rang. Dragging my sleep-deprived body out of bed, I tossed on a robe, pulled on a pair of thick socks, and padded to the front door. Batswin and Robbins stood on the porch. "A little early for a house call, isn't it, Detectives?"

"We came for the money," said Batswin.

I motioned them inside. "I wanted to give it back last night. Why now?"

"We were in the neighborhood," said Robbins.

I got the impression he and Batswin had rehearsed this encounter before ringing my doorbell. They had screwed up bigtime. Their visit to retrieve the money was Step One in their Cover Our Tushes cover-up.

Robbins unzipped his bomber jacket. The brown leather looked like it had seen combat back in Vietnam—if not Korea. Underneath, he wore an equally worn pair of jeans, a denim button-down shirt, and an Inspector Gadget tie. A Yankees baseball cap covered his balding head; brown leather gloves covered his hands.

Batswin wore a turquoise and emerald ski jacket, complete with a Hunter Mountain lift tag hanging from the zipper pull, over a pair of acid-washed jeans. No hat. No gloves. Silver and black onyx fetish bears dangled from her ears. She kept her jacket zipped.

I doubted Robbins' explanation. Westfield was out of their jurisdiction. Besides, they certainly didn't look dressed for duty. The detectives didn't want me handing the money over last night because they feared the Essex County cops would discover the phony Franklins used as bait.

Most likely, they'd taken the fifty grand without even signing for it. They probably planned to slip the money back into the evidence room this morning and not say a word about the missing two hundred dollars. After all, what were the odds of someone actually counting every counterfeit bill in each counterfeit stack?

"Where's the money?" asked Batswin.

"In the kitchen."

I headed down the hall. They followed. "I'd offer you a cup of coffee," I said, opening the freezer and pulling out the Burberry bag, "but Ricardo stole my coffeepot." Besides, I wanted them gone before anyone else woke. Explaining Batswin's and Robbins's presence held as much appeal as a day at the endodontist.

Neither commented on my hiding place. Robbins took the bag from me.

"What about the receipt?" asked Batswin.

I pointed to the tote. "Inside. Along with a signed I.O.U. for the money I borrowed."

She grimaced.

Without another word, they both headed back toward the living room.

I followed. "What happens now?"

"We'll wait for Ricardo to make the next move," said Batswin.

"What about the murder investigation? Am I still a suspect?"

They both paused at the front door and turned toward me. Robbins, his free hand poised on the doorknob, cleared his throat. "We're not at liberty to discuss that."

I glanced at the bag of counterfeit money dangling from his hand. I knew something that could plunge Batswin and Robbins into deep doo-doo. They knew I knew. Maybe that would give them incentive to get off my back and concentrate their investigation elsewhere.

I closed the door behind them and headed back to bed. Five minutes later the phone rang. "Hello?"

"Mrs. Pollack?"

"Yes?"

"This is Angie at the We Care Animal Clinic. You can pick up your pets this morning."

"They're okay?"

"Fine. Doc ran a few tests to be sure, but it looks like they were only doped with Dimetapp."

"Cold syrup?"

"It's got the same ingredient they put in over-the-counter sleeping pills. Apparently, your robber didn't intend to kill your pets, just put them to sleep for awhile."

"A real animal lover," I muttered.

Too bad Ricardo didn't extend the same consideration to higher order primates. I doubted he merely intended to slip my kids a Mickey and tuck them into bed. Not after trussing them up like a pair of Christmas turkeys and dumping them in the bathtub last night.

"By the way," said the receptionist, "the bill comes to three hundred twenty-seven dollars."

More good news. "Why so much?"

"Tests, boarding, and flea dip for all."

"They had fleas?"

"The dog did. We dipped the cat and parrot as a precautionary measure."

"Fleas in the middle of winter?"

"It happens from time to time. You'd better check your house, especially any of Manifesto's favorite curling-up places."

Just what I needed. I don't know why I should have been surprised, considering the current state of my Karma, or lack of it.

Have I mentioned that Lucille believes flea collars are a capitalist conspiracy to force hard-earned dollars from the hands of animal lovers throughout the country? When the dear Lord was handing out the Rational Gene, my mother-in-law must have been off protesting the use of *In God We Trust* on our currency.

So now her skewed sense of righteousness had cost me more of *my* hard-earned—not to mention bordering on nonexistent—dollars. Thanks to Ricardo's pilfering fingers, I could count on neither

Mama nor Lucille to kick in anything toward the vet bill. I had a few piddling dollars left to my name. I hung up, hoping I could spring the beasties with a post-dated check.

I also hoped that if there were any fleas residing in my house, they'd all hitched a ride on Ricardo as he helped himself to our possessions.

———

Mama and Lucille insisted on accompanying me to the animal hospital. I wanted to sneak off without telling them, but the dog and cat carriers were stored in the closet in their room. So the three of us, along with the feline and canine transporters and Ralph's birdcage, bundled up and shoehorned ourselves into the Hyundai for the fifteen-minute drive to the We Care Animal Clinic.

The car coughed and sputtered as I turned the ignition key and depressed the gas pedal. As the Hyundai chugged to life, the needle on the gauge dipped toward the red pump icon. I detoured into the first gas station we came to, pulling out two minutes later with five gallons of gas in the tank and less than two dollars left in my wallet.

When we arrived at the animal hospital, Lucille refused to place Mephisto in his doggie transport. "He hates the carrier, and he's traumatized enough after last night."

She clasped him to her chest and nuzzled the top of his head. The Devil Dog squirmed and whined. "See? Poor baby. Don't worry. Mother's here," she sang, clutching him even tighter.

He yelped.

One of these days she's going to love that dog to death with those Arnold Schwarzenegger arms of hers. I was too tired to argue about the carrier. I grabbed Ralph's cage in one hand and the empty dog carrier in the other. "Fine. Make sure he stays on your lap."

"Wait a minute," said Mama. "If that beast doesn't have to go in a carrier, why should Catherine the Great suffer? She has claustrophobia, you know."

Since when do cats suffer from claustrophobia? "Mama, it's only a fifteen-minute drive."

"She won't know that. Look at her. She's far more traumatized than that ... " She pointed to Mephisto. " ... that *mutt*."

Frankly, neither Mephisto nor Catherine the Great appeared anything close to traumatized. They both looked like they'd spent the night at The Golden Door Spa. "Fine, but it's up to the two of you to keep them separated and contained in the back seat. The last thing I need is a dog and cat fight while I'm driving."

"*Stand, stand and fight!*" squawked Ralph. "*Cymbeline*, Act Five, Scene Two."

Another county heard from. I raised his cage until we were eye-to-eye. "Don't you dare egg them on."

As it turned out, Mephisto and Catherine the Great behaved fairly well throughout the ride home. They only occasionally growled and hissed at each other. Too bad the same couldn't be said for Mama and Lucille. They squabbled and bickered non-stop.

Shades of he-touched-me/did-not/did-too arguments between a five-year-old and his seven-year-old brother flashed before my eyes. In retrospect, I think Nick and Alex were better behaved on their worst day than their grandmothers at their best. Relief surged through me as I turned the Hyundai onto our street.

Until I pulled into my driveway.

TWENTY-SIX

"Omigod!" I stared at the moving van parked in my driveway. "It's Saturday." The day Zachary Barnes was moving into the apartment above the garage. The apartment I still hadn't gotten around to emptying and cleaning.

"What's going on now?" asked Mama. She unlocked her seatbelt and wedged her head, shoulders, and half of Catherine the Great between the two front bucket seats.

"Move over. I can't see," said Lucille. She shoved Mama back and over to the side.

Mama jabbed Lucille with her shoulder. "Get your commie pinko paws off me!"

Annoyed by the jostling, Catherine the Great took a swipe at Mephisto. He bared his teeth and snapped at her. She jumped out of Mama's arms and bounded into the front passenger seat, landing on top of Ralph's cage. Ralph beat his wings against the wire mesh and let loose with a rapid-fire series of ear-piercing squawks.

"Who's that man with the police?" Lucille yelled over the din as she pushed Mama aside and shoved her own torso between the bucket seats. "Why is there a moving van parked in the driveway?"

My new tenant stood off to the side, clutching a cup of coffee. He appeared to be having an extremely animated conversation with the two cops who were supposed to be keeping an eye on my property.

I maneuvered myself around Lucille and one by one, pried Catherine the Great's claws off the bars of Ralph's cage, trying my best to hold each freed paw to prevent her from reattaching herself.

"He's renting the apartment above the garage," I told Lucille as I passed Mama's cat back to her.

"The apartment that by rights should be mine," said Lucille, "considering the exorbitant rent you're charging me. Extortion. That's what it is. My son never would have let you get away with taking advantage of me like this."

"Your son was the one who got my daughter into this mess," said Mama.

"Lies," said Lucille. "Nothing but lies."

I ignored her. When it came to Karl, Lucille lived in her own private world of delusion. She should only know he'd tried to kill her. And when that failed, how he stole her life's savings, killing three innocent people along the way.

But as much as I itched to tell her, I wasn't that cruel. Let her keep believing in Saint Karl—if Bolsheviks could believe in saints. I wished I had the luxury of assuming my husband was the man I thought he was.

"Oh, it's that handsome Zachary Barnes from the other night," said Mama, straining her neck for a better view. "If only I were a few years younger ..."

Lucille snorted.

Mephisto growled.

Catherine the Great yowled.

Ralph continued to squawk.

Zachary Barnes strode his angry Pierce Brosnan-George Clooney-Patrick Dempsey-Antonio Banderas good looks toward the driver's side of my car. The police followed close behind him. I exited the Hyundai to meet them.

Lucille grunted her way out of the back seat and hobbled toward the house, her cane pounding the frozen earth with each labored step. As she passed us, Mephisto growled at the officers. Lucille glared at all three men but zeroed in on Zack. "Thief!"

The officers turned to Zack. "Well?" said one, as Lucille doddered past them.

Zack opened his mouth to protest. "Look, I—"

"Ignore them." Mama, embracing Catherine the Great, rounded the car to stand beside me. She gestured with a jut of her chin toward Lucille. "They're communists. You know how *they* are."

All three men turned their heads to watch Lucille huff and puff her way up the back porch steps. "The dog, too?" asked one of the officers.

"Of course," said Mama. "French bulldog, my patootie. That dog's as Russian as the Kremlin."

I steered Mama toward the house. "Why don't you take Catherine the Great inside?"

"You may need me, dear."

About as much as I needed a migraine, sciatica, and a case of hemorrhoids all at once.

The back door of the house slammed behind Lucille. Zack transferred his attention to me. "For someone who was so worried that I'd back out of our lease agreement, you sure provided a strange welcoming committee. I arrived to find you not home and some of Westfield's finest accusing me of criminal activity."

I flinched. The man was one very unhappy camper this morning. But could I blame him? "We sort of had another incident last night."

"So I figured."

"And I sort of didn't get a chance to clean the apartment because of it."

From inside the closed car, Ralph continued to squawk. Even though I'd placed the door of his cage against the seat back, he'd somehow managed to rotate the cage enough to pick the lock and escape. He loudly berated us from his perch on the steering wheel.

The cops leaned forward and stared through the windshield. "I'll be damned," said the second officer. "A parrot!" He tapped on the windshield with his fingernail. "Polly want a cracker?"

Ralph hopped onto the dash and pecked at him through the glass. If it's one thing my Shakespeare-pontificating parrot hates, it's being reminded he's only a parrot.

Zack stepped closer to me, until our toes nearly touched. "Look, Anastasia, I don't care if you didn't get a chance to polish the doorknobs, okay? I just need to get my stuff into the apartment or the movers are going to dump it all in the driveway and take off."

"*Doorknob polishing*? Believe me, doorknob polishing is so low on my list of priorities that you'd need a bulldozer to unearth it."

Mama pushed me aside and stepped between us. "Now, Zachary dear, don't twist your knickers. You'll give yourself a stroke. Believe me, I know about these things. My late husband Seamus O'Keefe, bless his dearly departed soul, died of a cerebral aneurysm. You're far too young and handsome to follow in his footsteps. Not that Seamus wasn't handsome, mind you, but you never know if you're a ticking time bomb, as the doctors later told me—"

"Mama, please go inside."

"You know this man, Mrs. Pollack?" asked the officer who'd questioned Mephisto's political leanings.

"Yes. He's renting the apartment above the garage." I turned to Zack. "I'm sorry for the chaos. Please come inside and warm up."

Zack turned to the police. "You guys satisfied I'm not some serial killer?"

"Just doing our job," said the officer. He grabbed his partner by the arm and headed down the driveway. "We'll be in the car if you need us, Mrs. Pollack."

Zack called to the men sitting in the idling moving van. "You can start unloading the truck, fellas. I'll be out in a minute."

"About time," said the driver.

Before leading Zack into the house, I climbed back into the Hyundai and grabbed Ralph off the dashboard, tucking him under my coat to keep him warm.

"Why the police surveillance?" asked Zack. "Exactly what happened?"

"Long story."

"Some awful man taped us up and stuffed us in the bathtub last night," said Mama. "And he nearly killed Catherine the Great."

Zack looked at Mama as if she'd had one too many white Russians. "Catherine the Great died several hundred years ago," he said.

"The cat," I told him. "That's her name. And the vet said that creep only fed the animals enough cold syrup to put them to sleep, Mama. Climb down from your drama queen podium."

"Really, Anastasia!" She stroked her cheek against Catherine the Great's fur. "How would a deviant like that know how much cold medicine is too much? And why would he even care? He could have killed her. Poor sweet thing. And then to have to put up with that vicious Marxist mongrel trying to attack her. It's all been too much for her."

"Marxist mongrel? I think I'm going to need a scorecard," said Zack.

"He belongs to my mother-in-law. She's the one who called you a thief a minute ago. You didn't meet her the other night. She and the Demon Dog were off sulking in her room."

"They're communists," said Mama.

Zack gave her an odd look, but addressed me, "Speaking of thief, I take it your two-by-fours didn't do the job?"

"That sneaky Pete rang the bell," said Mama. "When I opened the door, he stuck a huge gun in my face. Can you imagine?"

"The bastard wiped us out," I said. "Down to our last jar of peanut butter and bag of cat food."

We entered the house, and I released Ralph from the confines of my coat. He flew up to the curtain rod above the sink window.

"I didn't notice the parrot before," said Zack.

"He was watching PBS in my bedroom. Ralph's a sucker for anything starring Helen Mirren. Reminds him of my Great-aunt Penelope."

"He has free reign of the house?"

"Not to worry," I assured him. "Ralph's housebroken."

"You're kidding! Is that even possible?"

"Ralph's a very unusual bird."

"*And show the world what the bird hath done*," squawked Ralph, as if to prove my point. "*As You Like It*. Act Four, Scene One."

"I'll be damned. A Shakespeare-quoting parrot. I'd say that qualifies as unusual."

"That's one word for it," said Mama. "If that bird-brained Penelope Periwinkle had spent half as much time finding a husband as she did fawning over that damn bird, she wouldn't have died a dried-up old spinster."

"Mama, I doubt Zachary is interested in your estimation of certain branches of our family tree."

I filled the tea kettle and placed it on the stove. "I hope instant is okay. Along with just about everything else that wasn't nailed down, the thief helped himself to Mr. Coffee." At least Ricardo had spared the pots and pans. I guess he had no use for eighteen-year-old dented Farberware and chipped Pyrex.

Nick and Alex barged into the kitchen. "Hey, Zack!" they both called out.

"Why didn't you guys tell the cops outside that you know Mr. Barnes?" I asked. "You invite him into the house when he's a stranger and leave him at the mercy of the police once you know who he is? Am I the only person who thinks this makes absolutely no sense?"

"Huh?" asked Alex.

"What cops?" asked Nick.

"The ones watching the house. They were about to arrest him."

"Thought I was the burglar, come back to finish the job," said Zack.

"What in the world have you been doing the past half hour?" I asked my sons.

"Jeez, Mom, it's Saturday. We slept in."

"Until Grandmother Lucille woke us up a few minutes ago when she came clomping down the hall," said Nick.

"Sorry, Zack," said Alex. He rubbed the still-red skin around his mouth. "We didn't hear anyone knock. I guess getting bound and gagged with duct tape yesterday kind of wiped us out."

"I know what you mean," said Zack.

"You do?" Both boys' eyes bugged out.

"I once stuck my camera where someone didn't want it. He had friends in low places."

I wondered if Ricardo was one of those friends. However, since I hadn't told either the boys or Mama about my dealings with Ricardo, I slapped an imaginary strip of duct tape over my own mouth.

"About the apartment," I said.

"What's the problem? I told you not to worry about cleaning it. I can sweep up after the movers bring the furniture inside."

"It's a little more than sweeping. Not enough hours in the day. I had planned to empty the apartment last night. Our intruder had other ideas."

"The movers have another gig to pack up later this afternoon," said Zack. "If they don't have enough time to bring everything upstairs, they'll leave my stuff sitting in your driveway. How much time do you need?"

"Thirty minutes. Forty tops," I assured him. Not that I had a clue how long it would really take. And when was I supposed to find the time to compile an inventory of all our missing possessions for the police and the insurance company? I needed those good hands guys to cut me a check ASAP.

I glanced at Mama to see if she could tell I was lying. She answered with the slightest raise of an eyebrow, but I had fooled Zack Barnes, and that's all that mattered.

I began issuing orders. "Alex, Nick, get dressed. You're on clean-up and hauling detail. Mama, you make Zack comfortable in the den."

"I can do more than that," said Mama. "And the Bolshevik can get off her fat rump and help as well if she wants to maintain her standing in the *Workers'* Party."

"Lucille can't climb more than a few steps, Mama." Besides, even if she could manage the stairs, Lucille would be more a hindrance than a help. I could do without her spewing forth a non-stop litany of complaints.

"How convenient. Laziest *worker* I've ever seen."

I ignored her, even though I agreed with her assessment of Lucille's work ethic.

"That woman's all talk, no action," said Mama. "Give her something to do that won't require climbing so many stairs. She's not the Queen of Sheba. What about the laundry? The hampers are overflowing."

"Hell, no," cried Alex. "The last time Mom asked Grandmother Lucille to do laundry, Nick and I wound up with pink underwear."

"Deliberately, no doubt," said Mama. "Devious old pinko battle-ax."

I turned to Zack and changed the subject. "I can offer you a selection of books and magazines while you wait. Unfortunately, you're out of luck if you want to watch TV or a movie."

"Or listen to a CD or play a video game or use a computer," grumbled Nick.

"He really cleaned you out," said Zack.

"Right down to Catherine the Great's kitty litter," said Mama.

"I'm not going to sit on my ass while you work," he said. "We'll get done that much faster if I help you."

"Now that's what I call a worker's party," said Mama. "That *prima donna* pinko should take a lesson from you, Zachary dear."

TWENTY-SEVEN

FOUR HOURS LATER MY studio had been moved from the apartment to the basement and Zack's furniture had been moved from the van into the apartment. It had taken Mama far less time to wrap Zack around her pinky, but then again, she'd already gotten a head start the other night.

Mama had always gone for men her own age or older, but they had a bad habit of dying on her. Maybe she'd decided she'd have better luck with someone younger. Much younger. I decided I wasn't cruel enough to tell her Zack already knew she was in husband-hunting mode and wasn't interested.

"If you're thinking what I'm thinking you're thinking," I told her after Zack offered to pick up pizzas for lunch—his treat, "you can forget it."

"Whatever do you mean, dear?"

"Don't feign innocence with me, Flora Sudberry Periwinkle Ramirez Scoffield Goldberg O'Keefe. I know what you're up to, and I'm telling you right now, no way am I calling that man *daddy.*"

Although, if I weren't so recently widowed and burned by a drop-dead gorgeous man, I wouldn't be adverse to calling Zack Barnes a few other things.

Mama fluttered her hand as if banishing my words into the stratosphere. "Honestly, Anastasia, I don't know where you'd get such a ridiculous notion. After all, my poor Seamus is hardly cold in his grave."

As was Karl, but I was still having certain totally inappropriate thoughts in regards to my new tenant. But that was Karl's fault, not mine. I wasn't the one who had screwed my spouse and kids, leaving us at the mercy of the likes of Ricardo.

Still, life would be simpler if I'd rented to a spinster piano teacher. Or a middle-aged gay couple.

———

Even though Lucille hadn't assisted with any of the packing or moving, she arrived in the kitchen at precisely the same time Zack returned with the pizzas. She grabbed four slices of pepperoni for herself and fed the crusts to Mephisto. So much for the Devil Dog's *delicate constitution.*

"Quite a zoo you have here," said Zack, scanning the kitchen.

Mephisto sat beside Lucille's chair, awaiting another crust offering. Catherine the Great had curled up on top of the refrigerator, and Ralph kept an eye on everyone from his perch on the curtain rod above the sink window.

"Hmm." I spoke around a slice of mushroom pizza. "*Casa Pollack's* very own version of Animal House."

"How do you keep the cat, the dog, and the bird from killing each other? They don't seem to get along very well."

"It's easier than keeping the grandmas from killing each other," muttered Alex out of the side of his mouth.

Nick laughed so hard he snorted root beer through his nose.

I scowled at both of them. "Apologize to your grandmothers."

"Why?" asked Nick. "It's true."

"They hate each other," Alex informed Zack—just in case he hadn't noticed this for himself.

I continued to glare at my sons until they muttered an apology to Lucille and Mama. "Only Ralph is a permanent resident," I said to Zack. "Catherine the Great and Mephisto are here temporarily."

"Manifesto!" said Lucille slamming her hand on the table. "His name is Manifesto."

"Either way he's the devil incarnate," Mama told Zack.

"Right-wing reactionary!" accused Lucille.

"Bolshevik!" shot back Mama.

Zack winked at the boys. "I see what you mean."

Lucille pushed her chair away from the table. She pointed a gnarled finger at Mama. "That woman is insufferable. And so is that mangy fur ball alley cat of hers."

"Why you ... you ... Stalin lover!"

"Fascist!"

"Truce!" I screamed.

Mama's mouth clamped shut.

Pounding her cane, Lucille stalked from the kitchen. As soon as she was out of earshot, Mama's tongue once again loosened and she began batting her eyelashes at Zack. "I want to hear all about your exciting life, young man. Don't leave out any details."

"Yeah, tell us about the guys who duct taped you," said Nick. "Were they Mafia?"

"Or terrorists?" chimed in Alex. "Were you shooting in Afghanistan or Iraq?"

"Nothing so exciting. Or dangerous. At least I didn't think so at the time. I try not to make a habit of winding up on the business end of an Uzi."

"Good," said Mama. "We've had enough excitement in this family to last a lifetime."

"But you did?" asked Alex, his eyes bugging out.

"Unfortunately."

Mama's hand fluttered to her heart. "My goodness! You must have been terrified."

"No way," said Nick. "I'll bet he Rambo'd 'em." He turned to Zack for confirmation. "Didn't you?"

"We could have used you here yesterday," said Alex. "Do you have a gun?"

Zack held up both his hands. "Easy, guys. I think you're getting carried away. I'm no Stallone."

No, you're more a Pierce Brosnan-George Clooney-Patrick Dempsey-Antonio Banderas hunk.

Where the hell had that come from?

I felt my face flush and glanced around to make sure the words had only popped into my head and not out of my mouth. Luckily, Mama and the boys were too fascinated by Zack to notice the inferno emanating from my cheeks.

I gave myself a mental rap on the knuckles. Newly widowed women—even those whose husbands had turned out to be lying, cheating bastards—shouldn't have such thoughts for near strangers. I took a deep breath and focused back on the conversation flying across the kitchen table.

"So where were you?" asked Nick.

"Why'd someone want to kill you?" asked Alex.

Zack leaned forward and rested his elbows on the table. "I was in rural Guatemala shooting a photo essay on Indian villages. There's little social or political unity among the Indian communities. They even have their own colorful styles of clothing. That's what I was focusing on for *National Geographic*."

Nick screwed up his face. "Sounds boring."

"Yeah," said Alex. "Who'd want to kill someone over native costumes?"

"Probably no one," said Zack, "but unfortunately, while traveling from one village to the next, I stumbled across something I wasn't meant to see."

"What?" asked Nick.

I answered for Zack. "Drugs."

"Exactly," he said. "Guatemala's major natural resource is its fertile soil. One of the villages had discovered they could make a lot more money growing marijuana instead of corn. The farmers mistook me for a drug enforcement officer. I was lucky they didn't shoot me on the spot."

"How ever did you get out of there?" asked Mama.

Zack flashed her a twinkling eye smile. "I used my immeasurable charm."

Of that I had no doubt. In no time at all my new tenant had woven a spell around both Mama and my boys. I was contemplating asking him to work his magic on Lucille when the phone rang.

"Quick! Turn on your television," said Cloris after I answered.

"I can't."

"What do you mean, you can't?"

"Excuse me," I mumbled to Zack, the boys, and Mama as I carried the portable phone into the living room. They paid no attention to me as Zack regaled them with how he talked his way out of a deadly situation—once his captors had removed the duct tape covering his mouth. "We were robbed yesterday," I told Cloris.

"Again?"

"Luck of the Irish."

"Since when are you Irish?"

"Since Flora Sudberry Periwinkle Ramirez Scoffield Goldberg became Flora Sudberry Periwinkle Ramirez Scoffield Goldberg O'Keefe."

"That doesn't count."

"I suppose not. Anyway, Seamus O'Keefe died trying to kiss the Blarney Stone, so how lucky can the Irish really be?"

"Anastasia!"

"What?"

"Stop babbling and listen."

"What's so important?"

"Vittorio Versailles is dead."

TWENTY-EIGHT

"Omigod! How?"

Through the phone line I heard Cloris take a deep breath. "A bullet to the back of the head. One of his peacocked goons found him at his apartment when he failed to show for some luncheon today."

Three slices of mushroom pizza flip-flopped in my stomach. "I'll call you right back." I clicked off, grabbed my cell phone, and headed for the back porch.

"Anastasia! What's going on?" asked Mama as I raced through the kitchen.

"Not now, Mama." I grabbed my coat off the hook in the mud room and slammed the back door behind me.

"Execution style?" I asked Cloris when she answered on the first ring.

"What was that all about?"

"Batswin and Robbins tapped my phone."

"Is that legal?"

"I gave them permission."

"Are you out of your friggin' mind? Why on earth would you do that? They're trying to pin Marlys's murder on you, in case you've forgotten."

"Believe me, I haven't forgotten. They gave me no choice. Tell me about Vittorio."

"The news mentioned the lawsuit he filed against Trimedia. And according to an unnamed source, the police are questioning several *persons of interest* at the magazine. The newscaster implied the police think someone at Trimedia took out a contract on Vittorio."

"I suppose whoever paid to get rid of Vittorio figured a hit man was a heck of a lot cheaper than an extended court battle."

"No guessing as to the outcome, either."

"But who?"

"Someone with balls. And connections."

The mushroom pizza solidified into a two-ton cannonball. "Hugo?"

"He fits on both accounts, doesn't he?"

According to the rumor mill, Hugo grew up in the shadows of organized crime, his father having been an accountant for one of the five New York crime families. Years ago Hugo had changed his name from the ethnic sounding Herschel Rosenbaum to the aristocratic sounding Hugo Reynolds-Alsopp. However, those same rumors claimed he still maintained ties with many of his father's associates and his own old friends from back in the day.

"We don't know that for certain," I said. "Besides, Hugo has no real power at Trimedia any more. He's nothing but a figurehead."

"What about that argument you overheard?"

I thought back to the angry voices coming from the other side of Naomi's office door. The out-of-character behavior exhibited by both Naomi and Hugo afterwards. Hugo's assurance that he'd handle everything. "If Hugo were leveraging a buyback of the company, Vittorio's lawsuit would put everything on hold."

"Or kill the deal if Trimedia lost the court battle," added Cloris.

"No Vittorio. No lawsuit. No problem."

"Bingo!"

"Now all I have to do is find out if Hugo was in negotiations with Trimedia."

"Still think he and Naomi didn't have anything to do with Marlys's murder?" asked Cloris.

"No, but I don't want to believe they did. Hugo maybe. He's got the connections. But Naomi? I just don't buy it."

"Maybe she didn't know."

"That would make more sense."

"So what's your next move, Sherlock?"

"I think I'd better keep that to myself. If my plan backfires, I don't want you getting hauled off to the slammer with me."

"You're planning something illegal?"

"Depends on your definition of illegal," I said.

"Forget my definition. How would Batswin and Robbins define whatever it is you're planning?"

"I think it would fall under one of those murky areas of the law."

"Be careful, okay?"

"I will."

What I planned was a search of Hugo's office. I wasn't certain I'd find anything incriminating—part of me hoped I didn't—but a reconnoiter of the office was easier than finding a way into his apartment.

———

The next day, after dropping Alex at the library and Nick at basketball practice, I headed for Trimedia. Even though I didn't expect anyone else to show up at the office on a Sunday afternoon, I decided to park my car across the road in the train station parking lot.

After letting myself into the building, I first headed for my office. I slipped out of my coat and hung it on the hook to the side of the entrance. In case someone else did decide to catch up on work today, I flipped on my computer and arranged my cubicle to make it appear that I was working on a project.

To add to the illusion, I slipped on my work smock and stuffed a few tools and supplies into the deep front pockets. In case the boys called, I grabbed my cell phone before storing my purse in the bottom drawer of my desk.

Hugo's office was situated on the fourth floor, the top story of Trimedia. Although he shared the marble-tiled, mahogany-walled floor with the other corporate stuffed shirts, the size and location of his office—a windowless, out-of-the-way closet of a space—reflected his status as a corporate Bottom Feeder.

However, power or no power, Hugo kept his office locked. I wasn't deterred. He shared a secretary with several lower level managers. I headed for her desk.

In the top drawer I found a set of keys, each contained a Day-Glo orange label with a letter of the alphabet hand-written in thick black marker. C, W, P, and H. Charles Zucker, Walter Montieth, Paul Horner, and Hugo Reynolds-Alsopp. I pocketed the keys and headed back to Hugo's office.

For a man who had no real function at Trimedia, Hugo's desk was extremely cluttered. Several mounds of manila file folders covered the surface. Another precarious pile filled the visitor's chair off to the side. Old issues of *American Woman* and various other publications he had once directed lay on the carpet, stacked neatly by year and title against the walls. The glossy columns of long forgotten issues stood silent sentry to a deposed potentate.

I glanced around the cramped office with its meager furnishings. Trimedia hadn't seen fit to supply Hugo with so much as a filing cabinet, let alone a computer. Hugo Reynolds-Alsopp had once controlled a publishing empire. Now he was exiled to a dismal hovel like an unwanted and unloved Cinderfellow. Was such a slap in the ego enough to make him turn to murder?

Clearing a space in the center of his desk, I settled into his chair and began skimming the contents of the first stack of file folders.

After two hours I'd found nothing to indicate Hugo was in negotiations to buy back the company and nothing that incriminated him or Naomi in the murders of either Marlys or Vittorio.

What I did find filled me with profound sadness. Hugo spent his days at Trimedia surrounded by the minutia of days long past. The files contained all the meeting notes, all the hard copy, all the blue lines, all the artwork, and all the financial statements from each of the magazines lined up against his wall. Over thirty years of the history of the Reynolds-Alsopp Publishing Company, from the day the first issues rolled off the presses. Nothing more.

Hugo was no murderer. He was nothing but an unhappy old man living in the past. Whatever his argument with Naomi had been about, it certainly wasn't anything that involved murder and mayhem. Or even the overthrow of the existing regime. Hugo had lost his publishing empire in a hostile takeover. He had neither the acumen nor the capital to reclaim his title and realm.

I mulled over what I remembered of Naomi's and Hugo's angry conversation.

"Don't be stupid. Everything will work out. I made a mistake. There. I admit it. Satisfied?"

"A mistake?"

"Yes, a mistake. Nothing more. It's over. Forget about it."

The *mistake* Hugo referred to was probably his affair with Marlys. It was over because Marlys had dumped him for someone with more power and deeper pockets. Not to mention the fact that Marlys was dead.

"Over? We're smack in the middle of a gargantuan dung heap."

"Not if we play our hand right."

"What are you suggesting?"

"That you let me handle things. Okay? We have a chance to set things back on track."

"Not with this new situation."

"A minor wrinkle. Trust me."

I filled in the blanks based on the clues spread out before me. Hugo had probably wheedled his way back into Naomi's good graces by convincing her he planned a buyback of the company. Naomi believed him because she needed to believe him. She hated

263

the new ownership and feared Marlys had planned to sleep her way into Naomi's job. The *dung heap* and *new situation* referred to Marlys's death which Naomi feared would stall or obstruct Hugo's buyback plans. Naomi had no clue that those plans were a mere pipe dream.

I left the office the way I found it, locked the door, and returned the set of keys to the secretary's desk. Shunning the elevator in hopes of shaving off a few of the donuts and brownies that had affixed themselves to my hips recently, I headed down the stairs.

As I opened the fire door leading onto the floor *American Woman* shared with several other publications, I heard voices coming from the direction of the Models Room.

The Models Room was actually a large walk-in closet at the northwest corner of the floor. We used it to store props and samples for past, current, and future issues. Since it's next to impossible to find plastic Jack-o-lanterns in April or ceramic leprechauns in September, we keep on hand a large supply of seasonal doodads and decorations for photo shoots. I also used the closet to store the various new products samples craft manufacturers constantly send me. Cloris gets samples of *foie gras* and Chambord-soaked pound cake; I get faux-fur felt squares and chenille stems.

But why would anyone be in the Models Room on a Sunday afternoon?

I crept closer.

"There's nothing but junk in here, Dicky. I don't know what you find so fascinating."

"Hey, one man's junk, yada-yada-yada."

"I thought you wanted to see my new office."

"I do, Sweet Cheeks. You're gonna give me the ten-dollar tour. Top to bottom. Every office."

Sweet Cheeks? I froze. Only one other person I knew had a fondness for that particular appellation. Ricardo. An iceberg twice the size of the Titanic killer broadsided me. A shiver coursed from my in-desperate-need-of-a-touch-up roots down to my in-desperate-need-of-a-pedicure toes. Could Erica's new boyfriend and Ricardo be the same person?

Dicky.

Ricardo.

The jigsaw pieces began to fit together. The resulting picture didn't paint Erica in such a sweet and innocent light. So much for following in the footsteps of Jessica Fletcher. Cloris had raised suspicions of Erica all along, but I'd pooh-poohed her.

"What's in these boxes?" asked Dicky. I heard scraping, as if he were pulling down one of the cartons stored on the top of the metal shelving. It hit the floor with a thud.

Erica winced. "Careful! You'll break something." The sound of tape ripping off cardboard echoed out into the hall. "Dicky, please. Don't open that. We shouldn't even be here. What if someone finds us?"

"Would you shut up? Jeez, I can't stand it when you whine. Grow up! Who's gonna find us? It's Sunday. Everyone's home in the 'burbs, playing mommy and daddy to the rugrats."

"I'm sorry." Erica's apology came out as a whimper. "What are you looking for? I'll help you. We'll get done much faster."

"Something that don't belong here. You'll know it when you see it."

"I don't understand."

Dicky snorted. "You ain't gotta understand. Just open the boxes. I'll do the understanding for both of us, Sweet Cheeks. *Capisce*?"

Even if Erica didn't have a clue, I had a pretty good idea what Dicky was hunting for. Actually, I had fifty thousand ideas. He probably figured if I hadn't hidden the money at home, I might have stashed it somewhere at work where no one would stumble across it.

No matter how much I protested to the contrary, Ricardo still believed I was pulling a fast one on him and had hidden the money somewhere. Probably because that's what he would have done.

I had to get back to my cubicle and out of the building before Erica and Ricardo discovered me. The most direct path took me past the Models Room. With the door open, there was too much chance of their hearing or seeing me.

My only other option was to slip downstairs, make my way across the length of the building to the stairwell at the opposite end, and come back up, approaching my cubicle from the other direction.

I turned toward the fire door.

"Anastasia?"

Shit! I spun around, feigning surprise. "Oh, Erica! Hi. I didn't realize anyone else was here."

"Neither did I. What are you doing here?"

"Just catching up on some work."

"I didn't see your car in the parking lot."

"I parked at the train station." I patted my stomach and laughed. "My new exercise regimen. Trying to walk off Cloris Calories since I can't resist those goodies she's constantly waving under my nose."

She glanced at her own stomach and giggled. "I know what you mean."

"What about you? Why are you here on a Sunday?"

"I wanted to show Dicky my new office."

At that moment, a man who looked like he could be in the cast of any number of Al Pacino gangster flicks stepped out of the Models Room.

Neither Mama nor Lucille had done justice to Ricardo in their description of him to Fogarty and Harley, although Mama had come much closer. Lucille definitely needed her eyes examined. Think Sylvester Stallone meets Steven Seagal meets King Kong, and you begin to get an idea. Right down to the forest of thick black hair covering nearly every inch of his exposed flesh.

Erica slipped her hand into Dicky's. "I'm glad we bumped into you. I've been wanting to introduce you to Dicky." She tilted her head back to catch his eye. "Dicky, this is my friend Anastasia. The one I've told you about."

Then she turned her attention back to me. "And this is my boyfriend Dicky."

I wondered how much Erica had told Dicky about me—not to mention everything else that had recently transpired at Trimedia. Had she told him about Vittorio's pending lawsuit? How scared she was of losing her job? She'd previously admitted having told him about Marlys.

My Jessica Fletcher mode kicked in. I now knew who had killed Marlys. And Vittorio. Motive? To help his girlfriend get rid of her Simon Legree boss and move from Bottom Feeder to the higher echelons of *American Woman*. Vittorio bought it because his lawsuit threatened to destroy Erica's newfound success. Talk about a supportive boyfriend!

I kept my hands shoved deep in my smock pockets and offered Dicky or Ricardo or whatever-his-name what I hoped came across as a friendly—and innocent—smile. "Nice to meet you, Dicky."

He stared at me without saying anything, only cocked his head in a semi-nod, his features remaining as vacant as the motels on the Jersey shore during a blizzard. Was he trying to figure out what I had overheard? Wondering if I suspected he was Ricardo?

His silence unnerved me. "Erica tells me you're an independent financial consultant?"

"You could say that."

I stretched my smile broader. "Well, I'd better get back to work and finish up my project. Have to pick my kids up in a little while. See you Monday, Erica." I waved as I started to head for my cubicle.

"I don't think so," said Dicky.

I turned around to find myself face-to-face with a very nasty looking gun.

TWENTY-NINE

DICKY CLAMPED ONE OF his hairy paws over my forearm and jabbed the nose of the gun into my ribs.

"My God, Dicky! What are you doing?" cried Erica.

"Shut up, Sweet Cheeks. Your friend here knows too much. I'm gonna have to take care of her."

"Knows too much about what? What do you mean *take care of her*?"

"Your boyfriend isn't a financial consultant, Erica. He's a loan shark and a murderer."

"No!" Tears swam in Erica's eyes. "She's wrong, isn't she, Dicky? Tell her she's wrong."

"Erica! For God's sake. Look at the gun! That's no Super Soaker he's poking into me."

"I don't understand," she whimpered.

"You don't need to understand nothing. Just do as I say," said Ricardo. "Unless you want to wind up just like your friend."

"But, Dicky—"

He spun around, jerking me with him. I tripped over his feet and fell to the floor. My knees slammed against the rock-hard Terrazzo. When he yanked me up, he nearly ripped my arm from its socket. I cried out from the pain.

"You're hurting her," said Erica.

Dicky waved the gun in her face. "So help me, you're really pissing me off, Erica. I'm gonna smack you good if you don't shut up!"

She sniveled as she backed up against the wall. Tears streamed down her cheeks. "I'm sorry. I didn't mean to make you angry, Dicky. Please don't yell at me."

He studied her for a moment, then grunted. "Okay. I forgive you. Go get that purple cord stuff that was on the shelf in there." He motioned toward the Models Room with his chin.

Erica stepped inside and came out a moment later with a spool of macramé cord. "This?"

"Yeah, that. Now we're gonna take your friend here out to the car. Nice and quiet." He poked the gun deeper into my side. "Got it, Sweet Cheeks?"

"Got it."

"Where are we going?" asked Erica.

"Never you mind." He jerked me toward the stairs. "You see anyone, you don't say a word."

I nodded.

He dragged me down the stairs. Erica followed.

My mind raced. If Ricardo had killed Marlys and Vittorio, he'd have no qualms about snuffing out my lights, as well. My only hope was that his greed overpowered his murderous tendencies. "If you kill me, you won't get your fifty grand," I said.

"Remember those friends I told you about, Sweet Cheeks? You're gonna work for them full time." He dragged the barrel of the gun down my torso. "Twenty-four/seven. No vacations. No benefits."

"What money?" asked Erica. "What friends?"

"None of your concern," he said.

If I was going to get out of this situation alive, I needed Erica's help. And the only way to gain that was to make her realize how high Dicky rated on the Creep-O-Meter. "I guess you didn't know your boyfriend helped my husband steal fifty thousand dollars from my mother-in-law, did you?"

"No, that can't be true. Dicky? Tell her it's not true." Erica's voice was a high-pitched whispery plea.

Ricardo squeezed my arm so tight it went numb. "That money belonged to me," he said. "Karl owed me. We had a business arrangement."

"Don't believe him, Erica. He tried to kill my mother-in-law," I said as he dragged me out the side door. A black sedan with New York plates was parked directly in front of the door, its massive trunk facing us. Scenes from *The Sopranos* flashed before my eyes.

"Grab my keys outa my left pants pocket," Ricardo ordered Erica.

"Erica, please! You have to help me!"

Refusing to make eye contact with me, she stared at the blacktop and mumbled, "I'm sorry, Anastasia." Then she reached into Ricardo's pocket and pulled out a set of car keys. "Here." She held them out to him.

"Do I look like I got a third hand? Open the goddamn trunk."

Erica pressed the remote. The trunk popped open. No way was I going in there without the fight of my life. I jerked and squirmed, flailing my one free arm and kicking Ricardo in both shins. "Erica, help me! He killed Marlys."

"Shut up!" He swung down with his gun hand, and everything went black.

———

I awoke in a nightmare, my body slamming and banging and bouncing back and forth, up and down, against the hard, rough sides of a small, cold, pitch-black prison. My head throbbed. I couldn't see, couldn't move. My arms were pinned to my sides, my legs bound together, my mouth taped. In the distance I heard voices. Shouting. Crying. I strained to listen.

"I gave you your big break, for crying out loud. Act a little grateful, why dontcha?"

"But, Dicky, you killed Marlys?"

"So? Everyone hated her, right?"

"Y … yes."

"So stop sniveling. She made your life miserable. I took care of it. Did you a huge favor. You should be thanking me, Sweet Cheeks, not bitchin' about the bitch."

"I know, but—"

"But nothin'. It's not like you ain't seen stuff like this before, being who's kid you are an' all. Watcha think I do for your old man, anyways?"

"But you tried to make the police think Anastasia killed Marlys. Why? She's my friend."

"Some friend. She tried to steal from us. Her husband was into me for fifty G's. So's now I owe your old man, and that ain't no good thing, Sweet Cheeks. Joey Milano don't like excuses. From anyone. Besides, that's fifty G's less you inherit some day. You wanna be friends with a bitch who'd steal from you?"

"N ... no."

"So's now you understand the gravity of the situation, right?"

"What are you going to do with Anastasia?"

"She's more trouble than she's worth. I'm gonna get rid of her."

Erica started sobbing. "Please, Dicky, please don't kill Anastasia."

"Would you stop with the blubbering!"

I heard a smack.

Followed by a gasp.

Then silence.

Erica couldn't take care of herself, let alone help me. She had stepped from a controlling, abusive father, right into the arms of a controlling, abusive boyfriend. And not just any father or boyfriend.

Erica *Milano*. From *The Bronx*. Home territory of the Milano crime syndicate, one of the Big Five New York crime families. Talk about a *duh* moment. She certainly pulled the polyester over our eyes, acting like the poster child for Naïveté Incorporated while hiding her true identity—the daughter of Murder Incorporated.

If I'd had a free hand, I'd have slapped my clueless forehead.

I was on my own, and the first order of business was freeing my hands. Ricardo had wrapped me like a macramé mummy. I rolled onto my stomach and felt the contents of my smock pockets jab me in the thighs. Shifting my weight, I discovered my cell phone still attached at my waist.

Dumb thug. He hadn't even frisked me before tying me up. Big mistake on his part. One I intended to make sure he'd live to regret.

Contorting my body, I squirmed around until I had dumped the contents of my smock pockets into the trunk bed. Then I scooted around in the dark, searching with my fingertips. Pencils. Markers. Assorted google eyes, sequins, and beads. A bottle of tacky glue. A spool of quilting thread. A roll of fusible webbing.

Bingo! My fingers curled around my trusty X-Acto knife. No girl should be without one. With the knife pinched between my fingers, I flipped off the protective plastic cap and set to work on the macramé cord.

As the car sped toward whatever spot Ricardo had designated as my final resting place, I hacked at my bindings. I also wound up slicing off half my skin in the process, thanks to Ricardo's breakneck speed, which sent me hurtling around the trunk like a pinball on amphetamines. Figuring I couldn't bleed to death from cuts made by a three-quarter-inch blade, I forced myself to ignore the pain and kept chopping away at my restraints.

After what seemed like forever, I freed my arms and ripped the tape from my mouth. Not bothering with my legs at this point, I reached for my cell phone and called Batswin.

"Batswin." She answered on the first ring, and I breathed a huge sigh.

"I'm trapped in Ricardo's trunk. He's going to kill me," I whispered.

"Who is this? I can't hear you. Speak up."

I whispered as loud as I dared. "Anastasia Pollack. I'm locked in Ricardo's trunk."

"Where are you?"

"I don't know. I was at Trimedia, but he knocked me out. I don't know how long ago. What time is it now?"

"A few minutes before three."

I remembered glancing at the clock on Hugo's desk as I straightened up his files. "Then we're somewhere within a twenty- or thirty-minute radius of Trimedia, but he's driving very fast."

"Can you describe the car?"

"A black Mercedes. New York plates."

"Any chance you caught the plate number? Or at least a partial?"

I squeezed my eyes shut, trying to remember. The entire percussion section of the New York Philharmonic was tuning up inside my head, compliments of Ricardo's conk to my noggin. I searched my memory.

"Mrs. Pollack? Are you still there?"

"Yes, I'm trying to remember. A vanity plate. He had a vanity plate."

"What did it say?"

I remember thinking how appropriate. And stupid. But why? The car hit a pothole. My head slammed into the top of the trunk, sending my teeth through my tongue. I tasted blood and groaned.

"What happened? Are you all right?"

"Sure, Detective." I spit out a mouthful of blood. "I'm having the time of my life—what's left of it."

"We'll find you. I promise."

"Great. You think you could maybe do it before I'm swimming with the fishes?"

"My partner's putting out an APB as we speak, but a tag number would speed things up."

"That's it!"

"What?"

"*Up.* The tag read UP2NOGD."

She snorted. "You're kidding."

"Hey, my brain is speeding toward a date with a bullet. Would I joke about a thing like that?"

"Sit tight. We're on our way."

Sit tight? Where the hell did she expect me to go? "One other thing, Detective..."

"Yes?"

"I know who—" Static blared in my ear. A moment later, my phone went dead.

There was nothing else I could do other than free my legs and wait. And hope the cops found Ricardo's Mercedes before he dumped my body in some watery grave.

At least the wait proved educational. Erica, sounding as though she had forgotten Dicky had moments ago smacked her hard enough to rattle her fillings—or maybe because of it—stepped into full suck-up mode. "You sure have the cops fooled," she said.

Ricardo guffawed. "Dumb *shmucks.* I sure got 'em chasing after their tails, don't I?"

"Except at one point I was scared they suspected me of killing Marlys."

"Hey, Sweet Cheeks, you know I wouldn't a let it come to that. Besides, I was always one step ahead of them, thanks to you."

"Me?"

"Sure. You did real good. You Bonnie, me Clyde, huh? Couldn't've set it up better myself."

"I don't understand."

"Remember the day you called all upset about that bitch boss of yours blaming you for something she wrote?"

"The article on Vittorio Versailles."

"Yeah. That one. You also mentioned the diamonds and her date later that night with what's-his-name."

"Emil Pachette."

"Right. Him. Anyways, that's when it comes to me. You know how I hated the way that bitch was treating you, making you do all her work and her getting all the credit. Not to mention the big bucks while you're making diddly-shit."

"Yes?"

"So's I figure nothing's gonna change as long as she's struttin' around like the Queen of the Nile."

"So you killed her for me?"

"Hey, what're friends for? And look where you are now. A big shit fashion editor. My Sweet Cheeks."

"No one's ever killed for me before, Dicky. I...I'm over-whelmed."

"Anything for my Sweet Cheeks."

"So tell me, how'd you pull it off?"

"Easy. I arranged for the fashion fag to leave town. Then I called the switchboard and left a message for the bitch. Pretended to be this Emil guy and told the operator to tell the bitch I'd send a chauf-feur to pick her up at the office." He laughed. "Only surprise! It wasn't a limo jockey who showed up."

"But how'd you get her to drink the doctored wine?"

"How do you think? I held a gun to her head."

"And then you made it look like Anastasia had killed Marlys because you thought she was holding out on you?"

He snarled. "Stroke of genius that hit me while the fashion bitch was drinking the Merlot. Originally, I was just gonna tie her up and secure a plastic bag over her head once she passed out. Then I thought, why not rattle the widow's cage a bit? Really spook her. And give the cops someone else to focus their suspicions on."

"Instead of me?"

"Right. By the by, Sweet Cheeks, I know your friend's got the dough stashed somewheres. Maybe when I tell her I'm gonna snuff out her kids after I dump her body, she'll have an attack of sudden remembering."

"Wh ... where are we taking her?"

"Delaware Water Gap. We'll toss the body over the cliffs into the river."

Hurry, hurry, hurry, I silently commanded Batswin and her posse. I tried my phone again, pressing *Redial*.

"Batswin."

"Thank God!" I whispered.

"Mrs. Pollack? Why'd you hang up? I was afraid to call you back in case he heard the phone ring. Stay on the line so you can help us track him."

"I didn't hang up. We must have entered a dead cell zone. But I know where he's taking me."

"Where?"

'The Delaware Water Gap."

"That means he's probably on Route 80. We've got state troopers all over that road, and I'm in a helicopter searching overhead."

"Best news I've heard all day. By the way, he just confessed to killing Marlys, and I'm pretty sure he knocked off Vittorio Versailles."

"Confessed? You mean he's with someone?"

"Erica Milano. Did you know that she's Joey Milano's daughter?"

"Of course. Was she in on all this?"

"Not intentionally, but it turns out Ricardo's her boyfriend, and she's been feeding him enough details to keep him outsmarting you."

More puzzle pieces fell into place. Erica had been standing outside the conference room while Batswin and Robbins were grilling me the day after the murder. She must have overheard me telling them about Ricardo and how I agreed to help trap him in their sting. That's why later she was so curious about the duffel bag. But at that point did Erica realize Ricardo was Dicky?

And it was Dicky—or Ricardo—who had given Erica an iPhone and suggested she copy all of Marlys's files to it in order to make dealing with Marlys's constant demands easier. I'll bet he downloaded those files to his own phone. Which would have given him access to all the e-mail addresses and phone numbers he needed to carry out his dirty work.

Ricardo continued to gloat about his success as I spoke with Batswin. I tried to listen to both of them at the same time, but the noise from the car made it difficult. "Hold on," I said.

"And you were responsible for the break-ins at Anastasia's house?" asked Erica.

"Yeah." He chuckled. "Piece a cake. I hit that place three times."

"Three? I only heard about the first two, but you didn't take anything, did you?"

"Sure I did. Not the first time, though."

"You went looking for the money?"

"Yeah, but some nosy buttinsky showed up. I trashed the place real good, though. Served her right for lying to me about the dough."

"You're sure she's lying? What if she really doesn't have the money?"

"Don't be stupid. She's got it, all right. Or she knows where it is."

"I don't know. What about the other times? Why'd you go back?"

"When you told me she and the cops were setting me up, I got the bright idea of planting a photo of that shmuck husband of hers with your bitchy boss. Make the cops suspect her even more of doin' in the bitch."

With everything else I had learned about my dearly beloved, at least he hadn't cheated on me. Well, at least not with Marlys. I might never learn what other secrets accompanied Karl to the grave, be they illicit activities or illicit affairs. And maybe that was a good thing.

I could have forgiven Karl his gambling addiction if he hadn't left us in a financial quagmire that ruined his sons' futures. After all, gambling is a disease, and I did utter that in-sickness-and-in-health vow. But gambling isn't covered by medical insurance, and all things considered, I would have preferred my husband contracting leprosy.

I also doubted I could have forgiven him for cheating on me. And then there was the business about trying to kill his mother. Even if Lucille was the commie from Hell, that's no justification for matricide.

"Anastasia figured someone doctored the photo and planted it in Marlys's apartment," said Erica.

"He wasn't such a bad lookin' dude, that Karl. Coulda happened."

"He was an auto parts salesman, Dicky! Marlys wouldn't look twice at a guy like that."

"Hey, Karl was hung."

"How would you know?"

"I seen him at the gym once or twice. Besides, high-class broads like to go slummin'."

"But if you knew Anastasia was working with the police, why did you go along with it?"

"Jeez, Erica! Don't go stupid on me. I needed to get them all out of the way long enough to hit the place again, didn't I?"

"Friday night?"

"Yeah, I wiped her out. Fenced the stuff to pay off your old man. But all that crap didn't make much of a dent in the fifty G's. Wasn't worth shit as far as your Uncle Nardo was concerned."

"Uncle Nardo? How's he involved in this?"

"Use your head, Sweet Cheeks. He's a fence, ain't he? Anyways, he claims what with eBay sellin' electronics crap so cheap and newer models coming out every day, it ain't worth the effort. I think he screwed me, though. Gave me all of five grand for the whole lot, but I had no choice. I had to dump the goods quick."

"But you had the diamonds, Dicky. Why not give those to Daddy?"

"You got boulders for brains, Sweet Cheeks? You know how much that ice's worth? I ain't turning them baubles over to Joey M. No way. I earned them diamonds fair and square on my own time, not on a job for the boss."

"But won't Daddy get real mad when you don't hand over all the money?"

"Why should I fork over my hard-earned dough when it's Karl who screwed me? And now his wife's trying to pull a fast one. Trust me. She'll cough up the whereabouts of the bread to save those kids of hers. Besides, I kinda figured you'd look real good wearing some of those rocks."

"Really?"

"Sure. Gotta get them reset first, though. Don't want anyone recognizing them."

"Maybe one of them could be an engagement ring?"

"Maybe."

"Oh, Dicky."

"Don't paw me while I'm drivin', Sweet Cheeks. Gets me too excited."

Erica giggled. "Dicky?"

"Hmm?"

"I just had an idea."

"Yeah?"

"Maybe we should stash Anastasia at Daddy's hunting lodge, and you could go get her sons and bring them there."

"Or maybe I should kill one first and dump his body at her feet. I'll bet she'd sing her little heart out to save the other one."

"Uhm … that would work, but why not kill him in front of her? More impact, right?"

"Yeah, even better. Hey, now you're talkin' like a Milano, Sweet Cheeks. Your old man'd be real proud of you."

"I'll stay at the cabin and keep an eye on her while you go get the kids."

"Sounds like a plan."

My heart now beat as loudly as the kettle drums pounding in my head. I could barely force the words out as I spoke into the phone. "Did you hear that? My God! He's going to kill one of my kids."

But Batswin didn't answer. We'd entered another dead cell zone.

THIRTY

"Shit! Where the hell'd they come from?"

Ricardo slammed on the brakes. I whiplashed from the front to the back of the trunk, adding yet another layer of bumps, bruises, and abrasions to my bleeding and battered body. The car fish-tailed; I flew from side to side. Now I knew what it was like to go a dozen rounds with Mike Tyson—and come up on the losing end.

I heard a loud smack as we sped off in the direction we'd come. "You back-stabbing bitch! You're working with them, aren't you?"

Erica screamed out in pain. "No, Dicky, no! I wouldn't do anything to hurt you."

"Then how'd they know to stake out the lodge?" Ricardo had gone ballistic. I couldn't be sure what he was doing to Erica as we sailed down the road, but by the choking sounds she was making and the repeated sickening thuds, it sounded like he had grabbed her by the throat and was smashing her head against the dashboard.

"I don't know!" she gasped. "Please stop! You're hurting me. I can't breathe!"

"Hurting you? I ain't begun to hurt you, bitch."

I heard a loud crunch. Then silence.

"Goddamn sonofabitch!" He slammed on the brake again. The car jerked to the side, spun, then flipped. My body bounced around like a load of wet laundry in a clothes dryer. My head continued to spin even after the car came to a rest, upside down.

I don't know how long I lay there. I think I may have suffered a concussion. Shouting voices and sirens surrounded me but like a dream that faded in and out of my consciousness. Finally, someone banged on the car. "Mrs. Pollack? Can you hear me? Are you all right?"

I never thought I'd be so happy to hear Robbins' voice. "I'm alive," I shouted.

"Hold on. We have to flip the car to get you out."

The Mercedes rocked back and forth like some mangled metal hammock. I swayed along with it, each to and fro more pronounced.

Someone yelled, "Here it goes."

The car flipped, slamming right-side up, and I followed, slamming my head yet again.

"Still with us, Mrs. Pollack?" yelled Robbins.

"No, I decided to step out for a Starbucks. This is a recording."

He laughed. Detective Robbins actually laughed! "While you're there how about getting me a double-shot mocha Frappucchino?"

A moment later I heard the unmistakable sound of ripping metal and saw the most glorious sight in the world—an Under Dog tie swinging from Robbins' thick neck.

He helped me out of the trunk and gave me the once over. "You don't look too good."

I swayed on my feet and nearly fell back into the trunk. He grabbed my arm to steady me.

"You think?" I said.

"We're going to get you checked out at the hospital," said Batswin, coming up behind us. A couple of EMTs, one wheeling a stretcher, followed her.

Robbins led me to the stretcher, but before I allowed them to strap me in, I scanned the area. Lots of cars with flashing lights. An ambulance. A fire truck. People milling around, some in uniforms, some not. A few holding rifles.

"What about Ricardo and Erica?" I asked.

Batswin jerked her chin toward a set of flashing lights receding in the distance. "The other ambulance already left with them."

———

Six hours later, after a stint of physical poking and prodding at the hospital, followed by several hours of verbal poking and prodding at the Morris County precinct, I sat in traffic on my way back to Westfield. Batswin drove, Robbins following behind in my Hyundai.

I had sustained a mild concussion from all the head-banging and several cracked ribs. My X-Acto knife stabbed, bruised, and battered body—covered in shades of reds, purples, blues, and greens—looked like an expressionist painter had mistaken me for a canvas. My head felt like it was hosting a rave, and it hurt like hell to breathe—let alone move. But I felt terrific.

"What's going to happen to Erica?" I asked. I had learned from Batswin that both Erica and Ricardo were listed in stable condition, having sustained numerous minor but few major injuries other than some broken bones. A testament to the advantages of seat belts and air bags, even when traveling at Mach One.

"She's cooperating. The Feds offered her Witness Protection, and she jumped at the chance. By the way, you owe your life to her."

"How? She couldn't have known I had freed myself and had my cell phone."

"No, but she had hers. She planned to call the police as soon as Ricardo left the two of you at her father's hunting lodge."

"And Ricardo?"

"He's angling to cut a deal, too."

"But he's a murderer!"

"I don't think the Feds will be interested. There isn't much he can tell them that they can't get from Erica. Ricardo is pretty low level in the Milano organization pecking order. My guess is he developed a relationship with Erica to curry favor with her father."

Poor Erica. She deserved a life of her own. No wonder she welcomed the offer of witness protection and the chance to get away from her family permanently. "So Ricardo was what? A mob loan shark?"

"Right."

I laughed. "Erica had us convinced *Dicky* was a financial consultant."

"Banker for a private financial institution would have been a more fitting description. He didn't lend *his* money. He lent *mob* money. And probably only about twenty-five thousand to your husband. The rest would have been the interest that had accrued on the loan."

"A hundred percent interest?"

"I think the going rate is something like twenty-five percent a week."

"Nice work if you can get it."

She turned her head toward me and raised an eyebrow.

"Don't worry, Detective. I have no plans to whittle down my debt by becoming a loan shark."

"Glad to hear that, Mrs. Pollack."

"Besides, I have no start-up capital."

"Right." Batswin chuckled.

Earlier I'd elicited a laugh from Robbins, now a chuckle from Batswin. Maybe the dynamic detecting duo was human after all. And to think, it had only taken me nearly getting killed to bring out the hidden Humor Gene in each of them. Who knew I had such talent?

"So Ricardo had to account to higher-up hoods for the money?"

"Every penny or they'd suspect he was skimming."

"Then bye-bye Ricardo?"

"You got it."

"I guess that's why he was so desperate. Even willing to kill for it."

"Kill or be killed with that group. But people kill for a lot less. Besides, your own husband committed murder for that same fifty thousand dollars."

I shuddered at the memory. Three innocent people dead because of Karl's greed. "I hope no further surprises materialize. I'd like to close the Karl chapter of my life and start a whole new book. Although, that seems unrealistic, considering I'll be paying off the debt he dumped on us for years to come."

"Oh, that reminds me," she said, shifting lanes to maneuver around a minivan, "while you were giving your statement at the station, we received a call from the Bronx police. Based on what you heard Ricardo admit, they raided Nardo Milano's pawn shop. All your stuff was still there. Once they're done using it as evidence, you can get it back."

The way the wheels of justice squeak and piddle along, that could be anywhere from six days to six years, but we'd manage. Somehow. We'd survived far worse over the past few days.

Half an hour later, Batswin pulled up in front of my house; Robbins parked my car in the driveway. We all piled out. "Nice," said Robbins, eyeing the two-seater silver Porsche Boxster he'd parked beside. "Yours?"

"Yeah, I only drive the rattletrap to work because of all the crime in the cornfields."

"That's what I thought."

All three of us laughed. "You're okay, Mrs. Pollack," he said.

High compliment coming from a man who only a few days ago wanted to slip a noose around my neck. "Yeah, so are the two of you." And I meant that. Batswin and Robbins weren't the incompetent country rubes I'd originally dubbed them. After all, they'd saved my life.

"The car belongs to my new tenant," I said.

I invited them in for cups of instant coffee, but they declined. "We still have reports to file," said Batswin, "but thanks. Maybe another time."

She and Robbins headed back to her car as I opened the front door.

"Keep it up, and I'll report you and all your cohorts to Homeland Security," screamed Mama. "I know what you're planning in those secret meetings of yours. You communists are as much a threat to this country as Al-Qaeda!"

"Me?" Lucille laughed derisively. "Who do you think supplied all those weapons to the Taliban? All *your* right-wing reactionary friends."

Mephisto barked.

Catherine the Great yowled.

Ralph squawked, "*Once more unto the breach, dear friend. Henry the Fifth.* Act Three, Scene One."

I turned to see Batswin and Robbins staring at my open front door. "Home sweet home," I said with a shrug and a wave as I closed the door behind me.

Life goes on. Eventually, I'd get past my anger over how Karl fooled and shafted us. I'd deal with Lucille, deal with Mama, deal with the debt, deal with getting Alex and Nick into college—and how to pay for it.

And then if I had any time or energy left, I'd deal with me. Maybe even dip my big toe back in the dating pool. You never know what's waiting around the corner.

Or above the garage.

THE END

If you enjoyed reading *Assault with a Deadly Glue Gun* read on for a glimpse of the next Anastasia Pollack Crafting Mystery

Mop Doll Murders

ONE

UPSTAIRS, THE FRONT DOOR slammed with enough force to register a five on the Richter scale. Dust dislodged from the exposed basement rafters and drifted down like polluted snow, settling over the basket of clean laundry I'd been folding. The ensuing shouting, barking, and yowling drowned out my muttered curse of choice and yanked my attention away from the now Dalmatian-spotted white wash.

"*Once more unto the breach, dear friends*," squawked Ralph, the Shakespeare-spouting African Grey parrot I'd inherited when Great-aunt Penelope Periwinkle died two years ago. "*Henry the Fifth*. Act Three, Scene One." He spread his wings and took flight up the basement stairs to check out the action. I raced after him, eager to prevent World War Three from erupting in my living room.

"Muzzle that abominable creature, or I'll have the pound haul him away," shrieked Mama. "He's traumatizing Catherine the Great."

"So shove some Prozac down her throat," said my mother-in-law Lucille. "What the hell are you doing back here? And don't you ever bother to knock? Just barge right in like you own the place."

"I have more right to be here than you. This is my daughter's house, you ... you *pinko squatter*."

292

As I hurried through the kitchen, I glanced at the calendar tacked next to the telephone. Mama wasn't due back from her Caribbean cruise for another three days. Damn it. I needed those three days to steel myself for the inevitable explosive reaction that occurred whenever Flora Sudberry Periwinkle Ramirez Scoffield Goldberg O'Keefe, my mother and the former social secretary of the Daughters of the American Revolution, locked horns with Lucille Pollack, my mother-in-law and current president of the Daughters of the October Revolution. I'd been swindled out of seventy-two hours.

By the time I entered the living room, Mama's and Lucille's voices had reached glass-shattering decibel range.

"Crazy communist!" yelled Mama. She stood in the middle of the room, cradling Catherine the Great, her corpulent white Persian with an attitude befitting her namesake.

Manifesto, my mother-in-law's runt of a French bulldog, stood inches from Mama's Ferrigamos, his bark having switched to growl mode as he glared up at his nemesis. With a hiss and a yowl, Catherine the Great leaped from Mama's arms. Showing his true cowardly colors, Mephisto, as we always called him behind his back and often to his snout, scampered to safety behind my mother-in-law's ample girth.

Lucille barreled across the room, waving her cane at Mama. "Reactionary fascist!"

"How dare you threaten me!" Mama defended herself with a French manicured backhand that would have done Chris Everett proud. The cane flew from Lucille's grasp and landed inches from Mephisto's nose. Demon dog yelped and dove between Lucille's orange polyester clad legs.

My mother-in-law's rage multiplied into Vesuvian proportions. Her wrinkled face deepened from a spotted scarlet to an apoplectic heliotrope. "You did that on purpose!"

Mama jutted her chin at Lucille as she rubbed the palm of her hand. "You started it."

"And I'm stopping it." I stepped between them, spreading my arms to prevent them from ripping each other's lips off. "Knock it off. Both of you."

"It's her fault," said Mama. She jabbed a finger at Lucille. Her hand shook with rage, her gold charm bracelet tinkling a dainty minuet totally incompatible with the situation. "And that vicious mongrel of hers. She sic'd him on us the moment we walked through the door."

Highly unlikely. "Mephisto's all bark and bluster, Mama. You should know that by now."

"*Manifesto!*" shrieked Lucille. "How many times do I have to tell you his name is *Manifesto*?"

"Whatever," Mama and I said in unison. It was an old refrain. *Mephisto* better suited demon dog anyway. Besides, who names a dog after a Communist treatise?

Behind me, Ralph squawked. I looked over my shoulder and found him perched on the lampshade beside one of the overstuffed easy chairs flanking the bay window. A chair occupied by a cowering stranger, his knees drawn up to his chest, his arms hugging his head. I glanced at Mama. Glanced back at the man. "Who's he?"

"Oh dear!" Mama raced across the room, flapping her Chanel-suited arms. "Shoo, dirty bird!"

Ralph ignored her. He doesn't intimidate easily. Mama was hardly a challenge for a parrot who had spent years successfully defending himself against Aunt Penelope's mischievous students. "Anastasia, I told you that bird's a reincarnation of Ivan the Terrible. Do something. He's attacking my poor Lou."

Her Poor Lou? Okay, at least the man had a name and someone in the room knew him. I stretched out my arm and whistled. Ralph took wing, landing in the crook of my elbow. *Poor Lou* peered through his fingers. Convinced the coast was clear, he lowered his hands and knees and raised his head.

"Are you all right, dear?" asked Mama, patting his salt and pepper combover. "I'm terribly sorry about all this. My daughter never did have the heart to turn away a stray." She punctuated her statement with a pointed stare, first in Lucille's direction and then at Ralph.

Lucille harrumphed.

Ralph squawked.

Mephisto bared his teeth and rumbled a growl from the depths of his belly.

Catherine the Great had lost interest in the family melodrama and dozed stretched out on the back of the sofa.

Before Mama could explain *Poor Lou*'s presence, the front door burst open. Fourteen year-old Nick and sixteen year-old Alex bounded into the living room. "Grandma!" they both exclaimed in unison. They dropped their baseball gear and backpacks on the floor and encircled Mama in a group hug.

"Aren't you supposed to be on a cruise?" asked Nick.

"Who's this?" asked Alex, nodding toward *Poor Lou*.

Poor Lou rose. He wiped his palms on his pinstriped pants legs, cleared his throat, and straightened his skewed paisley tie. "Maybe I should be going, Flora. The driver is waiting."

I glanced out the front window. A black limo idled at the curb.

"Yes, of course." She walked him to the door without bothering to make introductions. Very odd behavior for my socially correct mother.

"I'll call you tomorrow," *Poor Lou* told Mama.

She raised her head, batted her eyelashes, and sighed. *Poor Lou* wrapped his arms around my mother and bent her backwards in a clinch that rivaled the steamiest of Harlequin romance book covers. His eyes smoldered as he met her slightly parted lips. Mama melted into his body.

I stared at my etiquette-obsessed mother, my jaw flapping down around my knees, and wondered if she had eaten any funny mushrooms on her cruise. Out of the corner of one eye, I saw my two sons gaping with equally bug-eyed expressions. Behind me, Lucille muttered her disgust. Even Ralph registered his amazement with a loud squawk.

Over Mama's shoulder, *Poor Lou* stole an anxious glance toward Ralph, broke the kiss, and darted out the door.

Mama fluffed her strawberry blonde waves back into place, smoothed the wrinkles from her suit jacket, and offered us the most innocent of expressions as we continued to ogle her. "Is something wrong?"

"Wrong? Why? Just because my mother was doing the Tonsil Tango with a total stranger?"

Lucille stooped to retrieve her cane. "I suppose this means that trashy hussy is moving back into my room."

"*Your* room?" asked Mama.

"Hey, it's *my* room!" said Nick.

Poor Nick. He was none too happy about having to give up his bedroom to his curmudgeon of a grandmother. He didn't mind the occasional upheaval when Mama came to visit because he knew it was temporary. Besides, the boys and Mama had a great relationship. Lucille was another story. When she moved in with us to recuperate after a hit-and-run accident and subsequent hip surgery, none of us had expected a permanent addition to the household. Then again, I had suffered from quite a few delusions back then.

Lucille scowled at me. "You should teach those boys some respect. In my day children knew their place."

"Don't you speak to my daughter like that."

Lucille scoffed. "Look who's talking. A fine example you set."

"What's that supposed to mean?" demanded Mama.

"Strumpet." Lucille pounded her cane once for emphasis, then lumbered from the living room, Mephisto following at her heels. Lucille habitually pronounced judgment with a pounding of her cane, then departed.

"At least I'm getting some," Mama called after her. "Unlike a certain jealous Bolshevik who hasn't experienced an orgasm since Khrushchev ruled the Kremlin."

"Mama!"

Nick and Alex grabbed their middles and doubled over in hysterics.

Mama brushed my indignation aside with a wave of her hand. "For heaven's sake, Anastasia, I'm a grown woman."

"Then act like one. Especially in front of your grandsons."

She winked at the boys. "I thought I did. Besides, if they don't know the facts of life by now, they've got a lot of catching up to do."

I glanced at my sons, not sure how to interpret the sheepish expression on Alex's face nor the feigned innocence on Nick's. After the initial shock of seeing their grandmother in the throws of passion, both seemed quite amused by the drama playing out in our living room. "They know all about the facts of life. What they don't need is a graphic demonstration from their grandmother."

The corners of Mama's mouth dipped down. "Honestly, Anastasia, just because I'm over sixty doesn't mean I'm ready for a hearse. When did you become such a stick-in-the-mud, dear?"

I suppose right around the time she morphed from Ms. Manners into Auntie Mame. Other sixty-five year old women might behave this way in front of their daughter and grandsons, but up until today, Mama wasn't one of them. Was *Poor Lou's* last name *Svengali*?

Alex spared me from defending myself. "So who's the stranger dude, Grandma?"

"Lou isn't a stranger. He's my fiancé."

"Your *what*?" Surely I hadn't heard her correctly. Had some of that rafter dust settled in my ears? "What about Seamus, Mama?"

"Seamus?"

"Yes, Seamus. Remember him?"

Mama heaved one of those sighs reserved for children who need re-peated instruction and explanation. "Seamus died, Anastasia. You know that."

Of course I knew Seamus had died. He'd suffered a cerebral aneurysm while kissing the Blarney Stone. "But he *just* died. Three months ago." Within days of losing my own husband, Mama had lost hers.

"Well, it's not like we were married very long. He died on our six-month anniversary. Besides, I'm not Merlin. I don't grow younger with each passing year."

Ample justification for getting herself engaged to a total stranger, no doubt. "Where did you meet him?"

"On the cruise, of course."

"So you're engaged to a man you've known for all of one week?"

Mama shrugged. "Time is meaningless when soul mates connect."

Soul mates? The now-departed Seamus had been soul mate Number Five for Flora Sudberry Periwinkle Ramirez Scoffield Goldberg O'Keefe. When Mama finally met her maker, she'd have a line of *soul mates* waiting for her at the Pearly Gates. She'd better hope St. Peter allowed polygamy up in Heaven.

"Besides," continued Mama, "at my age, I have to grab happiness when it presents itself. Advice you'd do well to heed." She glanced down the hallway toward the bedrooms. "Unless you want to wind up like *her*."

"No, not that!" Nick grabbed his throat and made gagging noises. "Not my mom!"

Alex fell to his knees in front of Mama, his hands clasped in supplication. "Please, Grandma, save our mom!"

Comedians. I tossed them a mom-scowl. "If the two of you have so much time on your hands, you can vacuum and do a load of wash before dinner." Nearly seven and I still had to prepare a meal, finish a project for a photo shoot tomorrow, and figure out a way to rob Peter to pay Paul before the bill collectors came knocking. Again.

Alex grabbed his backpack. "Sorry, Mom. Got an economics paper due tomorrow."

"Bio test," said Nick, retrieving his backpack from the floor.

"Dibs on the computer," called Alex as he sped down the hall to the bedroom they now shared. The boys used to have their own computers, but Nick's died last month. A replacement would have to wait until I won Mega-Millions or Powerball.

Nick raced after Alex. Neither bothered with the baseball gear they'd dumped on the carpet. Apparently, it had become invisible to all but me.

I stooped to pick up the discarded duffels of sports paraphernalia. "I'm still in mourning."

Mama snorted as she followed me into the kitchen. "For a no-good gambling addict who left you without two nickels to rub together?"

"Karl and I were married eighteen years," I said softly as I hung the duffels on pegs in the mudroom off the kitchen. "He's only been dead three months."

Mama regarded me with an expression that hovered somewhere between pity and skepticism. "You don't still have feeling for him, do you?"

I grabbed the leftover chicken and broccoli casserole from the fridge. There was barely enough left for four, let alone five people. "Not exactly," I said, reaching for a box of mac and cheese to supplement the casserole. Not after what Karl Marx Pollack had done to his kids and me. I mourned for my former life. Before lies and deceit and death shattered the illusion of our perfect middle class world.

I brushed my desperately-in-need-of-a-styling-but-can't-afford-it hair out of my face and turned to confront Mama. "Besides, I don't have time for romance. I'm too busy paying off Karl's debts."

Three months ago, my husband of eighteen years had permanently cashed in his chips at a Las Vegas roulette table—after cashing in his sizable life insurance policy and 401(k), maxing out our home equity line of credit and numerous credit cards, *and* draining our teenage sons' college accounts.

Besides the mountain of debt, my dearly departed had saddled me with both Ricardo The Loan Shark and Comrade Lucille, the communist mother-in-law from Hell. Karl had also stolen his mother's life savings, thus leaving Lucille and Mephisto ensconced in Nick's bedroom where they'd remain—short of an act of God. Considering Lucille didn't believe in God and I had the luck of an excommunicated leprechaun, chances of her leaving any time soon were slim to none.

At least I no longer had to worry about Ricardo. He now resided at a federal facility. Permanently. No chance of parole, thanks to a trail of dead bodies three months earlier.

"A life without romance isn't worth living," said Mama. "Which reminds me, how's that sexy tenant of yours?"

"Zack?" asked Nick, bounding into the kitchen. He opened the refrigerator and began to survey the contents. "He's cool. Don't you think he and Mom—"

I cut him off before he could finish his sentence. "I thought you had a test to study for." I yanked his head out of the fridge and closed the door.

My sons shadowed Zachary Barnes like unweaned puppies. More often than not, I arrived home from work to find Zack sitting at my kitchen table, regaling Nick and Alex with his latest adventure. Lucky for me, the too-sexy-for-my-own-good photo journalist traveled frequently.

"I'm hungry."

"You'll have to wait until dinner."

He glanced at the clock over the sink. "Jeez, Mom, it's after seven. When are we going to eat?"

I tossed the box of mac and cheese at him. "If you're so hungry, you can help."

He tossed the box back. "Can't. Have to study." He snagged an apple from the bowl on the kitchen table and hustled out of the kitchen.

"So what's with you and Zack?" asked Mama.

When Mama first met Zack, she tossed her hair, batted her eyes, and preened in front of him like a svelte Miss Piggy trying to woo Kermit the Frog. When Zack didn't take the bait, she decided I should have him. This all took place within days of both of us entering the ranks of widowhood.

I handed her a half-empty bag of carrots and a vegetable peeler. "Nothing."

She raised an eyebrow as she began scraping carrots. "He's a very handsome man, Anastasia. Unattached. Good job."

"Forget Zack. Let's talk about you. Why are you home three days early?"

Mama had a knack for marrying grasshoppers—men who lived life to the fullest without any regard for tomorrow. When they died, as each of them had, they left her with fond memories of a good time and little more than pocket change. So between husbands, she camped out at *Chez* Pollack. Although also a grasshopper, Seamus O'Keefe had had the foresight to purchase a small life insurance policy prior to his and Mama's Irish sojourn—a life insurance policy Mama had discovered only by chance weeks after returning from Ireland. Behind my back she paid off twenty-thousand dollars of my inherited debt, then treated herself to a post-Seamus first-class cruise with the remaining five thousand dollars.

Mama waved a raggedly peeled carrot in the air. She was as useless in the kitchen as the rest of my brood. "The ship had some sort of mechanical problem in Antigua. Since there were severe storm warnings, Lou and I decided to fly home before the storm hit."

"And just who is this Lou?"

A dreamy look settled over her face. The corners of her mouth turned upward into a beatific smile as she exhaled a long sigh. "Lou? He's the answer to my prayers. And yours."

"Want to run that by me again?"

Mama rose from the table and tossed the carrot scrapings into the sink. "Lou is Louis Beaumont, Anastasia."

I waited. And waited. I crossed my arms, tapped my foot, cocked my head, and waited some more. "And?"

Mama's eyes grew wide. "Surely you've heard of Louis Beaumont."

"Can't say as I have."

"He produces *You Heard It Here First with Vince and Monica*."

That explained so much. I offered Mama a blank stare.

"The morning talk show with Vince Alto and Monica Rivers? Surely you've watched it."

"Television?" I laughed. "Right. Every morning while I loll around at the spa. In the afternoon I sip champagne, eat bonbons, and watch the soaps."

"There's no need for sarcasm, dear. It's a popular show. Even if you haven't watched it, I'd expect you to know about it."

"In case you hadn't noticed, Mama. I'm a single parent. I'm juggling a full-time job, two teenage kids, a house, a parrot who thinks he's the reincarnation of William Shakespeare, a semi-invalid mother-in-law, and her spawn of Satan dog.

"*And* when I'm not dealing with all of that, I'm trying to figure out ways to earn extra income because I'm up to my patootie in debt. I've never heard of Louis Beaumont. And you've heard *that* here first."

"Well, you'd better make an effort to watch *You Heard It Here First*, dear, because you're going to be a regular on the show."

© Robert Winston

ABOUT THE AUTHOR

Lois Winston straddles two worlds. She's an award-winning author of romantic suspense and humorous women's fiction. She's also an award-winning designer of needlework and crafts projects for magazines, craft book publishers, and manufacturers. Like Anastasia, Lois worked for several years as a crafts editor. A graduate of the Tyler School of Art, she often draws on her art and design background for much of the source material in her fiction. She and her husband live a stone's throw from Manhattan (assuming you can throw a stone across the Hudson).

Lois loves to hear from readers. Visit her at www.loiswinston .com, and check out Anastasia's Killer Crafts & Crafty Killers blog at www.anastasiapollack.blogspot.com.